Contents

Kate Westbrook

Kate Westbrook was born in 1970 and educated at Cambridge and Harvard. She has a doctorate in history, specialising in the emergence of post-colonial political structures. She has worked in Africa and Latin America and is the author of numerous articles, as well as two novels, as yet unpublished. She is a fellow of Trinity College, Cambridge.

The Moneypenny Diaries

Guardian Angel

Kate Westbrook

JOHN MURRAY

© IFPL 2005

First published in Great Britain in 2005 by John Murray (Publishers)
A division of Hodder Headline

Paperback edition 2006

A CIP catalogue record for this title is available from the British Library

ISBN 0 7195 6742 4
A-format paperback ISBN 0 7195 6777 7

Typeset in Sabon MT by Servis Filmsetting Ltd, Manchester

Printed and bound by Clays Ltd, St Ives plc

Hodder Headline policy is to use papers that are natural, renewable
and recyclable products and made from wood grown in sustainable
forests. The logging and manufacturing processes are expected to
conform to the environmental regulations of the country of origin.

John Murray (Publishers)
338 Euston Road
London NW1 3BH

To G. A. with thanks
K. W.

Introduction

The first entry I read was dated 6 July 1962, and began, '007 leaves for the Caribbean today. M returned from lunch on Monday at the American Ambassador's residence, called for Bill and issued a flurry of commands. "Send up the recent signals file from Station A, please, Miss Moneypenny . . . Get Head of Section C up here . . . Arrange a meeting with the armourer first thing tomorrow . . . and summon 007 immediately."'

The three packages from my aunt had arrived on 10 October 2000, exactly ten years after she died. They were delivered to my office in Trinity College, Cambridge. I had just returned from giving my first lecture of the term, and was settling down to a mug of tea and a small gas fire as the porter came in with the boxes. When I examined them – one large, two small, wrapped in brown paper and string and sealed with irresistible red sealing wax – I saw that each had a different postmark.

I opened the large one first. It was the size of a small school trunk, and heavy. The letter accompanying it was from a firm of solicitors on Queensgate, Inverness, and simply said that the box had been sent as per the instructions of their client, Miss Jane Vivien Moneypenny. I broke the seal and peeled back the paper to reveal a gunmetal-grey chest, securely fastened with a Chubb padlock. After a few fruitless minutes searching for a way in, I turned to one of the smaller parcels. It was a cash box, sent by another firm of solicitors, this time in Edinburgh. Again it was locked, but when I shook it I could hear the soft thud of some padded article inside. The third and last box had been sent by the engagingly named 'McTavish, McTwee & McTavish' of Portree, Isle of Skye. This one, thankfully, was only taped shut. I tore off the tape and opened the box, to find a small brass key. This fitted the lock of the second box, inside which I discovered, wrapped in layers of scarlet paper, the key to the large chest.

I unlocked it and peeled away more layers of the same brilliant tissue paper (so like my aunt – a dash of flamboyance in a discreet shell), to find neat stacks of identical red lambskin diaries, some forty of them, each carefully secured with a red leather tab. There was also a letter addressed to me in my aunt's familiar hand:

North Uist, 15th September 1990

My dear Kate,

First, please forgive the cloak and dagger arrangements I felt bound to make for the delivery of these books to you. Secrecy and subterfuge have become as natural an impulse to me as checking the rear-view mirror in a car, or watching for the heather to tremble before a storm. As you will soon understand, assuming you have the time or the heart to read this burden that I have laid at your door, I had additional reasons for care.

I hope you will not be upset when you learn how little I could ever tell you about my life. It was just not possible. Shortly after your mother and I came to England, I obtained a position as a

2

junior cipher clerk in the Secret Intelligence Service, and it was that organisation I served in some capacity for the next thirty years. As far as the world knew – and that included family, friends and lovers – I was a civil servant. I was taught to brush off any questions about my work with 'Oh, something in the Foreign Office, quite boring really.' That was as far as it went. I was happy with this. It was the nature of the pact to which I had signed my name, under a litany of official type, and to which I stayed true over the succeeding three decades. I am not a natural confider, and in any case I had few friends at that time in England. Those I made subsequently came from the same world and we were bound together by our secret lives. It only pained me that I could not share this with you then.

It is also the reason I never married. There were men I loved, but mostly they were not one of 'Us', not a fellow initiate to our secret world. There was one person for whom I could have forsaken everything, but it never came to that.

I wrote about my experiences. That was my sin, possibly my greatest one. From early childhood, I wrote my journals. Whenever I could, I would take a pen and one of these leather books – the first of which was my father's last gift to me, sent by ship from Scotland – up to an old acacia tree on the bank of our small lake, sit in the shade and write about the birds and beasts I had seen, about my dreams and feelings. At night, I would hide the book under my mattress. I wanted one day to be a writer, to travel the world in search of its wilder shores. This ambition, sadly, I had to relinquish after my parents died, for the rather prosaic need for financial security. But I could not break the habit of recording on paper the minutiae of my daily existence. It was strictly forbidden by the Office, of course. We were inculcated from the beginning with the impulse to destroy, to shred, to burn, to leave no trace of anything that could be of conceivable use to the enemy. For that reason, I could never take my diaries into work; when I went away, I left them behind, hidden as always in the safe I had built into the false wall between my bedroom and bathroom. Had my secret been discovered, even by our side, I would have lost my position, probably been prosecuted for contravening the Act that governed our daily existence. If They had found them, the consequences would have been considerably more serious.

Do you remember, many years ago, we laughed about a character in a book who was named Miss Moneypenny? You said something along the lines of 'Gosh, is that you, Aunt Jane? Tell me that you've been consorting with handsome secret agents and spies all along. Did you really love James Bond?' And we laughed some more, at the total preposterousness of it all, and never spoke of it again.

Well, my dear, yes, that was me. For nearly forty years now we have all kept quiet about a wonderful piece of literary piracy. But then we were good at secrets. Yes, I was personal assistant to the Chief, the man we called M. Yes, I knew James, as well as the other oo agents, and yes, they had a 'licence to kill' for their country. I had intimate knowledge of almost every detail of the day-to-day running of that extraordinary organisation. I was a party to events that will never be written about in even the most searching accounts of the time. But they happened, and in some cases they changed the course of history, as only a few know it.

So now, you see, I am faced with the dilemma of what to do with these diaries that I have hidden and protected for so long. I no longer need them; I have finally cured myself of the habit of writing; I feel I have little left to say. My first instinct was to destroy them, to build a grand old pyre and watch them burn to soft ash and fly into the deep-blue Scottish sky. I even went so far as to collect the driftwood. I don't know what stopped me; maybe some lamentable sense of vanity, an idea that you might be interested in what I was before I became an old island maid? Perhaps you would like to know about your grandfather and the true circumstances of his death, which I managed to uncover, but never to share with anyone, even my dear sister? Or was it merely to make you chuckle at the cloak and dagger world which is fast becoming a relic from the past?

So I have saved them. I am sure they can be of no interest now to either side; what I wrote of is already far in the past, and today is a different place. To make extra sure, I have instructed my solicitors to hold them back for ten years from the day of my death before sending them to you. By then, anyway, the official papers will have passed into the public domain, even if my experiences will still formally be bound by secrecy.

Whatever the motive, here it is, dearest Kate: my life, for what it is worth.

Enjoy yours, and please remember, the wind is never so strong that you cannot sail a little closer to it.

Your ever loving aunt,

Jane

How I wish I had known. When I first read the letter, I was filled with intense, conflicting emotions – excited, intrigued and upset almost in equal part. The excitement was easy to explain, but the sense of betrayal I found more surprising and harder to rationalise. It was almost as if a large part of my childhood – some of my happiest memories – had just been revealed to me as a chimera. I felt that I had been denied a role in my aunt's great adventure. In time, as I came to accept her parallel existence, I replaced this emptiness with a determination to get to know this parallel Miss Moneypenny – through her diaries – as well as I had known my Aunt Jane.

She had never talked to me about her work. It was not until her memorial service, in January 1991, that I had the first inkling that perhaps her working life was not as straightforward as I had supposed. My mother was already ill, so I had taken responsibility for organising the service. I realised that, close as I had been to my aunt, with a very few exceptions – her neighbours in Scotland, a handful of childhood friends from Kenya who had moved to England around the same time as she and my mother, Cambridge people she'd met on her frequent weekend visits to my parents – I knew none of her friends. And so, just as if you don't read newspapers when you're abroad you think the world has stopped, I had assumed she lived a quiet life. She loved travelling, and there had been occasional, oblique hints of men, but I had never met them and had no idea how to find them.

In terms of assembling the memorial service, my only point of reference – and a hazy one at that – was her work. I put a notice in *The Times* and the *Daily Telegraph*, and wrote to the Foreign Office. I didn't even know whose name to put on the front of the envelope. And so it came as a surprise when, on the day, St Martin-in-the-Fields was thronged with people: smart old gentlemen with watch chains and impressively crafted moustaches; ladies wearing gloves and hats. Elderly men chain-smoked on the steps outside. Some had lost an arm or a leg; others wore a patch over one eye. Many had faint Scottish accents and cold grey eyes. As a group, they seemed to have descended from a different world – from the palm court of a Cairo hotel in the 1950s, perhaps, or cocktails at the Café Royal.

6

They all came up to offer their condolences, but whether as a result of my state of sorrow, or because they mumbled, I caught few names. It was fortunate that Mark, my ally and sometime partner in crime, insisted on taking photographs, though at the time I thought it tasteless.

Those faces floated back into my mind as I picked up that first soft leather journal and started flicking through its pages. These were pale blue and gilt-edged, feint ruled, and crammed with words written in deep-violet ink. It was not a conventional calendar-type diary – there were no printed days of the week – and, as I soon saw, my aunt did not write with regularity. Nor did every volume begin in January and end in December. Some entries were many pages long; others no more than a few lines. Some were intensely personal; others related to the world of her work.

My dead aunt had led me to a hidden peephole through which I could spy on the most secret corners of power. As far as I knew, nothing of this sort had come into the public domain before; possibly nothing else like it exists – over the last few years I have searched hard. I once read about a young man's interview with MI6 at the beginning of the Second World War. He was given an address in Paris and told to report there for immediate duty. He carefully wrote it down in his diary, and as he made to put this away in his pocket his interviewer instructed him to hand it over. He opened it to the relevant page and tore out everything the young man had written, before handing it back. The young man never kept a diary again.

The journals awoke in me a curiosity to learn everything I could about this hidden world. Of the two British secret services – the Secret Intelligence Service (SIS or MI6) and the Security Service (MI5) – the former has always worn an extra cloak of secrecy. There have been histories written of MI5, former officers such as Peter Wright have published their own experiences (albeit against every effort of government), and a significant proportion of its archives has been declassified and filed in the National Archives. The same is not true of the Secret Intelligence Service – except, of course, in fiction.

The urge to find out the truth, to verify my aunt's diaries, hit me even as I was reading that first entry. It was the close link to a fictional world – or one that I, along with most people, assumed to be fictional – that had introduced a doubt. In other circumstances I would not have questioned my aunt; she was one of the sanest, on the surface most straightforward people I have ever met (five years ago I would not even have thought to qualify that description). Yet her diaries interleaved closely with the James Bond series of books by Ian Fleming, which I reread in tandem with the diaries. If what she wrote was true, then the Bond series was, at the very least, based firmly on truth. And if that was the case, then how did Fleming – never a member of the SIS – get his information?

I have spent the last five years – every spare minute I could squeeze between my academic duties – working on *The Moneypenny Diaries*: searching and researching, checking, rechecking and authenticating. I have travelled halfway around the world and delved deep into libraries and archives, submersing myself in a world of covers and code names, of shadows and mirrors, where much was not as it first appeared to be. In every place I have learned something. When I could not find the files I wanted in the National Archives in London, I found their counterpart in the National Security Archives in Washington, DC; where

Wright left gaps, Gordievsky and Mitrokhin filled them in. The more I discovered, the more it became apparent that Fleming had reported the events of the time with an alarming degree of accuracy. There was a real person called Goldfinger, and an organisation called SMERSH (or Death to Spies) – I visited its former headquarters in Moscow. There is an island off the north coast of Jamaica called Crab Key, and SPECTRE existed, as did Ernst Stavro Blofeld. I read the report on his death written by the representative of the Australian Secret Intelligence Service in Tokyo and sent to SIS headquarters in London. Which was not, however, in Regent's Park, as Fleming wrote, but in Westminster, nearer to the seat of power.

There were times when I felt I was swimming through a warm sea of truth, occasionally hitting cold spots of fiction. I didn't know where they were and when I might hit the next one. I was stunned to learn that Fleming had worked beside my grandfather – Jane Moneypenny's father – in Naval Intelligence during the war; how did that fit in? I would begin to doubt what I knew to be fact: I had little doubt that had I told anyone what I was doing, they would have laughed. For the first time I could almost imagine what it must have been like for my aunt to live in a world within a world. I started to seek out her former colleagues, and it was with one of them, after years of searching, that I finally experienced the flash of clarity. It was our second meeting; this person was close to my aunt, and our conversations had been full of emotion. After several hours, I asked about the Fleming books; how much was true? 'As much of it as he knew,' was the reply. I knew then that I was face to face with Fleming's source. We smiled at each other, and I made a promise not to reveal his identity while he was still alive. Now I am the safe guardian of another secret.

I returned to the diaries with a fresh eye and a clear mind. The line between truth and fiction appeared to draw itself as I followed it. Through his source Fleming had been given access to the inner sanctums of the Secret Intelligence Services, allowing him to report many of the great missions, successes and rare failures of the organisation, and in return he was careful not to reveal anything that would place the service in jeopardy. Some names and locations were changed, some dates were altered and emphases shifted, but essentially his stories are a near-accurate record of some of the intelligence service's more outlandish adventures.

At first, thoughts of publication were not at the fore-front of my mind. Throughout a lifetime of writing these diaries, my aunt never considered that they might one day be read – certainly not by a wider audience. Had there been even the slightest risk of that, I think she would have burned them immediately. Yet instead she entrusted them to me, and as her trustee I had no desire to betray her confidence.

I can pinpoint the exact time I changed my mind. It was a cold February day, and I was delivering a lecture to third-year historians on the Soviet/American nuclear arms race of the early 1960s. I started talking about the Cuban Missile Crisis. One of the students put up her hand. 'How did the Americans know that the Russians had nuclear weapons on Cuba? They only saw photographs taken from thousands of feet up. What if the Russians had just been bluffing, in an attempt to broker a deal with Kennedy that would result in America withdrawing its missiles from Turkey?' I felt as if I had been hit on the head by a spade. My aunt's 1962 journal had given me the answer to the student's question, but I couldn't reveal that, and even if I did I had no way to back up what I was saying. Suddenly I knew that the diaries had to be made public. The information contained in them would have to be released. I would do it, and, as a nod to the student who had asked about Cuba, I was going to start with 1962.

The events of 1962 were dramatic, but barely touched upon by Fleming. Presumably he, or his informant, thought them too sensitive. The stories he relates are among the more unusual adventures undertaken by Bond – events that are so far from our normal experience as to be plausibly fiction, and their publication of minimal security risk. My aunt's diaries, however, reveal a more gritty reality – and, in 1962, one of the most important contributions made by SIS, and indeed Bond, towards safeguarding world peace.

The decision to publish was easy to take on an intellectual level. I could justify it from almost every direction. There would be Official Secrets issues – my aunt had signed the Act on the day she entered the service, and even in death she was theoretically covered by it. But a colleague in the Cambridge law department advised me that the government would probably be reluctant to take issue with the diaries, particularly after the 2005 Freedom of Information Act, for fear of appearing to confirm their authenticity and with an eye to the negative publicity that would surround the suppression of information. I decided that I would take the risk, publish, and hopefully not be damned.

What was harder, however, was to rationalise the side effects of publication. *The Moneypenny Diaries* are not only a record of the inner workings, the key decisions – and deceptions – of a very secret organisation, they are also a private account of a private life. At the same time as I had been on a quest into the validity of received history, I had been making a personal odyssey – into the thoughts and dreams of someone I loved and admired. To reveal the first to the world would entail betraying the second, the secret history of my own family.

My aunt, Jane Vivien Moneypenny, was born in 1931 in Nairobi, Kenya. She had an apparently carefree early childhood on her parents' farm until the beginning of the Second World War, when her father, Commander Hugh Moneypenny, was recalled to London. A year later he was declared missing in action, presumed dead. A little over a decade after that, her mother was trapped in the crossfire between warring tribal groups and Jane, then twenty-one, and her younger sister – my mother, Helena – were orphaned and moved to London. Within months of arriving she had joined the Secret Intelligence Service.

As I discovered from her diaries, one of the main quests of her life was to find out the exact circumstances of her father's presumed death. It came as a revelation to me – from my mother I had always understood that my grandfather was a straightforward casualty of war. Over half a century later, my aunt – through her diaries – was able to lead me towards the truth. And that, in a sense, was thanks to him, my grandfather, who had sent Jane the first diary, along with his last letter.

That is the image I have in my eye now, of a young girl sitting in the lower branches of an acacia tree on the shore of an African lake. She carefully unwraps a brown-paper parcel to reveal a journal. It has soft leather covers and pale-blue pages. There is a letter from her father tucked inside, postmarked Aberdeen, in which he urges her to 'write down everything you see, every animal, bird and insect, and when I get back, we'll discuss them together'. She takes out a new pencil, licks the lead, and writes her name on the flyleaf: JANE VIVIEN MONEYPENNY. It is 18 October 1940. In one week her father will be reported missing in action in Europe. But for the next fifty years she will not forget his words.

Cambridge, 2005

1962

January

By the end of 1961 the world was precariously balanced on a political see-saw, with the USA and the Soviet Union vying to load greater weight on to either end. The Berlin Wall was newly erected, Yuri Gagarin had become the first man in space, and both superpowers were furiously devising, building and testing nuclear weapons. In his first year of office, John F. Kennedy had deployed nuclear missiles in Turkey, presided over a disastrous attempt to invade Cuba via the Bay of Pigs, and, in response to an escalation in Communist guerrilla activity, announced an increase in the number of 'military advisers' in South Vietnam. In political terms, everything was seen through the prism of the Cold War. It was either West or East; there was no middle ground.

This was the framework of my aunt's working life and the backdrop for *The Moneypenny Diaries*. It was in 1962 that Miss Moneypenny first stepped out from behind her typewriter to play a more active role in the service of the organisation for which she had worked, by that time, for nearly a decade. It also marked an important turning point in her ongoing search for the truth behind her father's presumed death, twenty-two years earlier.

The events leading up to 1962 were well documented by Ian Fleming in *On Her Majesty's Secret Service* (London,

1963). Where his account ends, my aunt's 1962 diary begins, in the closing stages of a Bond mission to track down and eliminate the elusive Ernst Stavro Blofeld, head of the Special Executive for Counter-Intelligence, Terrorism, Revenge and Extortion (SPECTRE) and long-standing foe of the British secret service. From *OHMSS* – and my aunt's diary for the previous year – I was able to get a fairly comprehensive overview of the operation code-named Corona. Secondary corroboration, however, was harder to obtain. The SIS has not, so far, declassified operation files such as this; the bulk of the treasure trove of agent reports, assessments and signals traffic remains in the jealously guarded Records section at its Vauxhall Cross headquarters. It didn't take long to piece together parts of the story from contemporary newspaper reports, both in England and in Switzerland. Background and colour emerged from a fascinating meeting with the Chief Herald, the 'Griffin Or' of the College of Arms, a charming man with the improbable name of Sable Basilisk, who had himself briefed Bond on the heraldic aspects of his mission back in 1961. But there were still significant gaps. It was only sometime later that it occurred to me to search the Ministry of Agriculture files. Here, at last, I found the corroboration I sought: the entire history of Operation Corona, including facsimiles of top-secret SIS documents and reports.

After many months on Blofeld's trail, Bond had learned that his quarry was living on the top of a remote Swiss mountain, with a new name and a new face. The self-styled Comte de Bleuville, keen to legitimise his title, had contacted the College of Arms in London. His request was passed to Basilisk, then a young herald, whose correspondence with the Count's lawyers was intercepted by the

Foreign Office. When the similarity between the phoney Count and Blofeld was noticed, Basilisk and Bond conceived a plan to infiltrate Bond into Bleuville's establishment in the guise of an heraldic emissary.

On 22 December 1961 Bond flew first class to Zurich on a Swissair Caravelle. The name on his passport was Sir Hilary Bray. He was met at the airport by the Count's secretary, Irma Bunt, and taken by helicopter to Piz Gloria, an Alpine research station dedicated to investigating a possible cure for allergies. There, between genealogical sessions with the Comte de Bleuville, Bond stumbled on a plot to bring Britain to its knees by wiping out the agricultural industry. This was to be done, unwittingly, by Bond's fellow guests, a dozen young farmers' daughters, former allergy sufferers. Each girl had been supplied with a deadly biological weapon, particular to the area of farming in which her family was involved, and, under hypnosis, had been taught how to administer it. All believed themselves to be working for the greater good, whether that be increasing the fertility of chickens or the yield of potatoes.

Bond managed to win their confidence and to compile a list of their full names and home counties, before his cover was blown and he was forced to escape. He fled down the mountain on skis, pursued by Blofeld's men. Bond evaded their fire and, at the bottom of the mountain, literally fell into the arms of his girlfriend, Tracy di Vicenzo (*née* Draco). Back on home turf, he delivered his report to his chief, M, before returning to Switzerland on an unofficial mission to flush out Blofeld, with the aid of Tracy's father. At the culmination of what turned out to be an incendiary affair, Bond chased Blofeld down a bobsleigh run, but failed to prevent his escape, returning instead to Tracy in Munich.

What Fleming does not record is the part played by my aunt in Operation Corona and its tragic consequences. From her diaries, it is apparent that Jane Moneypenny was far more closely involved in the life of the real secret agent whom Fleming named Bond than the books relate. Fleming changed the agent's surname as a security precaution, but otherwise his portrayal was remarkably accurate, from the thin scar that ran down his right cheek, to his licence to kill. In order to avoid confusion I have called him Bond throughout the published *Moneypenny Diaries*, though in the originals my aunt referred to him as James or the Commander, or by his number, 007. Despite my best efforts, I have thus far been unable to determine his real name.

Reading *The Moneypenny Diaries*, it is clear that my aunt was acquainted with every step of the operation to thwart Blofeld's scheme. She booked Bond's ticket to Zurich, and waved him goodbye on his mission. She welcomed him home on Christmas Day, when he returned briefly to get M's blessing before departing on the next stage of the operation. She deciphered his signals, filed the requisite fatality forms, and sat up half the night waiting for him to report the final results of the mission. And she was back in the office on New Year's Day, when the news came in that there had been some appalling aftershocks.

Tuesday, 2nd January

My heart breaks for James. Yesterday, within a few short hours, he became first a husband and then a widower. I hate to confess that I found both equally shocking. That it all happened on top of ten days of more than the usual fire-crackers did not dull the impact. He has certainly made it a festive season to remember, and although I am not too sure that the legions of policemen, civil servants and general mop-up people will thank him for ruining their mince-pies and Auld Lang Syne, the country has reason to be grateful.

My New Year's Eve had passed quietly. R* had taken me to dinner in a small pub on the river and we were driving back when the church bells started ringing. It felt apt, somehow, to be in motion while all around us clocks and calendars were clicking into a new cycle – a metaphor, perhaps, for us? I wonder. We swept by a succession of firework displays and glimpsed parties seeping out from between the chinks of backlit curtains. It was like a different world, one that I can't imagine rejoining. After a week such as we have had, it was all I could do to kiss R goodnight on the doorstep and clamber up the stairs and into bed. He understood – what a wonderful man.

M† had been invited to New Year's lunch with Prime Minister Macmillan at Chequers and I had promised

---

* Richard Hamilton – architect, and since October 1961, when they met on a rainy day under the half-built arches of Gaudí's cathedral of the Sagrada Familia in Barcelona, JM's suitor and consort.
† M – Admiral Sir Miles Messervy, aka the Old Man, or OM. Appointed head of the Secret Intelligence Service in 1956, after a successful career in the Royal Navy and Naval Intelligence. He wrote in green ink (a tradition emanating from the first chief), smoked a pipe (Old Havana tobacco), and favoured bow-ties (blue-and-white spotted). His hobbies included trout fishing, bridge, painting wild orchids, and the evolution of the naval cutlass.

Bill* that I would come in to catch up on the mountain of paperwork, which had been put aside while we dealt with the fall-out from 007's clash with Blofeld. I was at my desk, filling in the collateral fatality forms from 007's explosive adventures – he managed to dispatch a grand total of seven of Blofeld's men over his two visits to Piz Gloria – when Bill walked in, waving a cable and chuckling. 'Penny, you're never going to believe this,' he said. 'It's from Head of Station M [Munich station chief, Lieutenant-Commander Percival Savage]. Just wait until the Old Man reads it.'

He passed me the cable. It started in the standard fashion:

```
PROCOS EXMUNICH. NEW YEARS GREETINGS TO
YOU FROM STATION M AND THE NEWEST MEMBER
OF THE FRATERNITY OF HUSBANDS STOP THIS
MORNING EYE STOOD BESIDE 007 AS HE WAS
BETROTHED TO ONE COMTESSE TERESA DI
VICENZO AKA TRACY DRACO† DAUGHTER OF MARC-
ANGE DRACO COMMA CAPO OF THE UNION CORSE‡
```

---

* Colonel Bill Tanner – M's Chief of Staff (CoS), 007's best friend in the service, and occupant of the office adjoining JM's. Slight in build, with sandy hair and deep-blue eyes. Never married, he lived until his retirement from the service, in 1980, in a second-floor mansion-house flat in Earl's Court.

† Blonde beauty with a passion for fast cars and high-stakes gambling. In September 1961 Bond rescued her from the baccarat table in the casino at Royale-les-Eaux, where she was attempting to gamble with money she didn't have. They spent the night together, and the next day he followed her to the beach and prevented her from committing suicide.

‡ Tracy's father, a charming and powerful man, with a face like a creased walnut. Leader of the Union Corse, an underground organi-

STOP BOTH BRIDE AND GROOM APPEARED
SPECTACULARLY HAPPY AND I AM SURE YOU
WILL JOIN ME IN WISHING THEM MANY YEARS
OF CONTENTED DOMESTICITY STOP HE ASKS IF
YOU COULD BREAK THE NEWS TO M GENTLY AND
WILL REPORT BACK AFTER TEN DAYS OF
PASSIONATE LEAVE STOP AM OFF TO TOAST
THIS MOST UNEXPECTED PLEASURE IN FINE
MUNCHEN BREW STOP SIGNED 410

I must have looked quite as surprised as I felt, as Bill started
laughing again. 'How did he manage it, Penny? Only a week
ago he was down at Quarterdeck* persuading the Old Man
to let him stage a commando raid on Blofeld's mountain
fortress, and now he's married to a girl we've barely heard
of. She must be quite a cracker, but somehow I still can't see
007 settling down to two-handed whist and cocoa before
bedtime.'

Despite my current situation with R, I felt as if I had
been punched in the stomach. I know 007 is a professional
flirt, but I have always had a soft spot for him. He is not a
man to lose one's heart to – though it is not hard to imagine

_____

sation older and possibly more deadly than the Mafia, controlling
most organised crime – protection, smuggling and prostitution –
throughout France and its colonies. He arranged to have Bond and
Tracy kidnapped from the beach, then offered Bond £1 million to
marry his daughter and make her happy. Bond refused the money –
saying that Tracy needed first to go to a clinic to dry out – and instead
asked Draco for help in tracking down Blofeld.
* M's country residence, a small Regency manor house on the edge
of Windsor Forest, where he was looked after by Chief Petty Officer
Hammond and his wife.

how one could. He is tough on the outside, but I've always thought surprisingly vulnerable within. He's funny too, the original Devil-May-Care – with the emphasis on the Devil. I look forward to our irreverent banter and the occasional illicit swirl around my office. There has never been a married oo agent; I am not sure M would countenance it. He has enough problems with girlfriends 'hanging on to one's gun arm'; surely a wife would jam the magazine altogether? But 007 with a desk job? He wouldn't last the week. Why did he do it – was marriage perhaps for him the ultimate gamble?

Now he'll never know. Poor, poor James. It was only hours later that HoM [Head of Munich] telephoned through on the direct line. He sounded uncharacteristically agitated. 'There's been a terrible accident . . . No, not our man. His wife. Car smash. She took a sharp shock to the heart, died instantaneously . . . I'm going to the scene now. Don't know any details, but I'll report when I can.' Wham – I felt the second fist land on target. But I knew that 007 wouldn't appreciate the luxury of sympathy when what he needed was action. I was connected straight through to M at Chequers, who said to send Stoker Smith* to bring him to the Office. Then it was a matter of waiting to hear back from Munich.

M appeared unruffled, working through the signals tray with his usual efficiency. Perhaps he clenched his pipe a little more firmly between his teeth, puffed with increased urgency, but it was nothing that someone who was not sensitive to his every gesture would have noticed. However,

---

* Ex-Leading Stoker Smith was M's chauffeur and proud custodian of his 1946 black Silver Wraith Rolls-Royce.

when the signal came through, late that night, he almost snatched it from my hand.

It transpires that Tracy had been driving them from their wedding in her white Lancia. They were on the road to Kitzbühel when they were overtaken by a couple in a red Maserati, wearing white dust coats and linen helmets, their faces obscured by large, dark-green goggles. As they passed, 007 heard a shattering roar as the windscreen was blown out. The car careered off the road and smashed into a tree. A young patrolman found him cradling the lifeless Tracy in his arms, her blood staining his shirt. 007 looked up at him and said, 'It's all right. She's having a rest. We'll be going soon. There's no hurry. You see, we've got all the time in the world.' I cannot bear to think of that brave, proud man being hit at his most vulnerable spot.

It took HoM a good twenty minutes to prise him away and then only with the promise that he could accompany her in the helicopter to hospital. Once there, he was given a strong sedative and eventually allowed HoM to take him back to the Consul-General's house.

As soon as M had read Munich's report, he told Bill to organise a RAF transport plane to stand by to take him to Munich. Perhaps there is some of the milk of human kindness in the OM after all?

Thursday, 4th January

There was a postcard from 007 waiting on my desk when I got in this morning. It was dated 31st December, the day before disaster struck. I almost couldn't bring myself to read it. 'Dear Penny,' he had written. 'I've given up waiting for you to accept my proposals. By the time you receive this,

I will be married – I'll wager you never thought that would happen, did you? Seriously, I am as happy as a man could be and I know you are going to love Tracy almost as much as I do. We will be back in a couple of weeks and I look forward to introducing you then. Wish us luck. PS. I wish you could be here tomorrow to hold my hand.'

I wish I could have been there too, and I wish I could be with him now.

Saturday, 6th January

M back and opaque on the subject of 007. He came straight from the plane and shut himself in the office with the red light on.* An hour later, he called me in for the signals and sent out a couple of his own: to Tanqueray at Station WB [West Berlin] and Muir in Zurich. They were identical, both marked highest priority:

```
EXMAILEDFIST EYES ONLY MOST URGENT WANTED
FOR MURDER OF FRIEND STOP MALE AND FEMALE
BELIEVED TO BE BLOFELD AND BUNT† LAST SEEN
DRIVING ACROSS GERMAN AUSTRIAN BORDER IN
RED MASERATI STOP DESCRIPTIONS TO FOLLOW
STOP USE ALL POSSIBLE RESOURCES TO
APPREHEND AND BRING TO HQ STOP
```

---

* To indicate that he was not to be disturbed, M flicked a switch on his desk, which illuminated a small red light positioned over the outside door to his office. When it was on, only CoS and JM were allowed to interrupt him, and only on matters of utmost urgency.
† Irma Bunt, Blofeld's personal secretary and probable consort, was physically unattractive, with a square, brutal face, hard yellow eyes, and a smile like an oblong hole.

He ordered them to be sent by Triple X* via Geneva and Rome – two of our most secure routings. I waited for him to say something about 007, but he didn't. Mary† ambushed me outside the powder room, desperate for news. It wasn't until the OM had gone for the day that I was able to ask Bill. 'James is devastated, keeps blaming himself, says it should have been him, he should have been driving. He wanted to go after her killer but M's grounded him, temporarily suspended his licence. Accompanied him personally to Royale, where James insisted on taking Tracy's ashes to scatter in the sea. I imagine her father was there too; unsurprisingly, considering his position, M made no mention of it. Now he's given James a month's leave, with the proviso he takes it out of Europe. He brought him back to London himself, drove him to his flat and sat there puffing on his pipe while James packed a case. Then M almost frogmarched him on to a plane headed for Jamaica. I met them at Heathrow. He's given Ross at Station J‡ strict instructions to let him know as soon as he's landed. I sent Ross a cable to make sure he has someone to look after him.'

---

* The latest-generation cipher machine, incorporating three independent scrambler dials, which would be rotated to the appropriate settings as dictated by the daily code book. Messages were translated into ciphertext, then transmitted by radio in five-figure groups. The recipients would decipher them into plain text using an identical machine with identical settings.

† Mary Goodnight, secretary to the oo section. Replaced Loelia Ponsonby in 1961. Former WREN, with blonde hair, blue eyes and an hourglass figure. Non-smoker, she drank rarely and wore Chanel No. 5 daily.

‡ Commander Phillip Ross, RN – Head of Jamaica Station. Replaced Commander John Strangways, who was killed by the mysterious Chinaman Dr No in 1957.

Bill said that James is hell-bent on tracking down Blofeld and Bunt. 'He says he got a positive ID on them in the split second before Tracy was shot. It's highly probable. We traced Bunt to a hotel in Munich. She put a telephone call through to Room 310 of the Hotel Metropole on Lake Como on the 30th. The occupant of 310, who fits 007's description of Blofeld and drove a red Maserati, checked out soon afterwards, presumably headed for Munich. Unfortunately, they dumped the car outside Kitzbühel and we lost all trace of them. But James isn't going to let them go – if it costs him his life, he's going to track Blofeld down. He really loved her, you know. Tracy. Wish I'd met the girl who melted that heart of ice.'

I took Mary for a drink to Bully's, where I related the bulk of the conversation. I didn't dwell on Tracy. Whatever she says, Mary's half in love with 007 – though probably not much more so than with 006 and 009; in this business it's impossible not to get entwined with the people you work with so closely, not to mention with the business itself. Inevitably, we drifted into The Conversation. 'I'm not sure I can take it,' she said. 'Every time one of them disappears or gets in trouble, a little part of me goes with them. Either my heart gets broken every few weeks, or I get hardened to it. I'm not sure which is worse. Lil* said it would happen; she said three years in the oo section and then you have to get out, otherwise you never will. Well, I've practically just

---

* Loelia Ponsonby, former secretary to the oo section. Tall and dark, with an air of cool authority, she emerged unscathed from numerous assaults upon her virtue by 'her men'. She left the service in 1961, after becoming engaged to Gerald Gardiner, a member of the Baltic Exchange and heir to a dukedom.

begun and I'm already feeling it. But I can't leave – it's my dream job and what else could I do now? It was all right for Lil, she found Gerald. How on earth do you do it?'

But do I? How much of me has died along with the men and women we have lost over the past nine years I have worked here? Is that why I can't give myself unreservedly to a man, in case he, too, disappears one day? With R, for the first time, I feel the possibility – but as yet it is a faint one, and one that, I fear, I may be afraid to explore too deeply.

Sunday, 14th January

A wonderful weekend with Helena,* as always. Yesterday, we took some sandwiches and a flask and set off along the river towards Ely on our yearly pilgrimage for Pa.† He would have been fifty-nine today. It's nearly twenty-two years since he disappeared, two-thirds of my life. H and I indulged in our yearly fantasy of 'What if . . .' What if he

---

* Helena Moneypenny, JM's younger sister by three years, her closest friend and confidante. In 1953, aged nineteen, she moved with JM to London, where she finished her degree in Botany at London University. Subsequently worked in Cambridge, as research assistant to her then fiancé – later husband – Lionel Westbrook. Mother of Kate Westbrook.

† Hugh David Moneypenny, born 1903, Rhodesia, educated at Cambridge University and the Royal Naval College, Greenwich. In 1929 he married Irene Greenfield and was appointed naval attaché for the east coast of Africa, based in Nairobi. Qualified pilot, fluent German-speaker, renowned shot. Reported missing in action on 25 October 1940.

hadn't died; where would we be? What would we be like? How would our life have been different? As usual, we never mentioned the biggest 'What if' of them all – what if he isn't dead?

This year, I am determined to find out what really happened to him. I know that being unable to believe a parent's death is a common pathology – but when you never see their body, when they vanish into thin air and are simply 'presumed dead', surely one has some cause to wonder? I know I cannot permit myself even a sliver of hope, but I would dearly love to discover how and where he died.

I just can't get over the gaps in his service record. Nowhere is there any mention of active service, when we know he went to Madrid, at least, and to Lisbon – I have the postcards to prove it. And his last letter to me, I can't forget my promise* – just as I am still writing these diaries, as he desired. Sometimes, I wish I had never started – it would certainly make my life easier now. Every time I get out a journal, I feel the guilt of betrayal, but still I cannot stop, almost as if to do so would break that final bond with Pa.

Helena is in terrific spirits; she is my one sure connection to the world out there. Her wedding plans are still 'long term', which causes us considerable merriment.

---

* Dated 25 September 1940, received by JM 18 October and stuck into the front of her first diary. Hugh wrote to his daughter, 'I am going on a big adventure, like the one we went on to Turkana [lake in northern Kenya – the Moneypennys flew there in a borrowed seaplane for a weekend in 1938]. It will be tremendous fun. I should be back soon, but if I am gone some time, please promise me that you will look after your mother and sister, and don't worry. I am sure it will end with great success.'

Lionel* even finds it moderately amusing – he says that at his age he doesn't want to risk accusations of 'rushing into it'. I imagine that after six years of engagement, another few can't make a difference, and as H pointed out, she's not yet thirty, so there's still time for children – although whether Lionel will manage to give any child of his as much love and attention as he bestows on his beloved old bones remains to be seen.[†]

I didn't mention R. I want to tell H about him, but that would make it real, somehow. If I keep him a secret, perhaps I won't be forced into confronting the choice I know is looming?

I miss him. It's been over two weeks since we last saw each other – since then, he's been away and I've been buried under work. I wake early sometimes, wishing he was beside me.

Saturday, 20th January

A crisis averted. The *Sunday Times* has been inundating the FO with enquiries about the Swiss affair. Apparently, 007 was spotted in Zurich soon after Blofeld's empire exploded into the skies. Then one of the dead up there was identified as a known member of the Union Corse. The paper was on the point of printing an article linking the British intelligence

---

* Lionel Regis Westbrook (1910–91), fellow of Queens' College, Cambridge, Disney Professor of Archaeology, winner of the Huxley Medal, authority on East African cultural change, author of *Heat and Dust: An Examination of Early Kenyan Society* (Cambridge, 1992).
[†] He did. Almost.

services to the Corsican mafia, when M personally telephoned the editor and read him the riot act. The Permanent Secretary followed this with a dressing down in his office at the Ministry. If the piece had been printed – even unproven – it would have started a mountain of dirt-digging, questions in Parliament, all that sort of thing. Since it was an 'unofficial operation', M never told the PM about 007's involvement. If they'd been able to pin it on us, an organisation that doesn't officially exist, it would have become embarrassing.

M called a Cuba summit and asked me to take minutes since Bill was still busy mopping up the Swiss situation. Head of CA [Central America], A [America] and C [Caribbean] sections, with Ross over from Jamaica, Hughes-Onslow – our man in Havana until Castro kicked him out[*] – and Scott from Grosvenor Square [the American Embassy] sitting in. On the Agenda: (i) Lessons from the Bay of Pigs;[†] (ii) Local politics – do we have anything to fear?; and (iii) American action – what next?

I enjoyed the meeting. I find the idea of Cuba strangely alluring, probably something to do with the music, cocktails, the idea of dancing in the Havana night. I cannot help

---

[*] In late April 1961 the Cubans arrested and deported Peter Hughes-Onslow, correctly surmising that he was running a local intelligence network for the British secret service.

[†] Shortly before midnight on 16 April 1961, a US-backed invasion force of 1,500 men, mainly Cuban émigrés, approached the beach at Playa Girón on the south coast of Cuba. However, two of their ships ran aground and the planned landing was delayed, allowing the Cuban air force time to strike at dawn. The US refrained from air back-up, and by 19 April the invaders had been repelled by the Cuban army; 200 rebel soldiers were killed, and 1,197 captured. The US repeatedly denied any involvement in the coup attempt.

but feel some sympathy with the revolutionaries; possibly a *recherche* of my Kenyan student days? I would love to go there, but while I'm still working here – or until the Americans 'liberate' Cuba from Communism – that won't be possible.*

There was consensus that Kennedy would not walk away from Cuba – a case of saving face as much as defending his mighty land from the forces of Communism as represented by one small island. Why do citizens of the most powerful country on earth feel the need to flex their muscles so provocatively? The Soviet threat is undoubtedly terrifying, especially with their assumed nuclear superiority, but the Americans seem actually to enjoy getting wrapped up in McCarthyite paranoia. The politicians certainly find it expedient.

The main lesson from the failed invasion – not surprisingly – was the need for more humint [human intelligence] on the ground. If the Americans had had better intelligence from impartial agents in Cuba, would they have made the mistake of believing the dissidents' reassurances of a majority underground opposition, ready to rise up at the hint of American military support? Most probably not. Cousin Scott sat silently through all of this. Our Cousins† have nothing to be proud of. The official line is still that the Bay of Pigs was an independent dissident-led attack, and

---

* Employees of the intelligence services were prohibited from visiting countries under Communist rule, except on official business. This was essentially a security provision, based on the assumption that many intelligence operatives would be identifiable as such and therefore vulnerable to capture in hostile territory.
† Office jargon for the CIA.

although we know the truth – the world knows the truth – they have to stick to this blatant fiction.

He was similarly quiet when the discussion came round to any possible future American action. When asked, he just kept repeating, 'I am not authorised to comment on this.' He said it so many times that M became rarely irritated and banged his hands on the table, saying, 'Well, if you will not tell me, I will ask your superiors.' To which Scott simply shrugged apologetically and mimed his hands being bound.

Ross came by to say farewell on his way back to Jamaica. 'I have a message from our Commander friend; he asked me to give you a kiss and to say he wished you were there to tuck him up at night.'

'How is he? Really?' I asked.

'Not good, I'm afraid. Went to stay with him last week and he drank a bottle of Scotch before bed, then I heard terrible shouts in the night. I got up, expecting to see some intruder, but all I found was him pacing up and down, apparently berating himself. "Sorry, old boy," he told me. "Didn't mean to wake you." He looks like hell. I don't think he's even been out snorkelling.'

I asked him to convey my special best wishes and to say that all of our thoughts are with him. We need him back here. I think even the OM is missing him.

Wednesday, 24th January

Dinner with R last night. At last. I'd been looking forward to seeing him – but not without some trepidation. Somehow, whenever I glimpse that old Rubicon, I feel impelled to run in the opposite direction; maybe this time, with R, it will be different?

He had made a tremendous effort, booked Quaglino's and spruced himself up in a smart navy suit with a pale lilac shirt. He arrived with red tulips – in January! When I saw him, I felt a stab of pleasure and thought, This is going to be all right, I know it is. I was wearing my Sybil Connolly dress with the fine pleated linen skirt and new Frank Cardone blue and pink mod shoes. Had we bumped into anyone from the Office, I'm not sure they would have recognised me. It was raining hard when we got to the restaurant and when R came round to open my car door, water dripping from the spokes of his umbrella and over his spectacles, I had a scent of Barcelona and the exhilaration of our meeting.*

We were gay, with champagne and plenty to talk about. I told him about Helena and Lionel and the wedding that never is, and about *Inherit the Wind*,† which we saw at the Cambridge Arts Theatre. We started talking about the lengths to which one would go in the name of a job, the

---

* JM had a photograph of her and R in Barcelona, which she kept tucked into her Spanish phrase book. They are standing arm in arm in front of the cathedral. JM is dressed quietly, in a dark-green twinset and skirt, but her hair is wavy and tied back with a brilliant orange scarf. She is smiling at a tall, slim man, with slightly floppy dark hair, green eyes and tortoiseshell-framed spectacles, which give him a bookish air. At a glance, he looks unobtrusive, but in the diary entry describing their meeting JM wrote of the way his eyes sparkled with 'a hint of the Devil that I find enormously attractive'.
† A 1960 fictionalised celluloid portrayal, starring Spencer Tracy, of a famous 1925 courtroom battle in the American South about the right to teach the theory of evolution.

extent to which our work defines us. He was wonderfully eloquent on what it meant to him to build something and to be able to see the results in bricks and cement. 'If I couldn't work, I don't know what I would do,' he said. 'I'm not sure I would be me.' Perhaps I was a little quiet, because he stopped and took my hand. 'I know you like to keep your job and your private life separate,' he said. 'I respect that. But I also know it's important to you, and I want to share the important things in your life, though I've no idea whether you want to share them with me . . .' He trailed off, as if that possibility had only just occurred to him.

But I couldn't give him the reassurance he was seeking, instead muttering something about having been an orphan and how that made me wary of giving too much of myself to people, in case they are taken away from me. Which of course is only half the truth. I saw him looking intensely at me, as if trying to decipher what I was really saying. Sometimes, I wish I could sweep all the secrecy away.

Friday, 26th January

Blofeld's trail appears to have gone cold. 007 is due back in the Office any day, and we wanted to have something positive to give him. There have been suspected sightings around the world, some of which appear to have been genuine. It looks as if he and Bunt headed first to Prague – a couple answering their description were photographed leaving the Russian Embassy on 5th January. Unfortunately, by the time the report reached our head of station over there, they had vanished again. He immediately alerted the main exit points, put men in the airport and railway stations, but they saw nothing. A week later, Blofeld visited a document-forger in Istanbul, where we are sure he bought new papers. The forger is one of the best in the world, used in the past by the top echelons of SMERSH* and SPECTRE.†‡ Darko Kerim‡ sniffed him out years ago, but M decided that it would prove more profitable in the long run to leave him *in situ* and keep a more or less permanent watch on his premises (a shoe-repair shop deep in the Medina).

One of Kerim's sons – most of them stayed at Station T to work for the new head after their father was killed – recognised Blofeld immediately, despite the dark glasses and hat. He called the Office for instructions, and was told to concentrate on finding Blofeld's new identity, rather than on tailing him. Our chaps own the front-desk men in every hotel, and once his new name was known, it was thought we would be able to track him down soon enough. So Kerim junior let him leave, then went into the forger's rooms. Unfortunately, it was the wrong decision. Blofeld had made certain that no one would be able to follow his tracks. The

---

* The commonly used acronym for Smyert Shpionam, 'Death to Spies', the Soviet chief directorate for counter-intelligence activities, set up in April 1943. Thought to be responsible for the death of Trotsky. Purged in 1946 and restructured as five sections operating out of Moscow HQ.
† Special Executive for Counter-Intelligence, Terrorism, Revenge and Extortion: a private enterprise run for private profit by Blofeld, at the head of a group of twenty-two men – former members of SMERSH, Mafia, Gestapo, etc, experts in conspiracy, for hire to the highest bidder.
‡ Former Head of T (Turkey) Section, based in Istanbul and one of M's best operatives. Became close to 007 during an operation to depatriate a Russian Spektor cipher machine. He was killed in action on the Orient Express, 1956.

forger's throat had been cut. When our man arrived, blood was still draining from his severed arteries; he had faked his final document.

Wednesday, 31st January

A perplexing change in R. Over the past three days he has acted entirely out of character. On Monday, I received a message from the central switchboard, saying that a gentleman had telephoned asking for me. When, according to protocol, they informed him that there was no one of that name listed, he had persisted for several minutes, asking them to check. Ten minutes after ringing off, he had telephoned again, most insistent that I worked there, even describing me to them. He had refused to give his name, but they had managed to trace his number – would I like it?

He was at home when I telephoned that evening. I couldn't let on that I knew he had tried to contact me, but he seemed to be expecting me to call. He said he needed to see me, urgently. We arranged to meet on Friday night, but this evening, when I left work, he was standing in the street outside the Office. He must have followed me from home this morning – I should have picked him up, basic anti-surveillance drill, but I suppose my thoughts must have drowned out such instincts. Either that, or he is highly adept at tailing people. He made no effort to deny it, when I asked if he had followed me.

'I just wanted to see where you worked,' he said. 'I tried to telephone you on Monday, but they said that no one of your name worked for the Foreign Office. So I wanted to see for myself. I assumed you worked in Whitehall.' I told him that I normally did, but that I'd been seconded temporarily to one of our contractors and that my name had probably been taken off the telephone list while I'm here . . . I tried to make this prepared answer sound natural.

I took his arm and dragged him into a taxi. But not before I caught a glimpse of Troop* staring at us from the front door, and the last thing I need is for one of my colleagues – or indeed one of Them – to see me with R. We went to a bar off Oxford Street. Our conversation was not a comfortable one. He asked why I hadn't been straight with him. He wanted to know what I did and for whom I worked. He sounded confused, cross, even a little resigned. It is a conversation I have had a hundred times before – in my head. I was able to bluff my way through it; everything I said can be backed up by the FO Personnel Department if he asks any more questions. But it feels ugly to have to lie to him.

---

* Paymaster Captain Roger Troop, RN retd, chief administrative officer of the SIS.

February

The Secret Intelligence Service – the Firm, or the Office, as it is known to those who work there – is Britain's external security agency, responsible for obtaining secret information and conducting operations in support of the country's foreign-policy objectives. It has representatives or agents in nearly every country in the world, particularly those deemed to pose a threat to the security of the United Kingdom. These days, its headquarters is a showy building on the south bank of the Thames dubbed, not always affectionately, 'Legoland'. It is a London landmark, hard to miss, and its current chief, John Scarlett, is no stranger to public attention.

It was not always so. The SIS was originally part of the Secret Service Bureau, which in 1909 divided into two branches: MI5 and MI6 (Military Intelligence – sections 5 and 6). Under the command of Commander Mansfield Smith-Cumming – or 'C' as he and all subsequent chiefs were known, except for M, who chose to use his own initial – in 1922 MI6 severed ties with MI5, the domestic security service, to become a separate entity with the title of Secret Intelligence Service. There was little consultation and not inconsiderable rivalry with MI5. Each guarded its secrets from the other, almost as jealously as from the outside world. In most cases – apart from in the highest echelons – one had little idea of who worked for the other, or, indeed, on what they were working. Cumming died in his office in 1923, and the following year the SIS moved into an anonymous office building at 54 Broadway, opposite St James's Park tube station, which remained its headquarters until 1966. It was to here that Jane Moneypenny reported for work each day.

Until the Intelligence Services Act of 1994, the SIS did not officially exist. It was funded by the Treasury out of the 'Secret Vote', and all employees were bound by the strict terms of the Official Secrets Act. The officers were recruited straight out of university – primarily Oxbridge – and from other branches of the armed or intelligence services, being chosen for their sharp minds and discretion. The new recruits were sent first on a six-month introductory course, based at Fort Monkton, the SIS's secret training facility in Gosport, Hampshire, where they were instructed in the theory and practice of tradecraft: how to recruit and run agents, deal with notional defections, and conduct and resist interrogation, as well as the technical side of surveillance and photographic techniques. After this was completed, they would work in London for a further year and a half before being deployed to a foreign station, where they fell nominally under the aegis of the local British embassy or high commission.

Administrative staff comprised mainly well-bred and independent girls with a genetic aptitude for keeping secrets. Jane Moneypenny was not unusual in having a colonial background. It was held at the time that this conferred on the girls a certain toughness and adaptability that served them well in their duties, particularly foreign postings. Most had some sort of social or familial connection with the intelligence services; they were subtly sounded out by recruiting agents before receiving letters inviting them to an interview with the Foreign Office. Jane Moneypenny was picked out by Miss Oster, the eponymous head of an elite secretarial college in South Kensington, who also served as a respected scout for the SIS. Jane had signed up for a secretarial course soon after arriving in London in the spring of 1953 – and qualified top of her class in half the usual time.

As my aunt recalled in her journal of that year, Miss Oster had summoned her into her study after the graduation ceremony. 'She said she had a position that might suit me. "Your father worked for the Colonial Office in Kenya, did he not?" she asked. When I nodded, she continued, "Very well, this is along similar lines. Remember to wear a hat and gloves. Good luck."' My aunt was handed a blue application form to fill in and the time and address of an appointment for the following day. She duly presented herself at a smart terraced house in Victoria. There was no identifying plate on the door, which was attended by an ageing commissionaire in a black uniform with red piping. He called the lift for her, and pushed the button for the fourth floor.

'A middle-aged woman wearing a grey suit and pearls was waiting for me,' she wrote on 26 June 1953.

She ushered me into a room and told me to wait for Miss Stega. There were about twenty chairs ranged in rows facing the fireplace; half were occupied by girls of about my age. Most wore low-heeled shoes and subdued lipstick. They came from good backgrounds – you could tell from their faces, from the way they sat, tidily yet with confidence. A few talked to each other with the air of acquaintances rather than friends. Debutantes, probably, but from a very different stable to those who had whooped and danced on the tables of the Muthaiga Club in Nairobi.

An imposing woman walked through the internal door to stand at a lectern. She introduced herself as Pamela Stega, and explained that each girl had been recommended by 'someone who knows us and in whom we trust. I don't know how much was explained to you, but I suspect little,' she went on to say. 'You know that you have come for an interview with the Foreign Office. More will be revealed to those of you who are chosen for our training course.'

My aunt was more amused than bemused by this. Her name was called for an individual interview, and she found herself sitting in a straight-backed chair opposite Miss Stega, who was reading from an open file. 'She appeared to know a lot about my early life and educational past,' Jane duly recorded that evening.

She asked me why I wished to join the Service. I told her that I needed a job, that I wanted to do something interesting and challenging, and that I supposed I wanted to belong to some sort of family. It appeared to satisfy her, as later, when all the interviews were over, mine was among the ten names that she read out and asked to stay behind.

It was only when the lift gate had clanged shut behind the others that Miss Stega went on. 'Now, how many of you know what you are doing here?' she asked. Only one hand was raised. 'I am about to trust your discretion. I have talked to many young ladies who have come into this very room and I am rarely wrong. I can sense if they are suited to our particular line of work. If you are to proceed and take up a position in our organisation, then I must warn you now that you are not permitted to tell anyone –

not your friends or your family – where you work. For we are a secret intelligence service and any knowledge that leaks out is a weapon in the arsenals of our enemies. That is a considerable responsibility. Before I go on, is there anyone who thinks now that they might be unable to handle that kind of pressure?'

Two girls, rather shame-faced, stood up and walked out. The rest of us were given a copy of the Official Secrets Act and a few minutes in which to skim through it, after which we were handed a piece of paper to sign, saying that we had understood the Act and agreed to be bound by it. We were instructed to return tomorrow morning. I was filled with excitement as I walked home. It was not only the prospect of an interesting job, but the avenues that it might open for me to find out what had happened to Pa. Surely, if I am going to find a clue to his death, it must be somewhere within the secret service?

Wednesday, 7th February

007 came back to work on Monday. I had been looking forward to seeing him, but Ross hadn't been exaggerating when he said he was in a dreadful state. Beneath the thin veneer of a Jamaican tan he looked grey. His eyes were puffy and bloodshot and seemed almost to be out of focus, and nothing could disguise the tremor in his hands. His whole posture was deflated. Still, he smiled and gave me a hug when I said how sorry I was about Tracy. 'Me too, Penny,' he said. 'Wish you could have met her. Helluva girl. The Old Man wants to see me?'

He was only in there for ten minutes, but walked out in the same dazed state in which he had entered and left without a goodbye. M buzzed through: 'Make an appointment for 007 with Molony,* please, Miss Moneypenny.' It was a positive sign. At least M hasn't decided on the Shrublands† route again – I am not sure Rafiki‡ would forgive me another quarter's supply of hand-ground wheatgerm and Pettifer's Treacle.

I met Mary for lunch in the park. We had to eat our sandwiches with gloves on. On a winter's day like this, I envy her sunny halo of perfect blonde hair – it must be a cheering sight in the glass on a dark morning. It is always in February that my equatorial genes start to nag. I feel an almost magnetic pull to the south. February in Maguga,§ the flame-trees in bloom, the days hot and the evenings cool enough to sit outside and watch the fireflies skip over the water-hole. I wonder whether the old acacia is still there? One day I must go back – I think, at last, I am nearly ready for it.

---

* Sir James Molony, prominent English neurologist of the time and nerve specialist by appointment to the secret service.
† Following an attack of lumbago in 1960, M spent ten days at Shrublands, a health farm on the south coast, returning with crystal-clear eyes and the proselytising zeal of the newly converted. He gave JM a detailed account of his regime there, and ordered her tins of treacle and wheatgerm, which she fed to her dog. The following week M dispatched Bond to Shrublands in an attempt to curb his overdrinking and excessive smoking. Despite being almost stretched to death by a SPECTRE agent on a traction machine, he returned to work full of energy. Both he and M, however, lapsed after several weeks.
‡ JM's iron-filing-grey standard poodle. While she was at work he was looked after by Maura, a widowed Polish émigré living in the basement flat of JM's building.
§ The Moneypennys' dairy farm – in a wooded area fifteen miles west of Nairobi.

Mary is worried about 007 too. He doesn't even greet her with his habitual 'Good morning, Goodnight.' She says he's hiding a bottle of whisky in his desk. What should she do? I advised nothing and told her about the appointment with Sir James. 'He sorted him out after his tussle with Rosa Klebb.* I'm sure he'll do the trick this time. Let's see how he is by the end of the month. In the meantime, why don't you call May† and ask how he's doing at home?'

Personally, I think he needs distraction – a tricky assignment to get entangled in. Then he wouldn't have time to think. I'm not sure, however, that M would risk him in this state. Although I would never describe him as a gambler, M always plays by the odds – it is as if he has an internal calculator, primed to assess human risk,

---

* Colonel Rosa Klebb, former head of Otdyel II, the department in charge of operations and executions for SMERSH. A toad-like figure, recipient of the Order of Lenin, probable lesbian. She sent an operative to assassinate Bond on the Orient Express, as part of a plot to humiliate the British secret service. Bond survived and kept his would-be murderer's appointment with Klebb in a Paris hotel room, where he evaded her attempts to kill him with a gun disguised as a telephone and poisoned knitting needles. He managed to overpower her and call for reinforcements. However, as she was being led away, she kicked him with shoes impregnated with the deadly fugu poison, extracted from the sex organs of the Japanese globe-fish. While he made a rapid physical recovery, he remained mentally fragile until sent on another assignment, on Molony's advice. Klebb died thirty-three days later, while in British custody.

† May Davidson, Bond's housekeeper and 'treasure', a widowed Scotswoman with steel-grey hair and a handsome closed face, who looked after his flat in a tree-lined square off the King's Road. Fiercely loyal, she had known Bond since childhood, when she cared for his dying uncle.

and it is only if the odds are in his favour that he will contemplate action. But I am not sure how human frailty stacks up in this particular computation.

Saturday, 10th February

Bloody Troop. That man is beyond irritating. He is a nosy, small-minded prig. Yesterday, he sent me a note asking me to come to see him immediately about a 'vetting matter'. As I rode down in the lift to the fourth floor, my irritation must have been written all over my face; as the door opened, Sergeant Fletcher took his good arm off the controls and patted me on the shoulder. 'Don't worry about him, miss. He's got nothing better to do than make everyone's life miserable.' Most people seem to have this reaction when they come into contact with Paymaster Captain Troop. I remember when 007 had to serve on one of M's Committees of Enquiry into Burgess* and Maclean,[†] under Troop's chairmanship. I never thought it was possible to hang quite so many colourful adjectives on to one person. After the third day, I was a little concerned that James was about to draw his Beretta and kneecap him. 'That man is so small-minded, he'd have trouble finding his way around in an ant-hill,' he told me. 'Why can't he stick to counting lavatory paper and keep out of serious business?'

---

* Guy Francis de Moncy Burgess (1911–63), Cambridge-educated former BBC broadcaster and MI6 agent. Defected to Moscow in May 1951.
† Donald Duart Maclean (1913–83), British diplomat and double agent. Defected with Burgess in 1951.

I knew well what he wanted to talk to me about – that agreement I signed the day I joined the firm, pledging to 'divulge personal relationships of consequence'. Family members, spouses and other 'close friends' fall under that definition. The irony escapes none of us: that despite not being officially permitted to reveal our true occupation to our nearest and dearest, we are nevertheless supposed to offer them up to some sort of vetting-board before we are allowed to become intimate. Most people ignore these rules; we all know the boundaries and few of us trip over them. It's a form of self-regulation; no one is going to sleep with an enemy agent if they can help it – and if they can't, they're not going to admit it. Troop, however, is a self-recruited border guard and he feels that his official job description of Head of Admin allows him to pry into our personal relationships – whenever he catches us having them.

It was my first experience of this sort of attention from him, and I was not looking forward to it. I knocked on the door of the glorified broom cupboard that serves as his office and he barked for me to enter. When he didn't offer me a chair, I sat down anyway. 'Miss Moneypenny. You are doubtless aware that you are bound to declare your close personal relationships to the Head of Security.' It wasn't a question. 'On the evening of 31st January, I observed you outside this office with a gentleman who is not employed here. I do not have to remind you, of all people, that the location and business of this building is top secret, a matter of national security.'

'I'm sorry, Captain Troop. It was an unforeseen occurrence. That gentleman does not know what it is I do here. I can assure you I am very discreet.'

'Nevertheless, I subsequently pulled your file from Records and you have not declared any personal relationships, apart from your sister' – he consulted a file in front of him – 'Miss Helena Moneypenny, and a Dr Frieda Greenfield.* Could you please tell me the name of that gentleman and the exact nature of your relationship with him?'

'I would rather not,' I replied, already irritated not only by Troop's manner, but by his complacent assumption that he held some sort of dominion over me.

'I must remind you that under Section 5, Clause 2b of the terms of employment, I am entitled to insist on your telling me.'

'Very well then, his name is Richard Hamilton and he is a friend of mine.'

'A close friend?'

'You could say that.'

'Occupation and place of employment?'

'For God's sake, is this necessary? Yes, I suppose to you it is. He is an architect and he works for Dexter Eldridge Partners on Great Portland Street.'

Troop sneered a little as he made a note in his small, spidery hand; architects, apparently, trot arm in arm with academics along the bottom of his list of acceptable

---

* JM's great-aunt, her maternal grandfather's younger sister. Former fellow of Girton College, Cambridge, eccentric and collector of antique glass. When JM and Helena came to London in 1953, following their mother's death, they spent nine months living with Great-Aunt Frieda and her canary, Caruso. After moving out, they remained in close contact with her, frequently spending Sunday evenings in her Kensington basement apartment, enjoying her famous chicken soup.

professions. He then drew a packet of Senior Service cigarettes from his breast pocket, took one out and lit it. I made a point of coughing into my handkerchief, which he ignored and ploughed on with his list of questions.

'When did you meet and under what circumstances?'

'Barcelona, in October. It was raining; he offered me half an umbrella.'

'His family?'

'I've never met them.'

'Education?'

'For heaven's sake! Next you'll be asking for his primary school report card. Is this really necessary?'

On and on it went until I started fantasising that 007 had shot him. I could have produced some sort of retrospective licence to cover for it. I can't believe anyone would have mourned his absence; it seems inconceivable that a man like him could have a wife or family. At last, he reached the end of his list. He closed my file. 'I will be checking these details and you will hear from me in due course,' he said.

'And until then, I suppose I must refrain from sleeping with him?'

For once, Troop seemed thrown. He cleared his throat. 'Please be careful what you say and do not bring him to the Office or its immediate environs again.'

Any thoughts I might have had of ending the relationship with R – and it is not something I have properly considered – have been put on hold; I would not give Troop the satisfaction.

Tuesday, 13th February

M's words to our Cousins have borne fruit. Yesterday, Scott came back to see the OM and to deliver a file entitled 'Operation Mongoose'. M ordered it to be copied ('Do it yourself please, Miss Moneypenny; Red Star, Top Secret') and circulated to the 'Cuba Group' as it has been named, as well as to the oo section. 'Make sure 007 reads his, please. I want him in on these meetings. He is no longer on convalescence leave.'

Having been in on the birth of the Cuba Group, I was interested to read it. It did not disappoint. As M had suspected, Kennedy was not prepared to live with Castro as a neighbour. He needed to avenge the Bay of Pigs humiliation and was prepared to go to considerable – in my opinion, frequently ludicrous – lengths to do so. In November of last year, they launched Operation Mongoose,* a creeping campaign of destabilisation aimed at stimulating the anti-Castro Cubans (the same ones, presumably, who failed to stand up and be counted last April) into revolution. This time, the methods would apparently be more 'subtle' – if assassinating the President and destroying their crops could, by any stretch of the imagination, be described as subtle.†

---

* The name of the operation is not, as widely believed, a reference to Kipling's Rikki Tikki Tavi. Instead, it was initially conceived as a bluff. The CIA assigned a two-letter designation (a diaph) to every country in the world, and the code name for any operation in that country began with the appropriate diaph. In this case, seeking to confuse, the Americans chose to use the diaph of a country on the other side of the world from Cuba: Thailand or, in CIA doublespeak, MO. From there, 'Mongoose' was chosen at random.

† The proposed methods of assassination included drinks spiked with poisoned pills, booby-trapped seashells, a wetsuit infected with

Sometimes, I feel as if I'm working on the set of a boy's adventure yarn. It's exciting and easy to get completely wrapped up and involved in what we're doing, but if one was to take a step back on to the side-lines, one could be forgiven for thinking that it all stemmed from the racing imagination of a tuppenny novelist.

In Operation Bugle Call, for instance – and this is swathed in such impenetrable top secrecy that I can only imagine that they are taking it very seriously – 1,000 balloons are to be dropped over Cuba per month. Between them, they will carry up to 4 million leaflets and a wide variety of 'novelty items, such as "gusano libre" (the free worm – a twist on the name coined by Castro to describe those opposed to the revolution) badges, toy balloons in the

---

deadly germs – to be presented as a gift to the Cuban leader – and poisoned cigars, as well as the relatively prosaic high-powered rifle with telescopic sights. In addition, Mongoose detailed plans for political, economic and psychological warfare. Agent strength was to be built up, with Cubans in place, with Spanish-speaking CIA operatives and with possible third-country sources, particularly from those countries with a diplomatic presence in Havana. The main aim was to organise and incite small bands of anti-Castro Cubans to rebellion, as well as to undertake sabotage activities. The sugar harvest was a key target – attacking cane fields, mills, sacking and transport – as well as the contamination of essential imports into the country.

By February 1962, the Americans had already begun to tighten export controls and were embarking on what was called 'psychological exploitation of actions undertaken by the Project', to 'encourage world perception of the Cuban people as a "David", battling against the "Goliath" as represented by the Communist regime' ('Operation Mongoose: Program Review by the Chief of Operations, Edward Lansdale', Washington, DC, 18 January 1962).

shape of the "gusano libre", small plastic phonograph records, stickers, etc.' Could balloons and plastic worms seriously foment a movement capable of overthrowing a larger-than-life revolutionary?

Reading between the lines – and from Bill's reports of his conversations with the OM – our position is that we will support the Yanks in intelligence-gathering but, as things currently stand, are unwilling to contribute active assistance to the wetter side of any operation to destabilise the Castro regime. Somehow, I have problems imagining the typing pool being deployed to stuff party packs with toy worms, in order to overthrow a leader who, until a year or so ago, was one of our allies.* How the battlefield has changed! Still, M wants to be kept abreast of developments, in case Redland† gets involved in some way. To that end, Agent Scott has been appointed our official liaison officer, with a brief to be transparent.

Thursday, 15th February

I think at last I have a promising lead to Pa's disappearance. M returned from lunch at Blades‡ with an Australian named Sydney Cotton, a wartime chum. From the barely

---

* When Cuba was led by the corrupt Fulgencio Batista, Castro – still an undeclared Communist – was seen as a potential saviour and given support by the West.

† Jargon for the Soviet sphere.

‡ Private card club on Park Street, St James's. Formerly known as the Savoir Vivre (est. 1774), renamed Blades 1778. Membership was restricted to 200, with a £100 subscription for new members, and an annual fee of £50. There were permanent tables for high-stakes bridge,

perceptible glitter in his left eye, I suspected they had shared a bottle or two of that infernal Infuriator,* which, according to 007, has more in common with gasoline than with Château Lafite – I tried it once, just to see whether he was exaggerating. As they walked in, M said, as is his habit, 'Any messages, Miss Moneypenny?' Cotton stopped short. 'Moneypenny?' he asked. 'Any relation to . . .' At which M ushered him into his office. I'm sure it had something to do with Pa. I have always suspected that M must know the truth, but he would never give it up to me. When Cotton left, he smiled at me and I got the sense he was trying to convey sympathy. One gets these sorts of feelings round here; it is as if our antennae are permanently attuned to undercurrents.

It wasn't hard to find out where he was staying. With visiting war veterans it's normally The Senior,† and indeed one telephone call confirmed this. I cancelled dinner with R. Luckily I had brought my ear-rings and heels with me and I managed to slip them on and get out without the OM seeing me – it wasn't the moment for another frown at the 'womanly adornments which distract attention from the task at hand'.‡

---

poker and backgammon. Its kitchen and cellar were renowned, newspapers were ironed daily, and all banknotes were mint.

* M's usual tipple, an Algerian red wine of such inferior quality that the wine committee of Blades wouldn't have it on the wine list. Known as 'The Infuriator' in the Navy, for its propensity to send over-indulgers into a rage.

† The Services Club, 51 Piccadilly, favourite among serving and former high-ranking officers from the three recognised armed services.

‡ Other bees in M's metaphorical bonnet included misuse of service resources (primarily human), beards, beatniks, unpunctual trains,

I got away on time at six, for a change. I made my way to Piccadilly and found a small café with windows looking on to the club's entrance. For nearly an hour, I watched a stream of immaculately dressed gentlemen, polished shoes and umbrellas, walk up and down the steps and in and out of the heavy oak outer door. My subject, as I had begun to think of him, would be bound to leave at some point for drinks. They always did.

It was close on seven when he came out, tipped his hat at the doorman and turned left towards Piccadilly Circus. He wasn't hard to follow, he must have been a few inches over six feet tall, and he walked with the upright bearing of a soldier. It was fun, back to my training-course days.* When he got to the lights of Piccadilly Circus, he turned right and into the American Bar at the Criterion. Perfect. I gave him a few minutes to deposit his coat and umbrella at the door, then followed. He was sitting at the bar with a drink in his hand. I slipped into a booth, as surreptitiously as I could, my back facing his. I ordered a gin and

---

people who were totally bilingual, and anyone trying to exert pressure through family relationships with Cabinet ministers.

* New recruits to the administrative division of the secret service were put through a two-month training course. Mornings were devoted to traditional secretarial skills, afternoons reserved for more specialised training. One afternoon JM was given the task of following a man to see where he dropped off his secret message. She waited on the steps of St Martin-in-the-Fields until she identified her prey, a bowler-hatted man carrying a newspaper and umbrella, then shadowed him for half an hour until he made the drop – in the gentlemen's lavatory at Charing Cross station. She received a special commendation for this stage of her training activities.

tonic and got out my compact. Angled right, I could see him clearly.

My chance came when he got up and asked for directions to the gents. I carried my drink to a stool just two away from his and tried to look as if I had just arrived. When he came back to his seat, he glanced at me, then again. 'Hello, aren't you Miss Moneypenny?' he asked, with the unmistakable soft twang of an Australian accent. 'Why, Commander Cotton, what a coincidence,' I replied, looking surprised. 'I came here to meet a friend, but she left a message at the door to say she had to cancel. I couldn't face the rain quite yet, so I thought I'd treat myself to a drink. I love this old place, don't you? It was one of my father's favourites.'

'Ah Hugh, yes. I knew your father, you know. Good man. Terrible shame. Did we ever find out exactly what happened?'

I felt simultaneous euphoria and disappointment: I was right, he had known Pa, but not, unfortunately, his fate. Still, it was the best lead I've had in years and he might yet prove to be a link in the chain to the truth. Gently, I managed to steer the conversation around to his wartime activities. 'I flew reconnaissance for you guys. Special-ops stuff. Hush-hush, you know. Tell you the truth, I miss it. I'm finding civvie life a bit on the boring side. That's why I came over here, to catch up with old chums, relive a few adventures.' He was on his third large whisky and soda that I'd seen and I was about to ask where my father fitted in, when he stood up and excused himself. 'I've got dinner at Blades. Matter of fact another colleague of your father's. I think he was meant to be on Ruthless with him.' I was left hanging. Ruthless? What could that be? A ship? An operation?

I must find out who he was dining with. Porterfield* will tell me if I play my cards right.

Sunday, 18th February

A lovely day with R in Bath. Our relationship – if that is an appropriate description – appears to have pulled back from the brink. We caught the early train, went for a long walk around the city, then drank rather too much wine at lunch. We steered clear of talking about anything serious, but still had plenty to say. It was just on a few, fleeting occasions I got the sense that he wanted to tell me something. His eyes would go suddenly serious, his face blank – before he pulled himself back. They were momentary – perhaps I imagined them? Or perhaps he, as much as I, wants to paper over any cracks, to hold on to what we have without looking forwards or back?

I didn't mention the vetting and he doesn't seem to have noticed any unusual enquiries about him. When it's like this, there is no other person I would rather spend time with.

Wednesday, 21st February

007 came up, hoping to grab Bill for lunch, but he was cloistered with the OM. 'Come on, James,' I said, sweeping my sandwich into the drawer. 'I've got no plans. You can have

---

* Rodney Porterfield, butler at Blades, served under M as chief petty officer on one of his last commands.

lunch with me instead.' I had my coat and hat on before he could demur. We walked to a small restaurant in Pimlico, and no sooner had he sat down than he ordered a double vodka and a bottle of 1953 Château Talbot. 'You'll join me, Penny?' When I shook my head, he shrugged. 'Oh well, I'll have to drink it all myself. Can't let good wine go to waste.'

'How are you doing, James? Really?' I looked into those normally clear grey-blue eyes and could see nothing but a faint mistiness between the lattice of red capillaries. 'To tell you the truth, Penny, it's pretty bloody. I've been doing everything I can to try to forget it, but all I can think of is her excited expression when she talked about our future together. You know, for the very first time, I was prepared to give all this up for her. I'd have tried not to, of course, but if it came to it, and I had a straight choice, I would have chosen Tracy. I love the job, of course I do, but one can't keep on living like a cowboy for ever. I looked into her lifeless eyes and saw a whole damn funeral procession of people I've killed, starting with that Japanese cipher expert in New York, then the Norwegian double agent, half a handful of Mr Big's* hoodlums in Harlem and Florida and a score more, including the big man himself, when the boat blew up in Jamaica, right on through to Blofeld's apes on top of that bloody mountain. I've lost count, and that's only the ones I've had a direct hand in. How about Vesper Lynd?† Or Jill

---

* The most powerful black criminal of his time, and a member of the inner echelons of SMERSH. He was eaten by a shark after Bond had blown up his boat.
† Former PA to Head of S (Soviet Union), assigned to 007 – against his wishes – at Royale-les-Eaux in 1952 to aid him in his task to bring down SMERSH agent 'Le Chiffre'. Beautiful, with black hair, blue eyes and 'splendid protuberances, back and front' (Ian Fleming, *Casino*

Masterton?* Or Shaun Campbell?† I as surely signed his death warrant as shot him myself. What's the difference between me killing them and them killing Tracy? It's all part of the same game.'

I didn't say anything. What could I say that would make him feel better? That he's on the side of the angels and they deserved what they got? Where did that leave Tracy? That he was making the world a safer place for the rest of us? That he'd saved many times the number of lives that he'd taken? That we needed and valued and loved him? I let him rant on.

'Then I get back to this bloody Cuba stuff – the Americans meddling in other people's business. How many men died at the Bay of Pigs? How many more will go in Mongoose? It's anybody's guess. Maybe they're right; God knows I'm no fan of the Reds, but it's not always that cut and dried. I remember when Castro was our friend and we had an agent there who was one of his men and we couldn't get enough of him.

Royale (London, 1953)). She committed suicide while staying with Bond in a small coastal hotel, where he was recuperating from injuries sustained when he was tortured by Le Chiffre. He was distraught at her death. In her suicide note, she explained that she had been blackmailed into working as a double agent for the KGB. She took her own life to escape from her forced treachery.

* PA to the millionaire gold trader Auric Goldfinger. Bond took her back with him to New York as a 'hostage', after discovering that she had been helping her employer to cheat at cards. Goldfinger took his revenge by arranging for her to be killed by total immurement in gold paint.

† Agent Z2 – captured after infiltrating Blofeld's mountain hideaway. Recognising Bond, there under cover as Sir Hilary Bray, he appealed to him for help. Rather than betray his own cover, Bond pretended not to know Z2, who was summarily executed by Blofeld's men.

Now, suddenly, he's supping with the Devil. It's this bloody line between good and evil that seems to be getting a damn sight too fuzzy these days.'

He called the waiter over to order a double brandy. 'One for you, Penny?' 'No thank you,' I replied, 'and James, do you really think it's wise?' He took my hand and looked into my eyes. 'Thank you, Penny. I know I can always rely on you to have my better interests at heart, but I'm quite all right. Now, tell me, what's happening in your life?'

In an attempt to try to cheer him up, I gave him a blow-by-near-blow account of my confrontation with Troop. He began to look a little less miserable and even squeezed out a chuckle at my description of Troop's face when I outlined the nature of my relationship with R. 'Lucky man, this R. Do you love him?' he asked, at the end. 'Because if you do, either give all this up and marry him – or let him go. Don't try to combine love and this kind of work. It can only end in tears.' He picked up the wine bottle and poured the last few drops into his glass. 'Another bottle?'

Saturday, 24th February

I went into work this morning, on the pretence of catching up with the minutes of the last Cuba Group meeting. In truth, I was almost done anyway and after less than an hour had finished the typing and distributed copies to everyone on the circulation list. Then I wandered down to Records on the first floor, and after half an hour of chat with Alfred Brewis – the sole male presence in a stable normally full of neighing fillies – said I would be happy to hold the fort while he popped out for a sandwich. Saturdays are inevitably quiet and he didn't need much persuading. As soon as he was gone, I dived straight into the stacks and located Sydney Cotton's file. It was thick – and, as I discovered, he had led an extraordinary life. Born in Australia, he came to England and enlisted in the Royal Naval Air Service at the outbreak of the First War. He flew Channel patrols and invented a new, weather-proof flying suit before being reprimanded for insubordination and relieved of his command. The Australian Flying Corps rejected him on the basis of his record of having a 'difficult temperament' and deemed him 'unsuitable for employment in uniformed service'. Instead, he went into private business, in the new field of colour photography, and it was as a photographer that he became involved in the RAF – flying reconnaissance for British intelligence illicitly across occupied Europe in the early years of the Second War.

My eye was caught by the page detailing his work for Naval Intelligence in 1939/40. I'm fairly certain that Pa was involved in intelligence, as so many of his fellow Navy reservists were. It's the only logical explanation for his strangely anodyne service record. That was what was making my investigations so difficult. Cotton's acquaintance with Pa seemed to confirm this – there was no other mention in his file of naval work.

I was patting the file back into place when I felt someone approaching behind me. It was Dorothy Fields,* in her trademark little cherry-topped hat, working as usual. 'Why, Jane,

---

* Research officer (latterly senior agent-runner) and in 1962 one of only three women employed by the SIS outside administrative duties. After her retirement from the service, in 1985, she was awarded a peerage, and became an active member of the House of Lords.

I didn't expect to see you down here,' she said. 'Slumming it, are you?' I think I regained my composure in time, although it was hard to be sure; Dorothy's sharp eyes miss little.

Wednesday, 28th February

There's something queer afoot in the Office. I don't know what it is yet, but the OM has been unusually gruff without apparent reason. He shuts himself in his office for hours at a time with piles of old files. He has been to Downing Street twice in the last week and once to King Charles Street [the Foreign Office]. Then, yesterday, he called each of the section heads up to see him, one by one. Only Dorothy Fields stayed with him throughout.

Bill seems as much at a loss over what is going on as I am. When I asked him, he just shook his head and said, 'Our's not to reason why . . .' The second half of that phrase is dreadfully apt in this office.

Having exhausted this avenue of enquiry, I descended to the powder room. The PV* at six in the evening usually has a line on Office events long before they become official. But here, too, I found bewilderment, though most of the personal secretaries of section heads had also felt the tension in the air. 'CS [Chief of Soviet Section] has been buried under Red Star files for most of the day,' said Pamela, adjusting her beret in front of the mirror. 'He looked almost guilty when I brought in the signals.'

---

* The Powder Vine, or PV, was the informal gossip network among the secretaries and personal assistants, whose centre of power was the first-floor ladies' lavatory.

'CME [Chief of Middle East] has been on the scrambler to Beirut ever since he got back from seeing M,' added Janet d'Auvergne beside her. 'He told me to go home early, that he would finish up.'

'CSA [Chief of Southern Africa] left the office after his interview and I haven't seen him since,' said Amber. 'But then we all know he does that from time to time.'

'There's been a run on files over the last couple of days, that's for sure,' added a pretty young brunette from Records. 'We've been running up and down the stairs like nobody's business.'

'CNE [Chief of Northern Europe] looks as if he's been hit on the head with a ten-ton weight,' said Raine. 'I'm really worried about him. Jane, you must know what's going on. Is it really bad?'

I was forced to admit that I was as much in the dark as they were. At which point the door opened to admit Dorothy. We all fell silent as she went into a cubicle. When she came out, Janet nudged me, but I just continued washing my hands. If anyone knows, it's Dorothy, but despite using the same facilities, she's not part of the Powder Vine and she wouldn't appreciate being asked by any one of us.

I've only just managed to talk to Porterfield about Sydney Cotton's dining companion. I was cancelling M's lunch reservation and asked P whether I could talk to him about something confidentially. He told me to telephone back when he was off duty. So this evening, at half past six, I spoke to him. He did indeed remember Commander Cotton, of course. He had dined on the evening of the 15th with another tall man. 'I hadn't seen him before, Miss M,' he told me. 'But he was very much the gentleman. Well-cut suit, green eyes, fair hair brushed back. Definitely a military man. I'm just trying to recall his name. Something double-barrelled. A Commander too. They ate Beef Wellington and drank two bottles of our best claret – a '53 Château Calon-Ségur. Mind you, I wouldn't be surprised if it wasn't the Australian who consumed the bulk of it. Yes, that's it. A Commander Derring-Jones. I knew I'd remember it.' At that, P seemed to realise what he'd been saying and begged me not to mention his indiscretion. 'It's just that I feel I know you, Miss M. We've spoken so often now, I feel as if I do. And I would do anything for the Admiral.' I thanked him profusely and gave him my word.

Now I need to get back into Records to try to find Derring-Jones.

March

To adapt the well-known saying, 'You can take the girl out of Africa, but you can never take Africa out of the girl.' That definitely held true for my aunt, and also for my mother, though perhaps less so. The stories they told of their childhood in Kenya were tightly woven into the fabric of my own childhood. I would ask to hear them again and again: 'Aunt Jane, tell me about the time Grampa shot the wounded warthog,' or '. . . the time you got lost in the bush and were found by the Masai.' To a great degree, when I was younger, at least, I felt as though I had lived those same experiences, alongside my mother and aunt.

I can picture them now, sitting around our kitchen table in Cambridge, talking about the family farm near Maguga, their eyes shining a little more brightly, their laughs louder and longer. I remember my aunt once trying to describe to me what Africa meant to her: the sense it gave her of feeling more alive, as if her nerve endings were more exposed; of each day lasting more minutes and being clothed in richer colours. 'You feel in touch with the elements,' she told me. 'Every day you tread closer to the line between life and death than you ever would over here. It's not always pleasant. Sometimes it's terrifying and tragic, but it's impossible to feel nothing.' I made her promise me that one day we would go to Africa together; I wanted to see the farm where she and my mother grew up, the land they both loved so much. In 1988, thirty-five years after she had left, she fulfilled her promise and I was truly fortunate to be with her in Kenya as she retrod the footsteps of her childhood.

Jane Vivien Moneypenny was born in Nairobi General Hospital on 9 August 1931, and named after her paternal grandmother. Her parents doted on her, and recorded every detail of her early life in an annotated photograph album. There are pictures of her sitting on a beach examining shells, crawling on the floor grunting like a lion or barking like a baboon, and asleep in the dog's basket on the front veranda of their palm-roofed farmhouse. They took her everywhere, and treated her from the start like a mini-adult. On a camping trip down the Rift Valley, when Jane was a little over two years old and Irene pregnant with my mother, they were charged by an elephant, who skidded to a stop a bare fifteen yards from them – and Jane only giggled. She was a practical child, always outside, rolling in the sand, eating insects, happy on her own or with one of the farm hands or the women who worked in the house.

She was fiercely protective of her younger sister from the start. Even when Helena was too young to accompany her on adventures, Jane would make sure she was being well looked after, before disappearing into the bush to track wildlife. They saw other children infrequently. Their mother, Irene, did not care for socialising, and, apart from close friends and colleagues, preferred to stay at home with the family or to spend time with the black Kenyans she worked with, rather than venture into colonial society.

On the occasions when they did go into town – to swim at the Muthaiga Club, or for tennis parties at the homes of their father's government friends – the Moneypenny girls were noticeably more wild than their contemporaries, their skin more tanned, their deep-chestnut hair tangled and streaked with blonde by the sun.

When Jane turned six, her parents recognised the need for some kind of schooling, but, instead of driving her to the white schools in the suburbs, Irene organised for a retired teacher, Mrs Bisby, to come out to the farm three mornings a week, to teach her – and later Helena too – and whoever of the staff's children happened to be around and interested. The girls could already read, and did so voraciously. The house was full of books, and Hugh, in particular, loved to read to them – mainly long stories meant for older ears. Adventure books were their favourites: *Swallows and Amazons*, *Tom Sawyer* and *Kidnapped* were read over and over again. Hugh would also invent stories, based on the animal characters that lived in the bush around them. He taught the children to understand how the animals thought as well as acted. They would go for long walks, and he would point out clues to what had been passing through and when. From an early age, Jane developed a healthy regard for the wildlife, but she was rarely afraid: if you could read what they were thinking, they held no threat.

They loved their home. It was not a large farm, by Kenyan standards, but it was fertile and beautifully situated, on a ridge, with views down into the forests of Maguga on one side, and across to the great escarpment on the other. It was a happy place; the Moneypennys treated their staff with respect and kindness, and this was repaid with loyalty. Many of their workers, both inside and out, were with them from before the girls were born until the farm was eventually sold.

In early 1939 Hugh persuaded Irene that the girls would benefit from a more formal education and from the company of children their own age. They were enrolled at a primary school on the main road to Nairobi. Both took to it perfectly equably – Jane was a natural leader and soon had many friends – though they continued to maintain that they had learned more with Mrs Bisby.

Jane was devastated by the news that Hugh was to go back to England for the war. Several entries in her diaries recall the emptiness she felt the day he took her for a long walk around the farm and explained what he would be doing and why he was going. 'Look at what we have here, the freedom to go where we wish and live the kind of life we want,' he told her. 'I need to go and make sure that we – and others – continue to have those basic rights.' He promised to write every week, and asked her to look after Helena and keep an eye on Irene.

I remember Aunt Jane describing her father's departure. The whole family took the train down to Mombasa to see him off. He was wearing his naval uniform and carrying a stick made out of wood from the farm, which Josiah, the headman, had carved for him. It was his prized possession, and he waved it at them from the ship as it gave a last hoot and sailed off towards England.

Irene handled his departure with a breezy energy, which soon crumpled into fear and despair. Soon Jane had taken over many of the household duties; she would come home from school and talk to the farm hands, before cooking supper and putting her sister to bed. Often she would stay up late into the night talking to her mother, in a simultaneous effort to distract and reassure. She grew up quickly.

They lived for Hugh's letters. The girls would race each other to the postbox at the gate of the farm to see if one had arrived, and when one had they would shout for Irene and the three of them would go and sit on the grass under Hugh's favourite tree to read it. He was an entertaining writer, managing to make his life in England sound like an adventure – and to play down the perils of war. He made frequent mention of his new friends: Peter, Ian, Patrick, Euan and Sydney, as well as 'the warthog', their private code for Winston Churchill, at that time Hugh's ultimate boss as First Lord of the Admiralty. He made war sound like a boys' adventure, rather than the serious business of grown men.

He never told them exactly what he was doing, though there were hints. He sent one postcard from Madrid, another from Lisbon. Then, in October 1940, a letter arrived which, though cheerful in tone, was more serious in content, telling of the big adventure he was shortly to embark on. He wrote special messages to each of them. To Jane, he said, 'Remember, you are my eagle – please spread your wings and keep flying.' She carefully glued that letter into the front of her new soft leather journal.

Thursday, 1st March

I'm worried about 007. His depression doesn't appear to be lifting. He arrives at the office late and leaves early. According to Mary, on several occasions he has failed altogether to return from lunch and although he signs off on his files, I suspect he isn't really reading them. I know that M has progressed beyond sympathy and into irritation. Last week he summoned 007, and by the time he left, the OM was definitely angry. As the door buzzed open, I heard him saying, 'There's only a certain amount of slack I can cut you, 007. This is your last chance – next time I'll be forced to take your number away permanently. Miss Moneypenny, please ask 006* to come up straight away.'

That must have cut 007 to the quick. He's proud to be head of the oo section and would normally have hated the idea of another agent being given his assignment. 006 looked happy. Although they get on well, there's a tangible rivalry, a hangover from their service days. I know 006 gives 007 a bit of gyp about being a 'chocolate sailor' – because he was RNVR† in the war, while 006 was a marine commando. It's good-natured, of course, as 007's bravery has never been in doubt – rather the reverse – and his war record for daring missions is unparalleled. But the rivalry between them is definitely there. M does nothing to discourage it – he believes it gives them an edge.

According to Mary, 007 spent the rest of the day closeted in his office, probably with the whisky bottle. When 006 passed by, James said, 'Good luck, old boy. Watch out for

---

* Major Jack Giddings, born Camberley 1925, ex-Royal Marine commando and number two to Bond in the oo section. Blond hair, green eyes, expert in unarmed combat, with a workmanlike grasp of spoken and written Russian.

† Royal Naval Volunteer Reserve – also known as the Wavy Navy, after the wavy gold stripes on the officers' sleeves, which, it was sometimes noted, made them look like the man in the long-running Black Magic advertisements, giving rise to the flippant sobriquet of 'chocolate sailor'.

snipers in the second-floor window of the office building on the corner of Wilhelmstrasse, but otherwise you shouldn't have any trouble. I'll buy you a drink when you get back.' 006 flew that evening to Tempelhof. He goes over the day after tomorrow and, if all goes to plan, will be back across Zimmerstrasse with 625 by the end of the week.*

It is his first time across since the Wall went up. 007 has been once before, which was probably why M wanted him to go this time. It might have done him the power of good. He's going to have to take the next job the OM dangles at him, otherwise it's the long corridor for him and I'm pretty sure he would not survive that.

He has now spent nearly a decade in the 00 section, by far the longest-serving agent. I think the average is about three years – by which time they have normally burnt out, or worse. The pressure of living on the edge of death

---

* On the morning of 13 August 1961, Berliners had awoken to the presence of huge rolls of barbed wire strung around the ninety-six-mile border separating East from West Berlin. Over the days and weeks that followed, a permanent concrete wall was erected, which would become one of the most familiar landmarks in twentieth-century history. Much of the Berlin Wall's eastern side ran along Zimmerstrasse. Known as the 'death zone', it was patrolled by guards based in the 293 watch towers and 57 bunkers built to check the escape of refugees bent on reaching the West. From 1961 until the wall was dismantled in November 1989, a total of 192 people were killed trying to cross the border.

The 00 agents were routinely assigned as escorts across the border both for defectors from the Eastern Bloc and for British agents who had been undercover in the East. This involved either traversing the stretch of cleared land on either side of the Wall, often dodging bullets from snipers concealed in office buildings in East Berlin, or smuggling their charges through the checkpoints by vehicle.

must be profoundly affecting. I can hardly count the number of occasions on which he has nearly not returned from a mission. Even in the last year or so, he's been up against Blofeld twice and lost his wife as a direct result of his job.

And for what? A salary that is merely comfortable* and the prospect of early retirement on a meagre pension, if indeed he lives that long? Add that to the trauma he must have suffered from seeing so many people he knew and cared about blown to oblivion – indeed, having to kill others in the name of duty (I have lost count of the number of CFFs [Collateral Fatality Forms] I have had to file with the Ministry on 007's behalf) – and surely you have a recipe for breakdown? We shouldn't be surprised that he is suffering from some sort of extended hangover caused by excess death. Yet we can't afford to make too many allowances for it, for too long.

Sunday, 4th March

I can't bear it. Another weekend with R has disintegrated into conflict and accusations. I cannot believe it. On Friday night, I opened the door to Ennismore Gardens† and was immediately enveloped in the glorious aroma of simmering

---

* In 1962, a principal officer in the Civil Service received a salary of £2,000 p.a.
† Shortly after joining the service, using her share of the proceeds from the sale of the family farm in Kenya, JM bought a small, two-bedroom flat on the top floor of an elegant conversion in Ennismore Gardens, close to Hyde Park and the Royal Albert Hall.

onions. R appeared in the kitchen doorway, saying that he had borrowed my spare key from Maura and was going to cook dinner tonight. At the time, it was a wonderful surprise. Steak with béarnaise sauce and French beans, followed by baked apple with cinnamon and cream. There is no way I could ever concoct anything quite so delicious. I ate myself into a stupor – to the point where I was almost ready to pledge my life to him. Then we sat in front of the fire, listening to Brahms, until my eyes drooped. At midnight, when I woke, he was gone.

Yesterday morning, we packed Rafiki into the Mini* and drove to Henley, parked and walked for miles along the river until we found an unspoilt inn. We ate pub sandwiches and drank cider and it wasn't until the walk back that R asked me, quite out of the blue, whether I was committed to my work, if I ever thought about leaving. I was surprised, and answered that I hadn't. He looked at me for a minute, then changed the subject, asking about my family and what it was like to grow up in Kenya.

Perhaps because I was relieved to have left the work issue, I told him more about myself than I have ever revealed to anyone. We walked for hours and I talked about Pa and his disappearance, about Ma and her dreadful, painful end.† He listened quietly as I berated myself for

---

* To mark her thirtieth birthday, JM bought a second-hand red Mini, which she kept in a garage in Ennismore Mews.

† Irene Greenfield Moneypenny, born in 1904 in Liverpool, only child of two doctors, both émigrés from Latvia. She read medicine at Girton College, Cambridge, and while there met and fell in love with Hugh Moneypenny. While he was at naval college, she qualified and worked as a resident at a London teaching hospital. She continued to practise as a doctor when they moved to Kenya. When JM was born,

having failed to warn her about the real and imminent perils of Mau Mau, then put his arm around me and held me tight. 'Do you hate Kenya?' he asked. I had to stop and think for a second, before replying that yes, I did, probably to about the same degree that I loved it. I started telling him what it was about Africa that held me captive – the natural beauty, the huge skies that make you feel as if you can see heaven, the sense of time drifting by instead of charging away from you at full tilt as it seems to here. Once I started talking, I couldn't stop. I told him about the game that lived wild on the farm, about Evie, the meerkat, who would follow me everywhere, and about how we had been adopted by an orphan warthog – Pa had shot his mother after she turned on our dog – which we had christened Winnie, because he reminded Pa of Churchill. And I was suddenly filled with a longing to be back there. If the uprising hadn't happened, would I be there now? I might be following in Ma's footsteps, trying to help the Africans to help themselves – instead of raping and pillaging their God-given wealth, which is what the majority of our settler 'friends' seemed intent on doing.

R stayed quiet as I talked on and on. We drove back to London and after a cup of tea, I once again fell asleep on the sofa. The long walk, reliving those memories, had left

---

she gave up her job at the hospital to become involved in developing rural health initiatives, throwing herself into her work with the same passion she exhibited in all areas of her life. A fluent Swahili and Kikuyu speaker, she felt more at home in the tribal villages than at the Muthaiga Club in Nairobi, where, despite her husband's popularity, she still felt sidelined by her Jewish origins. She was at times a slightly distracted mother, but loved her daughters unreservedly. She was killed in the massacre at Lari on 26 March 1953.

me exhausted. But then I woke up with a start; I don't know why, I couldn't have been asleep for long. R wasn't in the room, and when I turned towards the kitchen I noticed a sliver of light under the study door. Thinking that perhaps he was reading in the study, waiting for me to wake up, I opened the door quietly. He was sitting behind my desk with, on either side, the bottom two drawers open, as if he was searching them. The colour drained visibly from his face as he quickly closed them. 'I was, er, looking for your passport,' he said. 'I needed the number. I wanted to take you away somewhere, as a surprise. Needed your passport number . . .'

We both knew he was lying. I just didn't have the energy to confront him. I suppose he was searching for clues about my work, not that he would have had any success at home. We have been happy; why does he have such a desperate urge to know more? He left soon after, saying he had work to do.

Wednesday, 7th March

I ran into that bloody Troop today. The timing couldn't have been much worse. At first I thought he was going to ignore me. I was all in favour of this, but after a minute's thought, it seemed odd. So I inched across to him. 'Captain Troop, hello. How's your vetting going?'

He gave a grunt and said, 'The wheels of the investigation are in motion. We are pursuing various angles. That is all I can say to you.'

Despite what had happened at the weekend, I was taken aback. I hadn't seriously thought it would take more than a minute to clear R. I searched through my memory for anything that might appear suspicious, but there was nothing. From what he had told me, he had a 'normal' upbringing; his parents were both teachers in Dulwich. He qualified at the Architectural Association. He likes travelling, loves his work, had nearly married a few years back, but it fell through at the eleventh hour. He has no apparent political bent – nor even, so far as I can tell, interest. But since the vetting procedure normally takes only a few days, it sounded as if Troop had found something not quite right. I can't imagine what it might be.

Friday, 9th March

I got back to my desk at lunchtime to find 007 pacing up and down the room. 'Penny, what's the latest on Blofeld? M's not telling me anything and I need to know. I think about that bloody man night and day. I can't bear the idea of him getting away with this. He's laid down the gauntlet and I can't just turn away like some kind of weakling. What am I doing, wasting time with this Cuba stuff and all the infernal paperwork when I could be out there looking for him?'

I reminded him gently that he had threatened to resign when he was assigned full-time to the search for Blofeld the last time he went to ground, after the Thunderball affair,* and had begged M for a return to active duty from 'routine police work'. 'This time you've turned down a mission and

---

* Blofeld orchestrated the hijacking of a NATO plane carrying two atomic missiles, which he attempted to ransom for £100 million. He was foiled by the combined efforts of 007 and CIA agent Felix Leiter.

want to go after him. I assure you that we've alerts out to every station and are doing all we can to track him down.'

'Do we have any idea where he is?'

I said he should really ask Bill about it. 'As far as I know, after Istanbul, he seems to have made his way to Mexico – we had a tentative ID from one of our agents in Mexico City, who thought he saw him walking around the medical district. It would make sense for him to change his physical identity again. We never found out where he had it done last time, but from what you said, they made a good job of it.'

James nodded. 'Yes, it was extraordinary,' he agreed. 'Even down to his ear-lobes.'*

'Well, we've had all our people in Mexico City working on it full-time, talking to all the plastic surgeons in town. The trouble is, of course, that most of them are working on the grey market, servicing American women who don't want to pay New York prices – as well as the occasional old Nazi on his way to a new life in Argentina, so they're not exactly talkative. Then, three days ago, we had another suspected sighting in Mexico, this one at the airport, boarding a flight to Madrid, but by the time we got the report, the plane had already arrived and the passengers disembarked. The Madrid station has been alerted, but so far, no news. Please, James, leave it to M. He wants Blofeld as much as you do.'

---

* At the time of the Thunderball episode, Blofeld had weighed twenty stone and had a pale complexion, black crew-cut hair, small eyes, the pupils completely encircled by white, a thin mouth and long, thin hands and feet. When Bond re-encountered him in Switzerland, he was a lithe twelve stone, with long, silvery-white hair, dark green eyes and full lips. Only his hands and feet looked the same.

'Penny, I love you.'

'I love you too, James, but I'm quite busy right now – if you could make an appointment we could discuss this in detail at a more convenient time . . . dinner would be good for me . . .' But he was already halfway out of the door. I'm sure he doesn't know the effort it costs me to be light-hearted in these exchanges. Even in misery, he is diverting.

Saturday, 10th March

An intriguing encounter last night. I had a ticket to listen to Isaac Stern and the LPO [London Philharmonic Orchestra] playing Brahms's Violin Concerto at the Royal Albert Hall. It's one of my favourite pieces and I'd been looking forward to it. R was meant to be coming with me, but after the débâcle of Saturday night, he obviously thought it wouldn't be a good idea, and left a note saying that he would have to work. It was a relief; I don't know quite how to confront his behaviour. So I telephoned the box office, who agreed to let me return his ticket. To cheer myself up, I wore my new Marion Foale lace dress – it's wonderful what a fillip new clothes can give. At the interval, I decided not to brave the bar and stayed in my seat instead. I was gazing idly at the wonderful gilt embellishments along the box edges, when the man beside me cleared his throat. 'Excuse me, please. May I look at your programme?' I smiled and handed it to him. After a few minutes, he passed it back. 'A wonderful performance so far, don't you think?' I agreed. 'It is the first time I have heard it in concert,' he continued, 'but I feel as if I know every note. I grew up in Africa and my parents had a wind-up gramophone which they would play every night. This was one of their favourites, and now one of mine too.'

I told him that I'd also grown up in Africa and asked where he had lived.

'My family had a farm in Tanganyika.* I am German – West German now, of course.'

I said that I'd thought his English was too perfect for an Englishman. He laughed. He had had an English governess in Africa, he told me. His parents were great Anglophiles. But that hadn't helped them after the war, when their land was reclaimed and they were forced to return to Berlin. He'd been a young boy at the time, but had never forgotten it.

The orchestra filed back to their seats, the conductor returned to a torrent of applause and the house lights dimmed. I sat back and concentrated on the music. But as soon as it had finished, I was aware of my neighbour; I was aware of wanting to talk to him some more, the old lure of a shared African experience. As I turned towards him, he said, 'Excuse me. Permit me to introduce myself. I am David Zach. I hope you don't think it is forward of me, but could I buy you a drink?'

We walked around the corner to the ground-floor bar of a small hotel on Queen's Gate. 'I'm afraid it's not very glamorous,' he said. 'I moved to London six weeks ago and I'm still trying to get my bearings. I haven't explored much outside the area around my flat.'

At the moment he's living in a serviced company apartment in Egerton Gardens, intended for visiting employees and important clients, while he looks for a place of his own.

---

* In 1964 Tanganyika was to merge with Zanzibar to form Tanzania.

He's planning to stay for at least two years in London, where he's setting up a new department for his company's London branch. He sounded almost ashamed to admit he was a banker.

'But perhaps I will never leave? Berlin has never really felt like home. I know I went when I was quite young, but I still feel like an outsider. I like it that way. To tell you the truth, I've never wanted to stay in one place for too long, and I've never had much reason to do so.'

We ordered drinks and moved to deep sofas near the front window. I asked whether he would consider returning to live in Africa.

'No, I don't think so. It has some sad associations for me. I have been to visit, though.'

'You have? I want to – it has taken me a long time to get to this point, but yes, I think I would like to go now, to see whether my childhood memories are real, or enhanced by the passage of time.'

He asked why I hadn't been before, and for some reason I ended up telling the story of Ma and Pa – for the second time in as many weeks. 'So you see, we were virtually orphaned,' I said, 'and those last years had changed my view of the country I thought I loved so passionately. I saw so much that was ugly and cruel, and I realised I was not a true African; I could only ever be an intruder, a representative of the ruling class, and that also shamed me.' My mouth opened in an involuntary yawn. 'I'm sorry, I have to go now. It's been a lovely evening, thank you. I enjoyed talking about Africa – it's rare to find someone who understands.'

He stood and held out his hand. 'Perhaps then we can do it again? Would it be a great intrusion if I were to telephone you sometime?' Feeling faintly guilty, I gave him my number.

Tuesday, 13th March

007 hasn't been into the Office for two days. Mary has no idea where he is. She telephoned May, who said that she was sure he was all right, and that she shouldn't worry. It sounded fishy to me – May is normally most concerned about James's safety. So this evening, after work, I went round to his place* and rang the doorbell. I would have recognised May even before she started talking: she looked exactly as I had envisaged her, from our occasional telephone conversations over the years. 'Miss Moneypenny, why it's a delight to meet you at last,' she said, after I'd introduced myself. She showed me into the sitting-room, which was lovely: masculine, yet immaculately stylish – an accurate reflection of 007. The walls were covered in navy rough silk, with walnut bookcases taking up the best part of three sides, and an ornate Empire desk in front of the broad window looking out over the plane-trees in the square on the fourth.

'I'm afraid the Commander's not here at present,' she said, looking a little uncomfortable.

I asked whether she knew where he was. 'I'm afraid I can't say. I don't exactly know, that is . . .' she tailed off.

'May, if you know where he is, please tell me. If the Chief finds out that he's taken off without permission, he could

---

* A small comfortable flat on the first floor of a converted Regency house, situated in a tree-lined square off the King's Road.

get in all sorts of trouble – perhaps even lose his job. If you give me some sort of clue, I'll try and track him down before that happens. Please, you've got to help him.'

She looked even more uncertain. 'Well, he didn't tell me exactly, but I did overhear him asking after flights to Spain, Madrid it was.'

I should have guessed. My fault. Now how to spirit him back before the OM notices he's gone?

Wednesday, 14th March

A meeting of the Cuba committee. I seem to have been appointed official secretary for the group – which makes a nice change for me and delights Bill. Apologies from Ross, who stayed in Jamaica, where he is looking into a series of unexplained fires in the sugar plantations. He suspects they might be arson, orchestrated by a freelance assassin based in Havana.* The Americans have stated categorically that they are not involved. 007 was not present – I made his apologies and explained that he was unwell. I'm not sure M was convinced. Bloody James – if I'm not careful, he could get me into trouble too. Why do I feel impelled to protect him?

---

* Thought to be Francisco 'Pistols' Scaramanga, also known as 'The Man with the Golden Gun', after his gold-plated, long-barrelled, single-action Colt .45. He worked predominantly for the KGB, but also as an independent operative for other organisations in Central America and the Caribbean. Based in Cuba since 1956, originally under Batista's protection, he switched allegiances and worked undercover for Castro until the revolution, after which he was appointed foreign enforcer for the Department of State Security. Born with a third nipple, two inches below his left breast.

Scott reported that the operational HQ for Operation Mongoose has been set up in the CIA station in Miami, known as JM/WAVE.* Based in a wooded compound on the south campus of the University of Miami, it sports a misleading brass nameplate identifying it as a technical enterprise. It's staffed by more than 250 Americans, running over 2,200 Cuban agents, most of them first-generation exiles, all directed towards developing and implementing a new strategy to overthrow the Castro régime. But, as Head of A pointed out, it's well known that the Cuban community in Miami is about as riddled with informers as a wheel of Emmental cheese; what's the betting that they've already infiltrated JM/WAVE?

The sabotage operations have begun. Teams of agents routinely open all freight bound for Cuba. With those containing machinery, they break crucial gears; additives are infiltrated into lubricating-oils so they wear out more quickly; foodstuffs are tainted with contaminants. At the same time, the Americans are supplying hardware to any of the hundreds of exile organisations based in the Little Havana area of Miami who can convince them they have plans to sail to Cuba. Sometimes, they're accompanied on their operations by an American agent or contractor, who

---

* JM/WAVE was the code name for the Miami operation. The head of station was Theodore 'Ted' Shackley, a senior and respected CIA agent, previously based in Berlin. In Miami, he became very involved in the attempt to overthrow Castro. Among the resources he had at his disposal were a multi-million-dollar budget, a navy of over 100 craft, including the 174-foot *Rex*, which was equipped with the latest electronic devices and 40-mm and 20-mm cannons, and access to F-105 Phantom fighter planes from the nearby Homestead Air Force Base.

81

supervises the blowing-up of sugar mills, oil refineries, factories and ships in harbour. 'We're hoping that the underground opposition forces in place are going to realise that they have significant support Stateside,' said Scott. 'Enough to stimulate them into action.'

'Have you considered the danger that this action might backfire?' M asked. 'Force Castro into seeking outside support?' Everyone turned to Scott to gauge his reaction, but he just shrugged.

I think M rather enjoys these meetings. They provide a chance, at least, to escape from whatever this big secret is that appears to have settled over his head like a thunderous cloud. He still meets Dorothy virtually every day and has been spending long afternoons locked up with Head of X.* I think he's told Bill, too, but if it is truly top

---

* X Section, devoted to cross-examination both of foreign spies, captured abroad, and of suspected double agents within the secret service. In 1962, X Section was located in a redbrick townhouse in Kensington Cloisters, west London, and staffed by a team of twelve trained interrogators and scientists. The basement was equipped as a series of detention cells (in one of which Rosa Klebb was held for over a month until her death, allegedly of a heart attack). The identity of the Chief of Section, known to all just as X, was a closely guarded secret and remains unknown to this day. What does exist, however, are several – heavily censored – documents generated by X, detailing best practice for 'soft' and 'hard' interrogation. The key to success in the former, according to X, is 'patience, a retentive memory and the interrogator's ability to mask his intellectual superiority and flatter his adversary to the point where he feels compelled to reveal how clever he is'. The inventions and concoctions of the scientists based in the first-floor laboratory contributed heavily to successful strong-arm cross-examination – along with a detailed knowledge of physiology and the limits of human endurance.

secret, it's a waste of my time to try to get anything out of him.

The Powder Vine meanwhile talks of little else. The section chiefs are still tense, with CNE apparently taking it all particularly badly. 'He cancelled his trip to Helsinki last week,' reported Raine. 'He's got terribly jumpy – I'm worried that he's heading for a breakdown.'

'The only thing I can think of is another mole,' said Janet. We all looked at her. It made absolute sense of the erratic behaviour. 'Look at the timing – there's that German defector singing away in Stockholm as we speak.* X came back from there midway through last month, which

---

Although torture is against the terms of the Geneva Conventions, it is clear that 'non-existent' organisations did not feel themselves to be bound by the same codes of practice that applied to the declared services.

* On 1 February 1962, a high-ranking officer of the Stasi, the East German secret police, knocked on the door of the British secret-service station chief in West Berlin and announced that he wanted to defect. He had with him his wife and daughter and three small suitcases. It came as a complete surprise. The German officer – known as Kingfisher – had been identified by the British as one of the Stasi high command and photographed visiting the Kremlin on several occasions. That night, he told his British counterpart that he had long been dissatisfied with the methods of his organisation and had become disillusioned with the ideological underpinnings of his country. He had been planning his defection for four years, during which time he had photographed and microdotted a mass of information that he believed would be of great interest to the West. When asked why he hadn't made contact earlier, he said he was afraid of arousing suspicion. Head of WB immediately contacted headquarters and arrangements were made to fly Kingfisher and his family to a secret location in Stockholm for intensive interrogation – to ensure he was a genuine defector instead of a Stasi plant primed with disinformation.

was when they all started acting as though a wraith was tapping on their shoulders. It was the same when Maclean was unmasked.'

I nodded. It explained why we were all being kept in the dark: the fewer people who know the inner workings of an internal investigation the better. If it was indeed the case, the months to come are going to be challenging, to put it mildly.

Thursday, 15th March

This is getting very awkward indeed. M asked me today whether 007 was back and had read the Cuba Group minutes. I said I didn't know, but would find out. I've spoken in confidence to Head of Madrid Station,* warning him to keep his eyes and ears open for 007 – he normally makes some kind of noise not long after hitting a city. Otherwise, what am I going to do? I can't go and fetch him myself. It's at times like this when I wish I had someone to confide in, when I feel very alone, in my sealed capsule of secrecy.

Friday, 16th March

I must be mad. I'm due to fly to Madrid tomorrow morning. Summers cabled this morning to say there had been an incident in a city-centre hotel. Apparently a man had broken into a suite on the penthouse level and, shortly afterwards, there had been an exchange of gunfire. There was one fatal-

---

* Patrick Summers, a young SIS high-flyer, who later took a sideways jump into the Foreign Office, quickly rising to ambassadorial level.

ity, a tall man who spoke with a pronounced Eastern-European accent, according to room service. Of the guest – who registered himself as Sverker Arneskans from Oslo and who was described by the desk manager as tall and pale, with long, thin hands and feet – there was no sign. Nor of the intruder. The police have initiated a citywide manhunt. Summers reckons that if it is 007 – and it certainly has his hallmark stamped all over it – he will contact the station at some point soon. 'We won't be able to shield him for long,' he told me when I telephoned this afternoon. 'We signed a non-violence pact with the Spanish security service, which we've already violated twice. If they find out it's us again, the station will be closed down. You've got to tell M.'

Of course that's what I should have done. But the consequences would have been all too certain; 007 was already on his last life. I spoke instinctively, almost before considering the consequences to my own career. 'I can't,' I said. 'Please help me to sort this out quietly.' I told him that I would come over myself.

What made me say that? I've never so flagrantly broken the chain of command before. Is 007 really worth risking my future for? I can't back out now. I only hope I can do something.

Sunday, 18th March

Home, thank goodness. By the time I got to the Embassy yesterday, James was already there and pacing up and down like a caged tiger. He looked more than a little surprised to see me. 'Penny, what on earth are you doing here?' he said.

I told him I'd come to take him home.

'On the Old Man's orders? He's going to have me strung up for this, but I was so close, I literally had him in my sights, but then his gorilla of a bodyguard jumped me and Blofeld slipped out on to the balcony. I went after him once I'd got the gorilla off my back.' I frowned at him and shook my head. 'Yes, I suppose I'll be needing one of your forms for him, Penny dear. But when I got on to the roof, he'd vanished. I came down the fire-escape, but I'd lost him. It's bloody frustrating.'

He looked momentarily taken aback when I told him that – apart from Summers and myself – no one knew where he was. 'You came by yourself to rescue me? Penny, you are a wonder.'

I tried to suppress a smile and hurry him along to the airport for the late plane back to London. 'We've got to get you out, before someone remembers seeing you in the hotel and the police issue your description.'

'Well,' he shrugged. 'I imagine Blofeld has long gone now. I went out to the airport yesterday in the hope of running into him, but I had no luck. The only hint of a clue was from a ticketing agent, who thought she might have sold a ticket to Singapore to someone answering his description. The plane had just left, otherwise I would have got on it myself. You don't think M would let me go out there to take a look?' He caught sight of my face and shook his head. 'No, I suppose you're right. Not a hope in hell.'

'You'd be better off keeping your head well down,' I told him. 'I'll see what I can do about Singapore.'

I'm more than relieved that we made it home without incident. Looking back, however, it's the first time I've seen 007 so animated since Tracy's death. Perhaps it was worth the risk?

There was an envelope waiting for me. I recognised R's handwriting but, right then, I hadn't the will to open it.

Saturday, 24th March

I'm not proud of what I have just done. I feel like a lowly sneak. 006 arrived back yesterday, with 625 in tow and a rubber chicken, which he presented to 007, with much hilarity. I love the festive atmosphere that greets an agent's successful return from a mission. They can be excused a modicum of bragging. I happened to be passing his office as he was recounting the events to Mary. 'Piece of cake,' he told her. 'A little sniper fire, but nothing I couldn't handle. I hope you weren't worried about me. Were you, even a little?' I don't think we're going to find anyone to bet against 006 being the first to bed her now.* She told me later that he'd invited her to dinner at the Ritz that night.† I resisted warning her to be careful.

I'd planned to spend today writing letters and sorting out the flat. But when I woke up, the sun was shining and I couldn't face the image of R sitting at my desk that assails me every time I open the study door. Instead, I went for a walk, somehow ending up in St James's Park, and when I saw the Office, just a hundred yards away through the

---

* When Mary Goodnight took up the job as secretary to the oo section, she became the subject of a sweepstake as to who would get her into bed first. Bond was initially a favourite, but dropped out of the running after he met Tracy.

† Although not officially encouraged, inter-office romantic liaisons were common and, from the service's point of view, preferable to out-of-office relationships.

trees, I succumbed to an urge that had been niggling me for the past few days. I went in and straight up to see Alfred in Records. He was talking to one of the research officers, so I just mimed going to get a file myself and he nodded me through. For the sake of my conscience, I went first to the Ds and pulled out the file on Commander Patrick Derring-Jones, RNVR,* which I had been meaning to do for weeks. There was a brief service record, describing his wartime career in what has now become a familiar lack of detail. Pinned to the back, I found a handwritten assessment of him written at the time by someone with an undecipherable signature. 'Derring-Jones has shown exceptional bravery in combat. He is unafraid to make decisions and, on occasion, to override those made by others. This has made him unpopular in some departments, especially when his judgement has been proven to be right. He may be just the man we need.' He had retired from the Navy in 1960, but there was an old address for him in Kincardineshire, Scotland, which I jotted down.

I replaced the file and then, with heart thumping, not really believing I was doing this, I went to the Hs.† Troop's evasiveness had been playing in the back of my head and I wanted to set it to rest. I looked quickly, not wanting to find his file – and I was more than relieved when it wasn't there. It goes to show that one should never give in to an over-active imagination, I told myself, as I almost ran from the building.

---

* Sydney Cotton's dinner companion, and former colleague of Hugh Moneypenny.
† She was presumably searching for the file of R – Richard Hamilton.

Monday, 26th March

The anniversary of the Lari massacre.* Helena came up to London and we met for lunch and talked about Ma. She says she would come with me if I wanted to go back to Kenya, unless I had someone else I wanted to go with. No, I told her, I don't.

I haven't seen R since the night I found him in my drawers. Last night, I found a note from him slipped under my door, apologising and asking whether I had read his last letter. I wrote back briefly, to say that I'd destroyed it before reading it. But nothing else. I didn't know what to say. I feel rather dreadful about it – my suspicions must have been unfounded. And I miss him, I miss what we had, and

---

* In October 1952, after widespread violence committed in the name of freedom, mainly by the members of a secret organisation which became known as Mau Mau, the colonial government of Kenya declared a state of emergency. Despite heavy-handed action by the colonial army and police, this did little to calm the situation. On the night of 26 March 1953, Naivasha police station came under attack. Half an hour later, a separate gang of armed Kikuyu warriors staged an ambush at Lari, a farming area just north of Nairobi and about twenty miles north-east of Maguga, near the edge of the high escarpment looking down into the Rift Valley. Their main target was the home compound of Chief Luka, a known sympathiser of the colonial government, where he lived with his eight wives, numerous children and loyalists. The results of the raid were devastating. The fighting spread over an area of forty square miles and when the authorities arrived the next morning they found piles of bodies, some burned, many mutilated. One witness saw a Mau Mau warrior slit the throat of a young boy and lick his blood. A total of 97 residents were found dead, 32 grievously wounded. Two hundred huts were burned, and 1,000 cattle maimed. Among the dead was the visiting health adviser, Irene Moneypenny.

what, for a brief time, I had dared to dream we might have. So many times I have picked up the telephone to ring him to try to patch things up, but then put it down again. Is there any turning back?

I returned home today to a more pleasant missive, a telegram from Patrick Derring-Jones.* It was short. He had known my father, he wrote, and would be delighted to talk about it. His wife was ill at present, but if I was willing to come up to Scotland I would be more than welcome to stay.

My hand was almost shaking as I wrote instantly accepting his invitation and proposing several dates next month. I'll have to catch the sleeper train up to Aberdeen on a Friday night, and return first thing on Sunday. But no journey is too far if, at the end, it unearths a vital key to the truth about my father.

---

* JM had written to him on 24 March at the address she had found in his file.

April

The telegram from the War Office shattered the fragile security of the Moneypenny women's wartime existence:

```
REGRET TO INFORM YOU THAT COMMANDER HUGH
DAVID MONEYPENNY RNVR HAS BEEN REPORTED
MISSING IN ACTION IN ENEMY TERRITORY STOP
EVERY EFFORT IS BEING MADE TO CLARIFY HIS
STATUS AND WHEREABOUTS STOP WE WILL KEEP
YOU INFORMED OF ANY FURTHER DEVELOPMENTS
STOP
```

I have seen the telegram. My mother kept it in her small wooden chest of treasures, along with the collected sentimental ephemera of her childhood. I imagine her and my aunt now, following their mother's death thirteen years later, packing up the family farm, trying to decide what was to be shipped to London and what given or thrown away. It must have been an extraordinarily emotional time – orphaned and about to take a giant step into the unknown.

My mother always told me that she didn't know what she would have done without her sister. She said she had large blanks in her memory following the two tragic defining events of her childhood, and that she knew only that Jane had led – probably at times tugged – her through them.

That my aunt was able to hold everything together, to be practical and rational not only for herself, but on her sister's behalf, is a testament to her extraordinary fortitude.

On 25 October 1940, the day the telegram arrived, the family's first reaction was of determined disbelief. 'He said he will be back and he will,' Irene insisted fiercely. That afternoon, Jane climbed the old acacia and wrote in her diary, 'The sun burns hot today in a blue sky, spoiled only by a single cloud the shape of a hippo. I can hear the hoopoe's cry and the distant bark of a Tommy [Thomson's gazelle]. Winnie is rolling in the dust and Mama says I may have a pet for my birthday. I think I want a meerkat to keep a watch out for Helena. I wish Pa was here. Please bring him back safely to us.'

From that day on, she wrote most days – always in the same spot, on the low-hanging branch of her father's favourite tree. She recorded everything, from the progress on the farm, to her family's increasingly dispirited search for clues to her father's disappearance. Some months after the initial telegram, one of Hugh Moneypenny's former colleagues from the colonial government drove out to the farm to see them. He said that Hugh had been classified 'presumed dead', and that they should not hold out hope for his return.

But they did. They still talked about 'when Pa gets back'; only Jane dared to think about the possibility that he might not return. She persuaded Irene to let them take the rest of the year off from school, enabling her to spend more time on the farm. One year became two as the faithful Mrs Bisby returned to her outdoor schoolroom on the veranda, looking out over the plains of Kenya.

Irene continued her quest for answers. She laid siege to

Government House in Nairobi. She peppered the ministry in London with letters, and when the war was over she went to England herself to bang on doors. But she returned empty-handed, with no answers, no clues even, to what her husband was doing when he went missing. She was told, again and again, that he had gone missing in action in enemy territory and that 'all evidence' pointed towards his having died.

Sunday, 8th April

A surprisingly lovely day. David Zach telephoned to ask me to accompany him to an exhibition of West African wood carvings at the Africa Centre. We met outside Covent Garden tube station. I hadn't appreciated before quite how good-looking he is. Tall and slim, with dark blond hair cut neatly, just over the collar line, and fine features. Almost too perfect for me – I prefer R's pale and rumpled air – but lovely to look at. From what Zach has said, he's probably about the same age as me, maybe a year or two older. He appeared to be pleased to see me and took my hand in both of his when he shook it.

The exhibition wasn't notable, and afterwards we strolled to a small café on Long Acre. It was warm enough to sit outside. He began to apologise for subjecting me to the exhibition and we fell naturally into a conversation about African art. He told me that he has several pieces that he had picked up over there. 'I find there is something almost elemental about it,' he said. 'It is so unforced, completely independent of fashion or current taste. It is funny how Africa brings out something in everyone it touches. Look at us, even. We have not lived there for many years, yet here we are, drawn together by a continent, and in many ways, a violent, pest-ridden place.'

We swapped horror stories, our shaves with danger and death, probably exaggerated, as most camp-fire tales tend to be, and then he asked again about how my father had died. He seemed genuinely interested and when I told him that his body had never been found, he was horrified. 'That is not good enough,' he exclaimed. 'People cannot just vanish, even in war it is unlikely. Do you ever think about the possibility that he might be alive, somewhere, perhaps with amnesia?' I laughed, before admitting that sometimes, in my secret moments, I indulged myself with the fantasy of finding him, but more than anything I wanted to discover what had happened, to lay the whole episode to rest.

We caught a bus to Richmond Park, admired the spring flowers and ate our first ice-creams of the year. Then we walked back into London, stopping on the way for an early supper. By the time we arrived back in Knightsbridge, my feet were aching. He accompanied me to the door, where he said a polite good-night. He's a charming man and I hope we will become friends. But Africa notwithstanding, I couldn't help but wish he had been R.

Friday, 13th April

The Friday reports* came in as usual. I'd like to have my own wall map, into which I could stick coloured pins, marking where each agent is operating, and the status of

---

* Each Friday, all agents in the field submitted reports to London HQ. The different station heads reported directly to their section chiefs,

their mission. Most are static, working for overseas stations attached to embassies or trade commissions. It's only really the oo agents who move about. Right now, oo6 is in Central America on the trail of a suspected drugs baron, oo9* is chasing the Blofeld lead in Singapore† and oo7 is sitting at his desk on the seventh floor, probably making paper aeroplanes, for all the good he is doing. I should be thankful, I suppose, that he's not getting into further trouble.

Instead of lunch today, Mary dragged me out to the stores. She's already getting worked up over what to wear for Lil's wedding, in two months' time. She's very keen on the Jackie Kennedy look and endlessly brings in magazine photographs of her, but somehow that tailored chic doesn't quite work with Mary's athletic build and English-rose complexion. We went into the big department stores where she tried on numerous dresses, but none met her exacting

---

who forwarded anything of importance to M, along with a weekly summary of events in the geographical area which fell under their responsibility. The oo agents reported directly to M. The communiqués came in by diplomatic bag, or were transmitted in code by radio to the Communications centre on the eighth floor, along the corridor from the Chief's suite. Still encoded, they were delivered to everyone marked on the distribution list by girls from Records, who kept a copy of all outgoing and incoming signals for their files. JM was responsible for decoding the urgent signals marked for M's eyes only – as well as for encoding the replies he dictated for her to send.
* Major Mark Carbon-Brown, an Old Etonian former SAS officer who had been earmarked as a future regimental Commander-in-Chief, before transferring unexpectedly to the intelligence services, reputedly at M's personal entreaty.
† The reported sighting at the airport in Madrid was attributed to one of the Madrid station's local informants – presumably with the connivance of JM and Summers.

standards. She hasn't told me so, but I strongly suspect that she's seeing 006 out of the office. If so, she's remaining admirably calm while he's away.

Friday, 20th April

The Cuba experts are beginning to take the situation more seriously. A report came through from Washington yesterday, to the effect that the US marines had successfully staged a mock invasion of a Caribbean island,* overthrowing a fictitious dictator. After reading it, Head of Section C sent round a memo to the Cuba Group: 'Looks as if it is a dry-run for another attempt at Cuba. Either that, or Washington flexing its muscles as a warning to Castro. After the Bay of Pigs, they cannot believe that Castro is going to turn tail and run. He is not the sort of man to be scared into submission, and this will only make him shore up his defences – or turn elsewhere for help. We must keep a close eye on the situation.'

Sunday, 22nd April

Lunch with R. A stilted affair. How can we have gone from intimacy to awkwardness in a matter of weeks? I had finally heard from Troop on Friday, a curious, ambiguous little note, typewritten, to the effect that 'We have been

---

* In April 1962, in an operation code-named Landphibex, 40,000 US marines, supported by four aircraft carriers and more than 50 warships, stormed the Puerto Rican island of Vieques.

unable to find verifiable evidence that Mr Richard Hamilton constitutes a security risk. However, you are reminded that it is contrary to regulations for you to reveal details of your occupation to him. Please notify the security department if there is any change to the current status of your relationship.'

It was hardly a whole-hearted endorsement – damn that man, it's patently not in his power to make people happy. If R is clear, then say it; don't leave room for doubt – there are no half measures here. It should have been something to celebrate; I wanted to tell R and laugh about it. I couldn't of course. I telephoned him and breezily suggested lunch. He came, but he was withdrawn, distant even. On several occasions I got that feeling again that he wanted to tell me something, but then he would shrink back, as though he had thought better of it. I wish we could wipe the slate clean and start again. But I fear it's too late, another candle snuffed out.

Tuesday, 24th April

The regular quarterly update from Q Branch.* It never fails to entertain – almost like a form of technology pornography. As usual, much of it was quite impenetrable to

---

* The 'Quartermaster' – the section handling resources and technical support, located in the basement. In 1962 it was divided into three sub-sections:
  I.   Gadgets – bugging equipment, lock-picking tools, jemmies, getaway cars, bikes, miniature helicopters and suchlike.
  II. Armoury – including the weapons store and firing range. Provided training and arms-maintenance services.
  III. Technical research – scientists (known as boffins) and analysts

non-boffins – a fact about which Head of Q* remains oblivious – and the rest, as always, reads as if it has been lifted from the back page of a boy's adventure comic. One section of today's report was entitled 'Miniaturisation: Key to the Future'† and went on to detail the new generation of tiny gadgets which will, apparently, become standard equipment to field agents. Somehow, I can't see myself wielding a lipstick pistol or hairbrush camera!

There was one entry, however, that caught my attention. In the section entitled 'Miscellaneous Field Protocol', I found advice on the prescribed method to search drawers: 'Always start with the bottom drawers. Then you can rest subsequent drawers on the one below, and do not have to waste time closing them.' I couldn't help but conjure up the image of R at my desk with the lower drawers open.

Friday, 27th April

It's crunch time for 007. M came back from lunch and asked me to summon him. But when I put the red telephone‡ call through to 007's desk, Mary answered. 'He's not here, Jane,'

---

invented and developed new weapons and devices for use by intelligence operatives and provided up-to-date information on the equipment in current use by the opposition.

* From 1952 to 1979, Dr Desmond McCarthy, an industrial engineer and inventor, who began his career with Marconi. Specialist in communications equipment and the miniaturisation of weapons.

† Included among several files of declassified Q Branch reports (1960–65), held in the National Archives and in part reproduced at the end of the April diary entries.

‡ The direct line between M's office and the oo agents' desks.

she said. 'He never came back from lunch. I've tried to get him on the Syncraphone,* but he left it in his drawer. He's not at home and the Bentley's† still here. I'll search the building.'

I had a hunch where he might be. A couple of times recently, I'd spied him sitting on a bench in the rose garden, just staring at the sky. 'I like it here, Penny,' he said once. 'The red ones remind me of Tracy.' It's been nearly four months since she was killed, but he's clearly living with it every day. According to Mary, he still arrives late most days with a bear of a hangover. 'I should have seen it, Penny,' he said when I found him this time. 'How did I let that happen to her? What am I to do now?'

I told him that what he was going to do now was to report in person to M, and that he had better pull himself together, as the OM sounded as if he meant business.

Together, Mary and I managed to get him brushed up and at M's door before he noticed he'd been waiting too

---

* A light plastic radio receiver the size of a pocket watch and similar in function to the modern pager, developed by Q:III and introduced as standard equipment for senior staff in 1961. If an officer was within a range of ten miles of Headquarters, he could be bleeped on the receiver. When this happened, it was his duty to go immediately to the nearest telephone and contact his office, using the prescribed incoming telephone number.
† Bond's pride and joy: a battleship-grey Bentley Mark II Continental, which he bought in parts for £1,500 and customised to his precise instructions, with a Mark IV engine, a new, convertible two-seater body, power-operated hood, and two large-armed bucket seats in black Morocco leather. It was meticulously maintained and referred to, by Bond, as 'The Locomotive'.

long. Despite his curmudgeonly ways, the OM is fond of 007. He would not have suffered this kind of behaviour from another agent, whatever the justification. He can't afford to.

Whatever he said had some effect – 007 came back through the baize door looking noticeably perkier. 'I'm off to the desert, it seems. Got to go home and pack my yashmak. Cheerio, Penny. Let's have dinner when I'm back.' Perhaps a blast of desert sand will do the trick? As he left, I raised my eyebrows at Bill. 'Some mission the Old Man's cooked up as a distraction from his misery,' he told me. 'We've had reports that a bunch of old Nazis are setting themselves up as an independent assassination agency, on hire to the highest bidders. They're purely muscle, but have more than sufficient experience in their chosen trade. They've apparently set up shop in Casablanca, so we've heard, and, according to our source, are meeting a prospective client next week. We don't know who that is, or where they intend to meet, or indeed whether or not this is a complete red herring. It's definitely worth chasing up, but 712 could have done it from Rabat. Still, it's not an easy task and, frankly, I told M that I wasn't sure 007 was up to it. But he'd made up his mind. He thinks a dose of adventure will help him to snap out of it. I think his patience is running thin, to tell you the truth. He equates what James is going through with losing one of his men in battle – terribly sad, but part of the job description. I fear it goes a bit deeper than that, though. I hope the mission will do him good; I just wish it could have been a little less risky.'

Monday, 30th April

A truly extraordinary weekend. I still cannot digest it. I caught the sleeper train to Aberdeen, then changed on to the branch line to Banchory. Patrick Derring-Jones was waiting, as planned, at the small station. I recognised him immediately – a tall man wearing a beautifully cut tweed suit, with an ice-blue shirt and striped tie. He must have been nearing sixty, but he looked much younger, naturally graceful. He greeted me warmly: 'My dear Jane Moneypenny. Yes, I can see you're Hugh's daughter, how very wonderful to meet you.'

As we drove to his house in a polished 1955 Bristol, he explained that his wife, Gilda, had cancer and was increasingly weak. 'I cannot tell you how painful it is for both of us. We met for the first time when she was just sixteen. That was before the war. All through the fighting, I was sustained by an image of her imprinted on my memory, and when it was all over we found each other again, and we have barely been separated for a week since then.'

The drive was beautiful. Spring was creeping up on northern Scotland and the hills were changing colour. In a matter of weeks, D-J explained, they would be purple from base to peak. We turned off the main road and on to a rutted track. He apologised for the bumps. 'I'm going to have them filled in this month – then at least I'll be able to take Gilda for drives.' After several miles, we rounded the base of a hill and saw, just above us, on a small foothill of its own, a pretty whitewashed house. I was saying how lovely it was, when he interrupted me. 'Just wait,' he said. 'The point of the house is at the back.' A gaggle of black Labradors ran out to greet us. D-J carried my bag to the house, calling out as he pushed open the unlocked door, 'Gilda, darling, we're here.' I caught my breath. In a straight line from the front door, I could see through the hall, through double doors leading into the drawing-room and out through a wall of glass, which overlooked a natural loch. I walked straight across. The trees on the far banks were almost sculptural, with the same flat tops as acacias. 'This is incredible,' I said. 'It reminds me of Africa.'

'I thought you might say that,' D-J replied, with a sad smile. 'Your father came to stay after a training course in the autumn of 1940. My parents were living here then. He looked out of that same window and said the same thing. He talked about you and your sister often. He was very proud of you both. When it was time for us to leave, my father drove us to the station in Banchory. We were early and while we were waiting we walked around the town – it was more of a village in those days – and Hugh stopped at the post office and sent the diary he had bought for you from Smythson's the day we left London. He said he thought one day you would be a writer. I wonder whether you ever received it?'

I nodded, too filled with emotion to speak.

'He was a wonderful man. I loved him dearly.'

As he said that, a tiny, bird-like woman walked into the room. She was dressed smartly in a yellow chiffon blouse and wide trousers. Despite her make-up and welcoming smile, she looked frail. 'Hello, Jane,' she greeted me. 'My husband has been so looking forward to your visit. As have I – you've given me a chance to get to know, at least a little, the great Hugh Moneypenny. But first, a drink? Tea? Something to eat?'

We chatted easily through the morning and into lunch. D-J told me how he had first met Pa. Both were RNVR, seconded into its intelligence branch. 'You knew that, of course?' I said I'd guessed, but found it hard to confirm. He smiled. 'Old habits die hard. I would have probably gone to my grave without uttering a word about intelligence, until Gilda got ill. Then other things suddenly seemed more important, like family, for instance. Come on, let's go and sit by the view. Gilda, my dear, we mustn't keep you any more. I'll bring you some tea. Excuse me, please, Jane.'

I sat looking out over the loch, filled with the tension of expectation. 'I have to apologise first of all,' he said on his return. 'I've thought of you – of Hugh's family – often over the past twenty years, but until I received your letter, it never dawned on me that you didn't know about Hugh's last adventure. I suppose, why would you? There were very few of us initiated into Ruthless. It was a brilliant scheme in many ways, but a mad caper in others. You have to understand that, for us, the war was like an exciting game. We cared passionately about the outcome and we were intensely patriotic, but we never lost the sense that it was a great adventure. We were lucky in that we – our close group at Naval Intelligence – never really had to suffer the most severe privations; we never fought on the front line, with our brothers and friends dying beside us.'

He talked for hours, describing in vivid colour life at the Admiralty, the missions abroad, the sense that the war could be won or lost by their actions. 'Each morning we would go first down to the Operations Room, where the whole picture of war was set out on charts, to catch up on the night's movements. We had a real sense of being at the centre of things.' A small group of them would meet for a weekly bridge game in Pimlico. 'It was at one of these evenings that Ruthless was conceived. I think four of us

were there: your father, Peter [Smithers], Ian [Fleming]
and myself. We'd been talking about the German naval
ciphers. They were widely thought to be unbreakable. Our
boffins at Bletchley* were brilliant, and had made great
progress reading Enigma† messages sent by the German
army and secret service, but the Kriegsmarine – that's the
Combat Navy – had its own version and we were getting
nowhere with it. Meanwhile, their U-boats were causing no
end of trouble. We needed a code book. Then one of us – it
was Ian, I believe – came up with this scheme. We would

---

* Bletchley Park, a former grand country house in Buckinghamshire,
which in 1939 was taken over by the Government Code and Cipher
School (later known as the Government Communications Headquarters – GCHQ). The code-breakers, operating out of makeshift
huts in the grounds, played a critical role in the eventual Allied
victory; once the Germans' signals could be read, their plans and
actions could be anticipated.
† The German coding machine, similar in appearance to a small
manual typewriter, encased in a wooden box, with three scramblers
positioned above the keys. When a letter of plain German was typed
into the machine, electrical impulses were sent through a series of
rotating wheels, electrical contacts and wires, to produce the enci-
phered letter, which lit up on a panel above the keyboard. Having
received the resulting code message and typed it into his own
machine, using the same scrambler settings, the recipient saw the
deciphered message similarly light up letter by letter. The rotors and
wires of the machine could be configured in 17,576 different ways; the
odds against anyone who did not know the settings being able to
break Enigma were a staggering 150 million million million to one.
However, using captured German code books, the code-breakers of
Bletchley, led by Cambridge mathematician Alan Turing, developed
the 'Bombe', an electro-mechanical machine that greatly reduced the
odds – and thereby the time required – to break the ever-changing
keys to the Enigma codes.

get hold of a German plane, dress up in Luftwaffe uniforms and crash-land it in the Channel. The Germans would be bound to send one of their new high-speed rescue launches over from Denmark to get us. When they arrived, we would knock them on the head, board the boat, sail it back to England and hand over the code book.

'It all sounded remarkably simple, especially after a few bottles of excellent claret. We set to work on planning the operation the very next day. First we needed a pilot – it was just the scheme to appeal to Sydney Cotton and he was soon signed up. Your father was fluent in German,* so he would be the radio operator. I was to be in the strike force, with Ian and Peter and a tough marine that Ian had somehow managed to borrow. Over the next few months, the plan started to come together. We managed to get hold of a twin-engined Heinkel III bomber, which had been shot down over the Firth of Forth and rehabilitated at Farnborough.† Peter went up to the store of captured enemy equipment at Cardington‡ and got us fitted out with Luftwaffe uniforms. Then it was just a matter of listening in to the regular air traffic to learn the call signs used by the Luftwaffe. We planned to broadcast the SOS in plain language anyway, so it was fairly straightforward.

'I have to admit I was nervous about the whole plan, but

---

* From 1913 to 1915, Hugh's father, Basil Moneypenny, served as British High Commissioner in Zanzibar. As the island was just off-shore from German East Africa, it was decided that the whole family would learn German – they hired a German governess, and spoke German exclusively at every meal for a year, by the end of which Hugh could speak the language near-flawlessly.
† Hampshire headquarters of the Royal Aircraft Establishment.
‡ RAF base, recruitment centre and equipment store in Bedfordshire.

Ian was supremely confident and carried us all with him. There were hitches, of course. I remember that Group Captain – what was he called? – Wilson, yes, who was responsible for the aircraft, was worried that a crash landing would collapse its Perspex nose, and water would flood in, drowning us before we could escape or be rescued. But we managed to solve that by getting the nose reinforced, and we found a way to inject oil into the exhaust to give the impression of a plausible engine fire. We were ready to go down to Dover when we hit the first major impediments. First Ian was prevented from participating by DNI,[*] who said he wasn't prepared to risk him being captured – poor Ian, he was fearfully disappointed, it was his plan, after all. Then Sydney was sacked from the RAF, which meant we couldn't really use him, however much we – and he – wanted to.

'We managed to get a new pilot, Miles Pitman, and we all went down to Dover in October. Then it was a matter of waiting for the right weather and reports of a suitable German ship in the vicinity. I remember, we stayed in this dismal little hotel. On the first night Ian, who had come along to direct operations, presented each of us with a knife that he'd designed with Lord Suffolk.[†] It was made out of one

---

[*] Director of Naval Intelligence – the position held from 1939 to 1942 by Admiral John Godfrey. Regarded as one of the Navy's most brilliant – if unorthodox – officers, he then commanded the Royal Indian Navy and retired in 1946, a year before the end of the Raj.

[†] Charles Henry George Howard, 20th Earl of Suffolk and Berkshire (1917–66), bomb and dirty-tricks expert for the Special Operations Executive (SOE), working out of its Baker Street HQ. Suffolk famously knew how to kill a man by biting him in the back of his neck.

piece of steel – a beautiful piece, but absolutely lethal. We were all issued with a gas-pistol disguised as binoculars and a Webley .455 six-shot revolver. It was immensely frustrating, sitting there waiting, playing bridge, trying not to think about everything that could go wrong. The clouds just did not clear. It must have been the cloudiest October on record. After about two weeks we were called back to London.'

D-J stood up. 'I must go and see if Gilda is all right. Is there anything I can get you? Please feel free to wander around, look at the garden, make yourself at home. Perhaps we can continue after dinner? Eight o'clock. No need to dress.' I walked to the other side of the loch and sat down with a pen and a notepad and wrote notes of everything he'd said. I didn't want to forget a single detail. I was filled with emotion that I almost didn't dare to feel. Then I walked up the mountain, slid most of the way back down and had time to bathe before dinner. We ate fresh salmon and talked about London, and I did my best to hide my impatience to continue the story.

At last, we were settled on the sofa with cups of coffee. 'We were back in London. Yes. We were there for barely a week. I remember we got a furious message from Bletchley, telling us to get on with it. They needed the key. Then one evening Ian phoned me in my office and told me we were going back to Dover that night. The forecast was good and we were due to take off the following morning. I don't think I slept. I'd been on missions before, of course – quite a few – but never with so little back-up and such a great sense of the unknown. I'll never forget that day. Gathering on the airport apron, all in our Luftwaffe uniforms. Your father with a bloody bandage around his head, Peter wearing a sling – in readiness, you understand, for when we were rescued. We took off as dawn was breaking. It was a beautiful sunrise, properly yolk-like. As we got midway across the Channel, your father called out to us all, "Ready, boys. I'm going to broadcast now. We're German from now on, not a word of English."

'It all went according to plan, at first; your father sounded genuinely in distress, Miles took the plane down and we set the engine alight. Black smoke was still belching out when we caught sight of a ship steaming towards us from the north. We had been sitting in complete silence. It was not until it got quite close that Miles said – and there was no German about this – "Bloody hell, it's a minesweeper. We're never going to get that." I remember thinking, We're done for. Anyway, there was no turning back. We just looked at each other and I think the same thought was going through all our minds: we would not surrender quietly. For me, it was a matter of escape or death. I did not want to be taken prisoner.

'They sent out a small launch with just two men aboard. Hugh was the first to get on and started jabbering away in German about the accident. He didn't stop talking, gesticulating wildly, poking the Germans in the chest, so they didn't have a chance even to look at the rest of us. The launch drew up against the side of the boat. It was a huge thing – probably ninety feet, with machine-gun stations at the front and rear. There were about six men on deck and probably a further four or five inside. One of the Germans climbed out of the launch on to the minesweeper, then held out his hand for Hugh, who climbed on to the deck, followed by Miles and the marine. Then the other German started to stand up; we were astonished that he should have left us on our own. Peter and I stayed rooted in our seats. I could see your father looking at us while he was saluting the captain. As the German was stepping on to the deck,

Hugh pulled out his gun, and shouted, "Go, Patrick, go." We hesitated. But a handful more Germans, alerted by his shouts, had rushed on deck, bearing weapons. Peter and I knew we had no choice. I gunned up the engine and drove away. They fired some shots at us, but our little boat was too fast. At a safe distance, we stopped and I got out my binoculars. But we couldn't see any of our men.

'As soon as we got back to England, we alerted our air-sea rescue boys, who went out in a small frigate, but the minesweeper was nowhere to be seen. All they found was the marine's body, floating in the water. There was no sign of your father or of Miles, and as far as I know they were never heard of again. After the war I tried to find out what had happened to them. I made all the enquiries, but there was nothing. They had vanished into thin air. I could only assume they had died soon after.'

I could see the emotion in D-J's whole body. I put my hand out and he grabbed it. 'I'm so sorry,' he said. 'We shouldn't have left them there. Your father saved my life. But for him, I wouldn't be here now. He was a true hero.'

We talked until late. The only question I couldn't bring myself to ask was what would have happened to my father. At one point, D-J just said, 'There can be no hope. He died an honourable man. He was a great patriot and a wonderful friend. I shall always miss him.'

Q BRANCH REPORT 1962:II

A. MINIATURISATION: KEY TO THE FUTURE

To evade detection, the tools of our trade must shrink. Our adversaries have been using miniature weapons for some time *(see Appendix A - The*

Methods of Smersh. No. 11: Special Weapons), but
our new-generation devices are smaller still.
    In the future, agents undertaking covert
    missions will be issued with:
A PIPE OR CIGARETTE PISTOL (to suit), or for
    ladies, the LIPSTICK PISTOL. All of the above
    are 4.5-mm single-shot weapons capable of
    inflicting fatal damage at close range if
    directed at any of the five most vulnerable
    spots (see Q Branch 1961:III/5/iv).
HAIRBRUSH CAMERAS. To replace out-moded fountain
    pen, cigarette-lighter and key-chain models. The
    workings of the classic Minox spy camera are
    fitted in the base, with pin-hole lenses,
    enabling easy sideways shots in a washroom
    environment. Spare film rolls can be stored in
    the usual manner in hollowed-out razors or
    toothbrushes.
COMPREHENSIVE BURGLARY EQUIPMENT SPECTACLES CASE.
    A new kit comprising a multi-function lock-
    picking tool, miniature electronic stethoscope
    for use on tumbler-type combination safe locks,
    and a key-casting and putty pad the size of a
    business card.
IN DEVELOPMENT: a new long-range radio
    transceiver, capable of sending and receiving
    signals both in voice and Morse code at a range
    of up to 1,000 miles. Expected to be operational
    September 1962.

B. MISCELLANEOUS FIELD PROTOCOL

SEARCHING DRAWERS. Always start with the bottom
    drawers. Subsequent drawers can thus be rested
    on the one below, saving time and unnecessary
    effort in closing them.
MODIFIED GETAWAY CARS. In response to increasingly
    thorough searches by border guards, who are

fully aware of the usual hiding places, we have
fitted each car in the new cross-border fleet
with one of the following: secure strapping
beneath the car (note: subject being transported
must be wrapped in a thermal blanket to mask
body heat and prevent detection by Soviet
temperature-scanning equipment); hollow behind
front grille — large enough only for a man or
woman below 5 ft 9 inches in height, who should
not be left there for more than 53 minutes, if
gasification is not to occur; on car rooftop in
hollowed out luggage.
SPY PLANES. The pictures we are receiving from
American U-2 spy planes are of increasingly high
quality. The planes have seven Perspex ports,
each linked to Hycon cameras specially developed
for the Central Intelligence Agency, which
combine an expanded focal length with a
precision-engineered lens which, using Kodak
high-grain film, theoretically allows details of
2 inches to be caught from a height of 70,000
ft. (N.B. Technicians require an advanced course
in deciphering these photographs for the
accurate identification of anything smaller than
a bus.)

May

The idea that some of my grandfather's compatriots and fellow initiates to Ruthless might still be alive did not occur to me until it was almost too late. By chance, I caught sight of Patrick Derring-Jones's obituary in the *Guardian* three days after his death on 12 October 2003; it detailed his wartime exploits while attached to Naval Intelligence, saying that he 'came closer than any other candidate to being the true-life original of Ian Fleming's Bond'. It was a case of truth and fiction having become seriously entangled: Derring-Jones served with Fleming – and my grandfather – in NI, and Fleming later wrote the series of books in which my aunt was depicted as a fictional character. Sometimes the intertwined connections threatened to short-circuit my brain.

Derring-Jones was ninety when he died; what if one of the others in that close group was still alive? Fleming, I knew, had died many years before, of a heart attack on 12 August 1964. Sydney Cotton followed him five years later, after a full and varied life. Hugh Moneypenny and Miles Pitman were both taken captive by the Germans and never heard of again. Which left one man: Peter Smithers. I typed his name into Google and came up with a string of results, mostly connected to horticulture and plant photography. This Peter Smithers, I learned, was born in Yorkshire and educated at Harrow and Oxford, emerging with a first in history, before signing up to the RNVR in the run-up to war, when he was seconded into Naval Intelligence. It had to be the same man.

The most recent website I found was that of a garden-lover's guide to Switzerland, which included an invitation to botanists to visit the private gardens of Villa Morcote, created by the renowned British horticulturalist Sir Peter Smithers. The address was there; I could find no mention anywhere of Smithers' death. In the summer of 2004 I wrote to Sir Peter.

He telephoned only three days later. Although he was ninety-one years old, he sounded as lucid and sharp as a much younger man. 'I would be more than happy to talk to you about Ruthless,' he said. 'I'm afraid I don't travel any more, but you would be welcome to come to visit us out here.' I did not need any further invitation.

On 15 August I flew to Zurich and transferred on to a train for the three-hour journey across the mountains to Lugano, on the Italian border. I was met at the station and driven to Villa Morcote, which turned out to be a stunning Japanese-inspired house, designed by Sir Peter after his retirement as Secretary-General of the Council of Europe, and lived in by him and his wife ever since. It was late evening when I arrived. I was greeted by a tall, slim man, wearing an embroidered kaftan, which somehow managed to make him look stylish and aristocratic, yet unmistakably British. From the minute he shook my hand, I was charmed. We sat on a sofa in front of large glass windows, through which I could see the lights twinkling around the great lake below. It was as though I had entered a different, magnolia-scented world, where the best of values were still upheld, where gentle intelligence would always triumph over ambition and pride. It was wonderful to feel that this man and my grandfather had been close friends.

He explained how they had first met: 'It was in the Admiralty, Room 39. I'd been invalided out of active service and instead attached to Naval Intelligence. I was called to an interview with Admiral Godfrey – we called him Uncle John, though never to his face, of course. I was shown into this large room. There were perhaps six or seven desks in those days, occupied by officers in uniform and probably two women secretaries. I was introduced to them in turn.' He recalled his first impressions of my grandfather – his warm smile and engagingly direct way of talking. 'It was also when I met Ian [Fleming] for the first time, at his desk in the far right corner of the room, immediately by the door to Uncle John's office. Over the next year or so, we would spend much of our spare time together, such that we had.'

He described lunches at Josef's, a small restaurant in Greek Street, where they would meet to discuss whichever of Fleming's schemes was the flavour of the day. 'He was always coming up with these quite outrageous plans – some were brilliant, others hopelessly impractical. Never dull. We all used to indulge him – in some ways I think we were quite in awe of Ian: he was a tremendously charismatic fellow. He would often ask some of his other contacts to join us. It was at Josef's that I met that man from Wilkinson Sword – I can't recall his name – who agreed to make me this.' He reached across to the coffee table, to pick up what looked like a long cane. With a glint in his eye, he grabbed one end and pulled out a slim, three-cornered blade. 'A naval officer off duty always carries a stick. Mine was just a customised version.'

His description of Operation Ruthless tallied in almost every detail with that given to my aunt by Patrick Derring-Jones. Sir Peter said he had asked himself over and over again whether they had made the right decision that day, but that they honestly hadn't seen any alternative; that my grandfather had made a marvellous sacrifice for Patrick and for him, and that by going back they would only have been captured themselves.

'What do you think happened to Hugh?' I asked. He shook his head sadly, and said he didn't know, but feared the worst.

Tuesday, 1st May

009 is back from Singapore. The lead to Blofeld turned out to have been a red herring; he found no evidence that either Blofeld or Bunt had been there. When Bill heard, he shook his head. 'It's been nearly seven weeks since the last sighting. Damn man seems to have dropped off the edge of the world. I suppose that's it, then. The Old Man will order the file to be put on the back burner; we can't afford to have men shooting around the world after ghosts – you know what he's like about wasting service time.'

James is not going to be best pleased to come back to this news. I think on some level he regards getting Blofeld as the only true recompense for Tracy's death.

Thursday, 3rd May

An unsettling experience. I got home from work yesterday, collected Rafiki and walked up the stairs to my door. It was locked, as usual, but when I opened it, Rafi started barking furiously. I was immediately on my guard, and stepped inside with some trepidation. At first glance, nothing appeared to have been touched. But Rafi was still on edge – rushing around the flat, in and out of every room, sniffing and barking.

I followed him, checking behind doors, opening every cupboard, but there was no intruder. Then I closed the front door and jammed a wedge beneath it and went to the hiding-place. My relief that it hadn't been discovered, that none of my indicators had been disturbed, was immeasurable.*

Feeling more relaxed, I was going into the kitchen to put on the kettle, when my eye was caught by the pad beside the telephone. When I'm talking on the telephone, I tend to doodle with my left hand – I've always wanted to be ambidextrous, for no particular reason, and practise when I'm talking. But the pad and pen were on the right. I froze

---

* In an earlier diary, JM describes the measures she has taken to detect whether her secret hiding-place has been discovered. These include hairs wedged into the door of the bathroom cabinet, behind which the secret cavity was located, and talcum powder on the inner rim of the cabinet handle and on the surface below, on which an intruder would have to balance in order to lift away the cabinet. The wall behind the cabinet was additionally covered in a false layer of wall-paper with an adhesive edge, which JM would replace after returning the diary to its secret niche, and the safe combination dial was coated in staining invisible ink which would be revealed under fluorescent light.

inside. I went over to take a closer look, but other than that, there was no sign of tampering. Then I went back to the front door and opened it to examine the lock. I felt a shiver down my spine when I recognised the tell-tale scratches that even the most talented lock-picker can't avoid.

Shutting it again, I drew across the chain and sat on the sofa, shaking slightly, thinking about what could have happened. I was almost certain that someone had been in my flat. And if that was indeed the case, what had they been looking for? At least they hadn't found the diaries. I thank every lucky star that my hiding-place held up. Writing these is a betrayal of all my training, all my ethics. It's a risk I take every time I get out my pen and open the cover. I know I should stop, but that would be a greater betrayal of Pa. So I live with the guilt every day and try not to think about the enormity of the consequences if they were found. Not only would my career be finished, instantly, but who knows how much damage would be wrought on the Office It takes something like this to force me to face up to it. And yet, at the same time, I feel compelled to reach for my pen to record my thoughts.

Apart from these, there is nothing in my flat that could get anyone excited. I can't believe that the African carvings and paintings would pick up much on the open market. Maybe one could get something for the wireless, or my mother's portable gramophone or Pa's old carriage-clock? But the photograph albums, Ma's Kenyan journals, my modest wardrobe and several shelves of well-thumbed books would have little value to a stranger. Looking around me, it seems like a pretty modest haul for more than three decades of living. My few pieces of real jewellery are in the bank – I was wearing my pearls, and the rest is paste. Nothing, apparently, to interest this intruder.

But presumably he had been through everything? The private effects of my life? The thought of it makes me feel sick – but even worse is the motivation behind it. Why me? Have I been targeted? And if so, why? I'm filled with unease. The idea that I have stepped through the looking-glass; from being a hunter, I have become one of the hunted. It's almost too bewildering to take on board. Of course, we are all targets, juicy morsels of enticing information, potential bonanzas to Them. But me? I'd never considered it. To all intents and purposes I'm a secretary, a civil servant, an anonymous woman. I cannot have come to Their attention.

My first instinct was to call the Office. I went across to the telephone, but then stopped myself. What would I say to them? That my dog had barked? That the pad was on the other side of the telephone and there were some tiny marks around the lock? And what if they decided to come and search the flat thoroughly themselves? It would be a horrible irony if my secret were to be discovered by my own side.

Instead I called an emergency locksmith. By the time he had left, it was late. I telephoned Helena, and told her all about my visit to Scotland – the idea of waiting until I had something more concrete to report suddenly seemed selfish. I shouldn't have worried about raising her hopes – she was excited by the news, but warned me that I shouldn't expect too much. We talked for a long time about Pa and those days at the far frontier of our memories. I ended up saying nothing about the break-in for fear that she would worry. Sleep not being an option, I bundled Rafi into the Mini with no particular aim, and in due course found myself driving along Edgware Road and towards Marylebone. R's place.

It's been almost two weeks since we last saw each other, and although we have spoken a few times, they were stilted conversations. Even a month ago, my instinct at a time like this would have been to telephone him; he would have rushed straight over and I am sure we would have ended up treating it as another experience to notch up on the bed-head of life. Despite the awkwardness of our last meeting, I still found myself wanting to see him. It was past midnight, but he wouldn't mind being woken.

I parked outside his building and Rafi bounded ahead of me up the stairs. I knocked on the door and it was opened almost immediately. R was fully dressed. 'Jane, are you all right?' he asked. His embrace seemed almost tentative. 'Yes, fine. We were just passing. Neither Rafi nor I could sleep.' He looked at me. 'Has anything happened?' We went through to his drawing-room and sat down (there were three empty coffee cups on the table, I noticed). I told him about my fears that my flat had been broken into. He asked if anything had been taken, and when I said no he asked more and more questions. Whom had I seen recently? Who might have known where I lived?

I was beginning to get irritated. I told him I really hadn't come round to talk about it. Then, I suppose, I lost control. 'Why are you so interested anyway?' I asked.

He looked at me. 'What are you implying?'

'Nothing, just that you also seemed to be very interested in my personal things.'

'Oh come on, Jane. That isn't worthy of you. Are you comparing me to a burglar? This is crazy.'

I left without a word. Thank goodness I had Rafi with

me. He tried to climb on to my lap on the way back and when we got home he jumped into my bed and showed no inclination to leave. I felt enveloped by shame; I wish I could have taken back what I said. I took half a grain of Seconal and fell into merciful oblivion.

Sunday, 13th May

Dinner last night with Zach. A perplexing occasion. I lay awake almost until dawn turning over in my mind what he had said, exploring every nuance from one direction and then the next. He'd taken me to a small Italian restaurant called Nino's, off the King's Road, a busy place, staffed by cheerfully shouting Italian waiters pushing dessert trolleys.

It was, he told me, the first restaurant he had come to in London, when he was a young man. He'd got himself in a spot of trouble and his father had come over here to bail him out, followed by dinner at Nino's and a strict talking to. Zach looked at me carefully before apologising: 'Was that insensitive of me? You never had a father to get you out of scrapes.'

I smiled and told him not to worry, that I had rarely got myself into any kind of serious trouble.

The waiter came over with our food. It was delicious – tender veal marinated in lemon with buttered spinach. It wasn't until we'd finished our main courses and ordered coffee that he started talking about my father again. 'I've been thinking about what you said about your father. It all sounds very familiar. I am sure I have heard someone talking about him. Maybe it was in Tanganyika? Or maybe

Berlin? I can't be sure. But Hugh Moneypenny: it's a name that is not easily forgotten.'

I was too surprised to say anything. Pa has been upper-most in my mind since Scotland, but it was the last thing I'd expected to hear from Zach. I must have looked amazed, as he went on. 'Yes, I'm sure I could find out more. If you want me to, that is. Come to think of it, I don't believe it was in Africa. Not unless it was on one of my recent trips. But why would your father have come up in conversation? Who would I have talked to about him? No, it must have been in Berlin.'

I was still shocked, but not so much that I didn't notice him looking at me intently. I returned his gaze, but couldn't read anything in those pale grey eyes. It was as if an iron shop-front had been lowered over a jeweller's window. Was he humouring me? Trying to grab my atten-tion? Or was this something altogether more complicated?

'Yes,' I said eventually. 'Of course I would love to learn anything I can about my father. Yes, yes, of course. I would be very grateful for any memories about him. I'm sorry I seemed so stunned. I suppose he must have met so many people in his life. He had a full life before I was even born. It's just funny . . .' I realised I had been gabbling and stopped myself abruptly.

'What's funny?' he asked.

'Nothing really. It's just that I have been thinking a lot about my father recently. It comes in phases.'

And then the conversation veered back to other matters, the shutters were raised and Zach was as charming and amusing a dinner companion as I could have wished for. We had another cup of coffee before he walked me to the Brompton Oratory. He wanted to see me to my door, but I insisted I could make my way through the mews myself, that I enjoyed late-night walks alone. He laughed. 'You are certainly an extraordinary woman. What other idiosyncrasies do you have, I wonder? Do you enjoy swimming in Arctic streams, or riding racehorses backwards? Please let me take you out for lunch one weekend soon so I can find out more about them.'

Last night, as I lay in bed, I replayed that short conversation about Pa over and over in my head. What was it about it that had started the alarm bells ringing? Probably nothing, just an excessive sensitivity towards anything that smelt of tradecraft: how to hook an agent, then reel them in. That on top of the suspected break-in, which I have almost convinced myself must have been in my imagination. This is the real world, though; most people live their lives without deception. That Zach had heard my father's name must have been a coincidence – the world is a small place. But why would he have heard about him in Berlin, of all places? As far as I knew, he had never been to Germany. It was impossible.

Monday, 14th May

My first shooting lesson. When I mentioned to Bill, in passing, that I was worried about burglars, he insisted I learn to defend myself. He buzzed straight through to Major Boothroyd* in the Armoury and set it up there and

---

* Major Godfrey Boothroyd, head of Q:II, armourer to the secret service and internationally renowned small-arms expert. Sandy-haired, with wide-set, clear grey eyes, he worked as a consultant to

then. I can't quite see myself keeping a gun under my pillow in Ennismore Gardens, but I used to be fairly good with a rifle in Kenya* and I've always wanted to try my hand at target shooting.

There were four of us – three new male officers and me. We reported to the basement at nine sharp and were led into the briefing-room, a windowless dungeon set up like a classroom with desks and chairs. Major Boothroyd stood at the front, a diminutive figure in a navy blazer with regimental buttons and tie. 'Firearms are formidable weapons,' he told us. 'Used properly, they are extremely effective both in attack and for self-protection. However, it is not just a matter of pointing them at a target and firing. With a gun comes responsibility and it is this, as well as the rudiments of shooting them, that we will teach you over the weeks that follow.'

Five guns were laid out on the table in front of him, and he went through them one by one, describing each of their capabilities, strengths and weaknesses. The names were almost mythical in their familiarity: Enfield .38, Colt .45, Walther PPK, Beretta, Browning HP. 'Now, I want you to go

---

the service long beyond his official retirement age. Author of four manuals on the gun lore of close-combat weapons, and designer of the new firing range at Bisley.

* JM was just seven years old when Hugh Moneypenny put a small rifle into her hands while they were out hunting game for their dinner. As she recalled in a later diary, he had told her it was important that she didn't become sentimental about the wildlife, that one day she might need to kill in order to eat or to defend herself. He taught her to aim and fire, and, although she failed to bring down that first gazelle, before long she was having more success. After his death, she frequently shot wild game for the family pot.

through to the arms store and each draw an Enfield – Miss Moneypenny, I think perhaps the Beretta for you. It's a lady's gun, .25 calibre, too light to do serious damage at a distance, but quiet and effective at close range.'

I liked the feeling of a gun in my hand. Though light by gun standards, it felt reliably solid. The grip of cross-hatched wood was cool to the grasp, the dark metal barrel not much thicker than my middle finger. It was the gun, I knew, that 007 had carried for many years,* to the amuse-ment of 006 and 009, who favoured heavier models. 'Now, before we let you loose on the range,' Boothroyd continued, 'you need first to learn how to look after your weapon. This is every bit as important as being able to shoot the heart out of a moving target, because if your gun jams while you're in action, you're dead.' He smacked his left fist into his right palm.

The next half an hour was occupied with stripping, assembling and cleaning our guns. It was when we learnt how to load the magazines, and how to switch the safety catch on and off, that I began to feel a little uneasy. Handling the bullets; they were heavier than I had expected, more sinister to look at, and I found the loading mechanism stiff and the process slow to complete. And once the gun was loaded, the reality of what I was doing bore down on me, and I found myself holding it more than a little gingerly. Boothroyd was advising where best to

---

* After a decade of faithful service, Bond's Beretta misfired while he was grappling with Rosa Klebb. M ordered him to change his per-sonal weapon, and Boothroyd equipped him with a Walther PPK 7.65 mm, a .32 calibre weapon, still light but with considerable stopping power.

carry our weapon. 'I would always advise tucking it inside your belt or waistband, on your hip or behind you on your shooting-hand side. I know shoulder holsters have a certain fashionability – they don't spoil the line of your suit, for a start – but to my mind they prevent a fast draw. I've known men get shot while they're removing their weapon from a shoulder holster.' The idea, right then, of secreting a charged weapon anywhere against my body was distinctly unappealing. 'Right,' he continued. 'We have only just begun, but the rest can wait. I imagine you're keen to get to the range. I have to go now, but will leave you in the capable hands of Corporal Hedges[*] and his crew.'

Earmuffs and eye-shields on and standing in a cubicle looking down the range at the target – a body shape painted to resemble a German soldier – with Hedges at my shoulder zeroing my sight, I felt a flutter of excitement mixed with nerves. I released the safety, raised my arms, trying to keep them steady, and looked down the sights. At the command 'Fire', I squeezed the trigger. It was stiffer than I had anticipated, and although I had heard a thousand shots before, I still gave an involuntary start after firing. However, with no noticeable recoil, it didn't affect my aim and to my satisfaction my first shot landed only inches from the centre of the target. I managed to place the remaining five in a neat cluster around it.

I felt both exhilarated and slightly sick. The power contained in that small metal case was terrifying; the thought of what might go wrong, beyond comprehension. Still, I

---

[*] Corporal Ken Hedges, Boothroyd's number two, in charge of the day-to-day running of the firing-range.

couldn't disguise a small smile of pride when our target sheets were collected and compared and I found I had fared the best. 'Well done, miss,' said Hedges. 'You gentlemen are going to have to up your game to match that shooting. It may surprise you to learn that the ladies often shoot better than the gentlemen, especially at a stationary target. They tend to be calmer, and have a steadier hand. We'll have to see how you all fare next session with the shoot/no-shoot targets.'

Friday, 18th May

M called in oo6 this morning and when he came back through the baize door he looked excited. 'I'm off again,' he said. 'Up to the North Pole this time. Keep an eye on Goodnight for me, will you?'

According to Bill, it will be a testing mission – that was his little joke. 'M wants him to verify those reports that have been coming in about a massive nuclear test at Novaya Zemlya* last year. The Yanks are getting very het up about it. Their birds† haven't been able to confirm anything, and we could all do with an accurate head count on missile numbers and types up there.'

oo7 sent a cable from Casablanca reporting that he'd managed to track down a few old Nazis, but as far as he

---

* In 1954, the Soviet Union established its largest weapons-testing grounds at Novaya Zemlya, a pair of Arctic islands separated by a narrow channel and located off the north coast of European Russia (between 70° 31′ and 77° 6′ N, and 51° 35′ and 69° 2′ E).

† From January 1958, when *Explorer I* was launched into earth's orbit, the US had been receiving pictures of the earth's surface taken from satellites – or 'birds', as they were colloquially known.

could see they were more interested in doing experiments into cross-racial pollination than in assassinating Westerners. 'A bloody wild-goose chase after a bunch of toothless has-beens' was how he described it in his – unedited – report; I made sure that M did not receive that version. He said he had a couple more leads to check out, before heading back to HQ.

Perhaps, in view of the telephone call I received last week, he would be safer staying away a little longer. Sable Basilisk at the College of Arms* contacted me. He was extremely apologetic, but said he needed a little guidance. He is apparently being inundated by calls from a girl called Ruby Windsor,† who is desperate to get in touch with 'Sair Hilary'. 'She just won't stop telephoning for him, and then last week she turned up at the College asking to see him. Luckily, I was passing through the hall and heard her and was able to take her aside. I told her that Sir Hilary Bray was on an assignment abroad. She insisted that they were . . . er . . . practically engaged and that she needed to contact him urgently. I said I would see what I could do. She's now ringing me every day. I'm not sure what else I can do.'

---

* The official repository of the coats of arms and pedigrees of English, Welsh, Northern Irish and Commonwealth families. On request – and for payment – a herald at the college, such as Basilisk, could undertake genealogical and heraldic work for private clients outside its normal geographical orbit.
† One of Blofeld's guinea pigs at Piz Gloria, the daughter of chicken farmers from Lancashire. She was 'cured' of her allergy to chickens after answering an advertisement in the *Poultry Farmer's Gazette* seeking volunteers to come to a Swiss research institute working on allergy correction.

Basilisk sounded embarrassed. I don't imagine they get too many lovelorn girls battering at the great wooden doors of the College of Arms. Unfortunately, we do, particularly where 007 is concerned, and it's usually up to me to mop up the mess. I told him to give her my number when she next telephoned and that I would ensure she stayed out of his hair in the future, for which he thanked me profusely.

When the call came through the following day, I was ready. 'Miss Windsor,' I said, adopting a haughty tone. 'Sir Hilary asked me to pass on his warmest regards and to ask whether you had received your family tree. You did? I'm so pleased. He's terribly sorry that he can't talk to you himself, but he's been called away on urgent business to Japan. I shouldn't tell you, but he's working with the Emperor over there. Very hush-hush. If it works out, it'll cause quite a stir. We expect him to be there for some months. Lady Amanda is going out to join him. Have you met her? No? Lady Amanda is his third cousin once removed. They're to be married later this year. The invitations haven't been sent out yet; it all depends on how this job goes. He's a very important man, you know. They've been betrothed to one another almost since birth. Now, is there anything I can help you with? He very specifically asked me to make sure you were all right.'

Thankfully she said no. There have been occasions when I've had to meet the young girl in question, and even, once, to arrange a discreet doctor's appointment. I don't know what it is about the oo agents which makes them seemingly incapable of completing a mission without melting some poor girl's heart on the way. They're all as bad as each other, though I suspect 007 has the edge. Or had, anyway. There was that exotic fortune-diviner from Haiti.* I rather liked her. She came through London a couple of years ago with her fiancé, an American magician she'd met in Las Vegas. James was away, so Bill and I took them to dinner at Simpson's. Then there was Tiffany,† the diamond girl. Quite another story. She stayed around for some time – May was always phoning Lil or me to complain about her – said she stayed in bed until noon eating chocolates and leaving the wrappers strewn over the floor. I never met her, but saw them once walking into the Savoy. She was beautiful, but not exactly classy. She proved that when she ran off with the American marine from the Embassy – that must have hurt 007's pride somewhat, though I doubt it did lasting damage.

The Russian, Tatiana Romanova.‡ We all met her, of course. 006 had to go to Paris to bring her back after 007 was kicked by that dreadful Klebb woman. I felt sorry for Tatiana. She was an innocent. She had come to rely on

---

* Solitaire, real name Simone Latrelle, black-haired daughter of a French colonial slave-owner in Haiti. When her parents died, she worked as a fortune diviner in a Port au Prince cabaret, where she was discovered by Mr Big. She helped Bond evade Mr Big's wrath, then escaped herself from his clutches and into Bond's arms.

† Tiffany Case, croupier and diamond-smuggler. Her mother kept a brothel in San Francisco. When Tiffany was sixteen, after being gang-raped, she ran away from home, ending up in the employ of the Spang brothers, gangsters based in Las Vegas. She encountered Bond when, posing as a small-time criminal, he offered his services to her as a diamond 'mule' from London to New York.

‡ Corporal in the State Security Department and Greta Garbo look-alike, selected by Klebb to lure Bond into an assassination trap by professing her love for him. Unaware of the dark subtext of her assignment, she genuinely fell in love with Bond on the Orient Express between Istanbul and Paris.

James during the train journey back from Istanbul, and I think she truly believed he liked her for more than her cipher machine.* She never had a chance to find out; she came back here to a full debriefing by Head of S, the Signals chief and even M himself, before being whisked off to a safe house in the country, given a haircut, a new name and a decent job at GCHQ,† I believe. It took 007 a few months to recover from the Klebb foot, and as far as I know he never tried to track Tatiana down.

Honeychile Rider.‡ That's a name one doesn't easily forget. She's still sending James Christmas cards – Mary came to me with last year's one, wanting to know who she was. I filled her in on the Dr No mission. I think James was truly fond of Honey, as he called her, but in a paternal way. He arranged for her to go to see a plastic surgeon in Philadelphia to fix her nose, and the last thing we heard she had married the doctor and they had two children. Then there was the physiotherapist from Shrublands – she was the one who got into trouble – and heaven knows how many others. And now poor Ruby.

---

* The Spektor – offered to Bond as an enticement to walk into the KGB trap.

† Government Communications Headquarters, since 1952 based in a heavily guarded complex in Cheltenham, Gloucestershire. It has two main missions: sigint (signals intelligence – the monitoring and deciphering of enemy wireless transmissions), and information assurance (keeping the government's information and communication systems safe from outside interference).

‡ Beautiful blonde shell-collector with a 'figure of Venus' and a broken nose, encountered by Bond on Crab Key while he was on the trail of Dr No. They managed to escape together from No's fortress and returned to her home in Jamaica.

He may make these girls feel they're special at the time, but a man like 007 lives for adventure and if they're part of it then when that particular adventure ends so does their involvement. In the end, it is to M that 007 returns. To M and to the Office – and to me, I suppose.

Sunday, 20th May

R is leaving the country. I arrived back from the park this morning with Rafiki to find him sitting on the steps outside my flat, clutching a large bunch of flowers. He stood up as he saw me. 'Oh Jane,' he said. 'I had to see you once more. And I couldn't go away without saying goodbye to Rafi.'

'Go away? Where?' I asked. As he said it, I felt the bottom drop out of my stomach. I thought I'd come to terms with the end of our relationship, but the idea of him leaving the country was suddenly hard to bear.

'West Berlin. I've been offered a job by a very good firm, with a shot at a partnership if it all goes well. There's an enormous amount of exciting work out there and I . . .'

He tailed off. I suppose what he was going to say was that he needed to get away from me. 'West Berlin,' I started. 'That would be a wonderful place to visit, but to live? With all that's going on over there now – it might be cut off at any time.'

'Is that the official Foreign Office line, then?' He laughed. 'No, I think I'll be all right. One has to take risks sometimes, don't you think?'

We went to the Brompton Grill for lunch. It was not a good choice: it was there that we had met that first Sunday after our return from Barcelona and, inevitably, the memories rushed back to envelop me. The Gaudí cathedral, the rain, rushing for shelter and being rescued by a tall man with an umbrella. A coffee, which turned into a drink and dinner that night. And the next and the next. We had so much to talk about, it seemed. I was drawn to the look of intelligence in his eyes, his long, slender hands, his passion for architecture, the way he seemed to find the laughter in everything. For the rest of that weekend, we acted like a young couple in love for the first time – and maybe for me it was?

Back in London, at first our lives seemed to mesh together neatly. For once, I didn't feel crowded and, I suppose, somewhere in the back of my being, I dared to dream that this time it might not have to end. But it did, and it has, and despite the ugliness of the last few months, I shall miss him.

We embraced goodbye. He held me away, looked into my eyes and told me to be careful. I have a funny sense that he knows something that he hasn't told me.

Friday, 25th May

A horrible, horrible day. At lunchtime I found Raine in a dreadful state, rushing along corridors asking everyone if they had heard from CNE.* He didn't show up for work this morning. She called his house and his wife said he hadn't come home last night – she had assumed he'd stayed at the office. I asked if his car was here. 'No,' said Raine. 'He left the car-park at 8.15 last night. What is so awful is that his

---

* Chief of Northern Europe, a career intelligence officer named Clive Mostyn.

office is so tidy. It's impeccable. There are no papers on his desk, his wastepaper basket has been emptied, and you know what chaos it is normally.' I took her by the arm to tell Bill. Somehow, whenever there's a crisis, I turn to him.

He looked immediately concerned when he heard. He told Raine to go back to her office and telephone all of CNE's regular haunts. 'I've done that already,' she said. 'Then do it again.' As soon as she'd left he buzzed through to M's office. Then he asked me to call Vallance [Assistant-Commissioner Ronald Vallance] at Scotland Yard. 'Ask him to put an APB [All Points Bulletin] out urgently, please, with special vigilance at the national exit points. Then call the Watchers* and tell them to keep an eye out for Mostyn at Kensington Palace Gardens [the Soviet Embassy].'

We heard from Scotland Yard shortly after four. Vallance called M directly. When he opened his office door he looked suddenly ten years older. 'I'm afraid we're too late, Bill,' he said. 'CNE was found inside his car on Hampstead Heath. He's dead, I'm afraid. Looks like suicide. Miss Moneypenny, could you go and break the news gently to his secretary. Make sure she gets home safely. And please ask Miss Fields to come up here now.'

By the evening, the news had spread through the whole office. Everyone was walking around in a state of shock, not knowing quite what to think. Poor CNE. I suppose it must

---

* Attached to A Branch of MI5, the domestic intelligence – or security – service, the Watchers provided surveillance of foreign embassies, consulates and trade commissions. They photographed people going in and out and checked their identity against a mugbook of known diplomats and suspected intelligence operatives. On occasion, they tailed agents of particular interest, from suitably anonymous cars fitted with souped-up engines.

mean that our speculation was founded, that there had been a mole, and that it was he. I would never have suspected poor old Clive Mostyn. He always seemed such a gentle man, so completely dedicated to the Office.

Saturday, 26th May

News of CNE's death was reported in *The Times*, in a short article that managed to allude to his true profession without stating it categorically. Someone from this place has obviously been talking. M is not going to be best pleased. I can't help but feel sympathy for Mostyn's family – I believe he had young children and now they're going to have to grow up with a pall of suspicion hanging over their father's death.

Sunday, 27th May

Lunch with Zach. I'd been looking forward to it, a welcome antidote to the tragedy at the Office. We arranged to meet outside Harrod's and I'd just arrived when he swept around the corner in a new car. It was a soft-topped, two-seater silver Mercedes 300 SL, with a wonderfully throaty growl. He was wearing a navy cap and cream scarf and looked very dashing. He certainly made the Knightsbridge ladies' heads turn. I had on my Jaeger silk tea dress, and couldn't suppress a shiver of pride that it was beside me that he stopped. The car had been delivered just two days ago, he told me. 'I've been waiting for it for weeks now. That was why I didn't ask you to lunch before. I thought we would go to the country, if that's acceptable to you.' I had no objections and sat very happily as we barrelled along the Great West Road, my hair whipping against my cheeks. While we were moving, conversation was impossible. He turned every now and then to smile and I noticed, for the first time, that he had exceptionally perfect teeth. I found them rather off-putting. Post-war dentistry in Tanganyika must have been superior to what we had to endure in Kenya.

We had a lovely lunch at a small pub in Maidenhead, then went for a walk along the river. The last time I had been there was with R and I felt a momentary pang of sadness for what could have been, as well as a sliver of guilt that I was enjoying it now with another man. It was a beautiful late-spring day and we sat down to feed the ducks and swans with our purloined bread rolls, when Zach brought up the subject of Pa again. I have to admit I was half longing for it and half dreading it. Replaying it now, I am forced to admire the easy way he dropped it into the conversation.

'You love animals,' he said. 'You must miss that about Africa, your pet meerkat . . .' It was as if a red flag had gone up; I was sure I hadn't mentioned Evie to him. But I said nothing and he continued, leaning a little closer. 'I was intrigued by what you said about your father last time we met. I searched through my memory and managed to track down the person who had mentioned him to me.'

I asked if he was sure it was my father.

'I am sure. Hugh Moneypenny. He disappeared on 25th October 1940.'

I was sitting up straight now.

'I've found out a considerable amount about him. Things that will surprise you and, I hope, please you.' He paused, before dropping the thunderbolt. 'Your father did not die

135

in 1940. He survived Operation Ruthless and was taken back to Berlin as a prisoner. I spoke to someone who had met him. It was this person who told me about your meerkat, Evie, I must confess, and the warthog you named after Winston Churchill. Your father called you Janey, didn't he?'

I nodded, unable to speak, desperate to make some sort of sense of what he was saying. He just looked at me. Two questions were spinning round and round in my mind, but it took what felt like a long time to be able to form my mouth around them.

'When did he die? Is he still alive?'

Zach shrugged. 'It is certainly possible. My contact seemed to indicate that this might be the case. I can do more, if you want me to. But it will require some considerable effort. My contact is not going to tell me this sort of information easily. I will need something from you in return.'

I started to feel icy fingers tip-toeing up my back, as he continued. 'Don't worry, it's not that I want to go to bed with you – although of course I do.' He smiled.

I looked straight back at him. 'I want to know more than anything what happened to my father and will give you what I can. But what does your contact need? I'm not a rich woman, but I have some savings.'

He shook his head. 'Not that. No, I need to know a bit more about what you're doing . . . I know where you work.'

I must have let the shock and horror show on my face. He put his hand on my arm and I snatched it away. 'There's nothing to be afraid of,' he said. 'I promise this will remain our secret. You are good at keeping secrets, I think. Come on, let's head back now. You must think about this – I just want to help you and I won't be able to do so unless you give something back. We will meet again in one week and talk about it some more.'

We drove back to London in silence. I can't even begin to sort out the conflicting emotions that are raging around my entire body at the moment. I'm lost and there's no one I can turn to. Can I ever trust my instincts again?

June

At the peak of the Cold War, each side was engaged in a constant quest for inside information about the status of its enemy. They thirsted for knowledge about everything from details of nuclear programmes to the chemical composition of ink used by junior intelligence officers. Code books, passwords, staff structure, policy determination – all were prizes more valuable than gold. And the best way to gain access to most of these was through a mole. In the 1950s and '60s the presence of spies and traitors within the intelligence structures of both East and West was a subject that both obsessed and terrified all who lived and worked within those organisations.

The main objective of an intelligence officer working abroad was – and is to this day – to recruit agents. It is an art – of seduction and coercion. The best recruiters possess an almost supersensory ability to recognise a potential double agent, combined with an instinct as to how best to hook him – or her. Their prey might be motivated by political concerns: either a belief in the philosophies of the other side or a disillusionment with the practices of his or her own. For some it is a question of greed: the promise of a better life, money, status. For others there is little choice: they have been lured into a compromising act then threatened with exposure if they do not switch sides. According to a former member of the SIS whom I talked to, 'If an officer brings in two good agents in his career, who stay "in place", then he has made an enormously important contribution.'

Even a successful recruitment might not be what it at first seems. During the Cold War, the organisations of both East and West were occupied as much with feeding their enemies false information and supposed double agents who turned out to be triple agents, working for their initial employers all along, as they were with delving for the truth themselves. It was a world of suspicion and counter-suspicion, information and misinformation. And the Secret Intelligence Service was at the heart of it.

Since 25 May 1951, when Guy Burgess and Donald Maclean disappeared on the night boat from Southampton, with a final destination of Moscow, the SIS had been under the international microscope. The unveiling of the first two members of the Cambridge spy ring had resulted in a loss of face in the eyes of its allies – particularly the Americans, despite their own leakage problems – while its enemies looked on with a secret smile. By the turn of the decade, however, the proverbial boot had swapped feet. First, Polish intelligence officer Michael Goleniewski defected and subsequently pointed a finger at an MI6 officer then stationed in Berlin, George Blake, who on 3 May 1961 was sentenced to forty-two years' imprisonment for treason. By this time the West had a new mole, a GRU (Russian military intelligence) colonel named Oleg Penkovsky, who revealed, among other things, details of the physical appearance of Soviet missile launch sites. Later in 1961, a new KGB defector, Anatoly Golitsyn, revealed that there were five members of the Cambridge spy ring – prompting further frenzied introspection.

But it was not only those in the higher echelons of their organisations who were targets for turning. Anyone with even the most seemingly minor role was regarded as a potential mole. The diplomatic circuit at home and abroad was a cauldron of suggestion; cocktail-party chatter disguised furtive attempts to milk opposite numbers for information while feeding them disinformation and sounding out potential sources. Many were approached, in a variety of ways, on numerous occasions throughout their careers. Most managed to recognise and parry what were often merely exploratory advances and to laugh about it afterwards. It was all part of the Great Game of espionage.

Monday, 4th June

My second shooting lesson. I'm enjoying this now, though I still treat the gun with the respect it merits. We spent less time in the classroom and more on the range this session, but I find the theoretical aspects equally involving. I had never before given much thought to bullets; now I appreciate that the ammunition you choose is as important as the weapon. Full metal jacket – where the lead core is entirely enclosed in its copper casing – is standard. Soft points, where the copper doesn't cover the tip, mushroom inside the target, causing greater internal damage, though they have a shorter range. Modern bullets are increasingly pointed, so as to pierce body armour – just listening to the thwock as the bullet leaves the weapon and instantaneously punctures the target is enough to make one doubt even the possibility of surviving a bullet wound. Major Boothroyd is a repository of gun knowledge and he really loves his subject. You have only to see him fondling a weapon to know how much he reveres it.

In the range, we started with another session of shooting the 'Huns'. I was pleased to see that my accuracy had not diminished and I still scored better than the men. I shouldn't have been so proud. My fall was to come with the fabled shoot/no-shoot targets. They were set up sixty feet away, at the end of the range. At the signal, one would flip around, Corporal Hedges explained, and we had three seconds to determine whether or not he was carrying a weapon. If he was, we should shoot; if not, hold fire. It was a test of reactions and nerve. 'Come on, Miss Moneypenny, you're out in front so far, let's see how you fare. Remember, many of these people are innocent civilians. You don't want their blood on your conscience.'

The first one was easy: the picture flipped and it was a man in a balaclava pointing an automatic. I shot and he fell down. So far, so good. The next was also armed to the teeth. I missed with the first round, but got him with the next. 'Fire your initial shot at the largest part of the target, probably below the stomach, the second into the chest area,' Hedges said, as I waited for the next figure to reveal itself. But this one was a woman carrying a baby, and although I recognised her as such instantly, I nearly fired anyway. It was like a reaction I had trouble controlling. I nearly shot the next one, a teenager with a violin, too, and when the first man whipped around again I hesitated and only managed to let loose a wild shot as he was flipping back.

This went on and on, figures flipping to and fro. I could feel my shoulders getting more and more tense as my accuracy and speed diminished. When, at last, all my magazines were spent, I found I was shaking like a leaf and could barely place the gun down on the counter in front of me without dropping it. There was no way I could have reloaded again, not at that time anyway. I had managed to get away without shooting a civilian, for which Boothroyd himself congratulated me. 'But you were far too slow. You would have been shot by the oppo ages ago. What you have to learn is to let go of your head – stop trying to second-guess the targets and act on reflex. I promise, your instinct rarely lets you down.'

One by one, I watched my fellow students face the same challenge, as slowly the feeling of seasickness in my stomach began to subside. They fared more or less as poorly; one young man, currently a junior researcher in the Caribbean Section, almost broke down after he shot the mother. 'I can't do this. I don't want to do this,' he said.

'Don't worry,' Boothroyd reassured him. 'You'll probably never have to use a gun in anger. Most people facing the shoot/no-shoots for the first time do just as badly. In fact, we've had less than a handful who've managed perfect scores first time out, and they've all at one time had offices on the seventh floor.' I doubt that any of us are destined for the oo section.

As I was leaving, Major Boothroyd called me into the arms store. 'Miss Moneypenny, come and look at this. I think it might interest you.' He pulled a tan-coloured, leather-bound book from the shelf. It was slightly battered, with gilt-edged pages. He lifted the front cover; inside nestled a tiny, snub-nosed gun with a mother-of-pearl handle, small enough to fit in the palm of my hand. 'It's a Baby Browning.* A pretty little number, but effective too. It's a favourite with the Mafia for executions. Your target is sitting in a restaurant, you walk up to him, you bend down as if talking to him and jab the Baby into his waist. Pop pop. You fire twice and walk away. The noise would be just loud enough to make people look up from their dinner, but they probably wouldn't guess what had happened, or where. Meanwhile, a .25 bullet is ploughing through your target's vital organs, liver on one side, kidneys on the other. He has only a tiny chance of staying alive. It's a nice little gun for a lady's handbag.'

Wednesday, 6th June

007 arrived back from Morocco today, with little to report. He looks fitter, but there is still a blankness in his eyes and a certain lassitude to his gait that I find disconcerting. He came out of M's office and raised his eyes to the ceiling. 'I hope you're holding the first dance at Lil's wedding for me,' he said. 'Of course, James,' I replied. 'But you'd better confirm soon. I'm not sure I can keep the competition at bay for long.'

It was familiar banter to both of us, though this time I had a sense that we were just going through the motions.

This afternoon, we all went to Clive Mostyn's funeral. The moment he died, he lost his initials, and now there's

---

* Browning .25 ACP, 6.35-mm miniature pistol, first introduced by Browning in 1905 and since then copied by numerous gun manufacturers.

another CNE sitting in his chair. It was a moving affair; his wife looked devastated, the rest of his family bewildered. Still, I sensed a slight release in M's tension. CNE's suicide has, perhaps, given M an escape route from scandal.

Thursday, 7th June

R has gone. I received a letter in yesterday's post, telling me he would already be in Berlin by the time I read it, that he wished me luck and that everything could have turned out differently. It gave no forwarding address. I honestly don't know what I feel and am trying my best not to think about it.

Friday, 15th June

Still no word from oo6, but this was to be expected. The likelihood of his having found a reliable channel of communication from the Arctic wastelands of Novaya Zemlya back here was always slim, and as Bill said, if they were to catch him, they wouldn't miss the chance to rub it in our faces. If all goes according to plan, he should be back within a few weeks.

Sunday, 17th June

This has turned into a truly dreadful mess. I've never felt so torn in my life. I've had my dearest dream dangled in front of me, but only in exchange for something that is not mine to give. And yet. And yet.

I met Zach for drinks in a small restaurant in Soho on Friday night. I'd cancelled last week, but it wasn't something I was going to be able to escape for ever. Again, he had found a quiet alcove. He was as charming as ever, but this time there was no pretence that we were pursuing anything but a business relationship. It was as if he'd exchanged the hat of suitor for that of mentor and guide. In view of the circumstances, I found this distasteful, but I suppose the alternative was less appealing. He was at pains to maintain that everything was for my benefit – that the situation had only arisen after I'd expressed interest in finding out the truth about my father, but we both knew that was not true. We are professionals, even if I'm straying far from my normal domain. I can't quite bring myself to grasp the enormity of what he's asking me to do. He says it's nothing important, but we both know that there's no return from that first step towards betrayal.

How did I get myself into this situation? What is more important to me: my career and country, or my flesh and blood? If I am to believe what Zach has said   and deep down I want to, desperately – I now have real hope, for the first time in two decades, that Pa could be alive, somewhere, perhaps being held as a prisoner. Certainly he did not die on 25th October 1940. Zach could not have known what he does otherwise, surely.

'*Swallows and Amazons* was your favourite book when you were growing up,' he said, after our drinks had arrived. 'You used to sit and read it on the lower branch of an old acacia tree overhanging the lake at the bottom of your garden at Maguga.'

'Yes,' I replied slowly. It was an eerie feeling: both that my father was rising from the dead, and that a stranger knew these private things about me.

'Have you kept up your diary that he sent you from Scotland? The red one with the pale-blue pages?' he asked.

I just looked at him and shook my head slowly. I begged him not to make me do this. Couldn't he just tell me about my father? It all happened so long ago. He knows I want to know what happened to Pa, but I can't betray my work. In any case, I told him, I really don't know anything important. I'm just a secretary at the Foreign Office; they don't tell me their secrets. I spend most of my time typing routine reports, forms, nothing that could possibly be of interest. As a cover, it is believable, but not, clearly, to Zach.

He shook his head this time. 'Miss Jane Vivien Moneypenny, I know who you work for. I know an extraordinary amount about you. I know that you eat one piece of wholemeal toast and half a grapefruit for breakfast every day, that you don't drink coffee and prefer cold milk. I know where you spent your holiday last year. I know the name of your sister and her fiancé, Professor Lionel Westbrook, of your dog, Rafiki, and the kind lady Maura downstairs, who looks after him while you are at work. I know where you have your hair cut, that you are allergic to eggs, and that your favourite lunchtime sandwich is ham and strong mustard washed down with a glass of milk.'

I felt physically sick, violated, surprised, ashamed and threatened, all rolled together. He flashed those perfect teeth at me. 'Come on, we are partners in this. I can help you to find your father through my contact – and in return all I need to give him is some very basic information, nothing that will put anyone in jeopardy. You still don't need to proceed if you don't wish to. All my contact wants to know is how the British believe the situation in Berlin is going to play out, whether they are making preparations to act militarily if the Russians carry out their threat to turn their quarter over to the East.* That's not so very difficult, is it? It's not going to compromise anyone.' 'I can't,' I replied. 'I made a promise when I joined the organisation that I wouldn't reveal anything about my work. I signed my name to it.† I can't do it.' I shook my head, determined not to succumb to tears.

'Don't worry,' he patted my hand. 'By doing this you'll be helping your country. If we all worked together in a more constructive and transparent fashion, we'd have a far greater chance at peace. Instead, there's secrecy and skulduggery. We have to guess at each other's plans, and sometimes we make the wrong decisions, based on the wrong information – decisions that we might not have reached had we known the real facts.' I put my head in my hands. The waiter came over and I couldn't help but notice Zach's composure as he joked with him and smoothly asked for the bill.

---

* At the end of the Second World War the city of Berlin was divided into four zones: American, British, French and Soviet. The first three comprised West Berlin, essentially an island, situated 100 miles into Soviet-occupied East Germany and connected to the West by a narrow corridor. Soviet premier Nikita Khrushchev was keen to see a peace treaty between the West, the USSR and the two Germanys. When the Western powers refused to accede to his terms, he threatened to sign a unilateral treaty with East Germany, leaving the East Germans to decide for themselves about the future of Western access to the divided city.

† New recruits to the Civil Service who might one day have access to 'sensitive' material have first to sign the Official Secrets Act. Passed into law in 1911, the Act comprises two sections: the first dealing with espionage, and the second making it illegal to disclose any information, on any subject, without authorisation – except when such disclosure is in the interest of the state.

'Now, Jane, I am leaving this in your hands,' he said, as the man went away. 'If you decide you want to track down your father, it can be done. But first you have to fulfil your side of the agreement. You're in a position to make copies of the briefing papers – you know the ones I mean. I want you to take them in a sealed envelope to Brompton Oratory in exactly one week's time. Go into the church through the Brompton Road entrance. Just to your right is an altar, a memorial to the war dead, with a copy of Michelangelo's *Pietà* in front of it. On the floor below the statue are the words "Consummatum est". You'll see two large marble columns close to the wall just to the left of the altar as you face it. Make sure no one is watching and then leave the envelope in the small space behind the column nearest to the wall. Don't leave the church immediately as it could appear suspicious, but walk around as if you're a tourist, then leave at your leisure. I'll contact you once the material has been collected, with more news of your father. Don't worry, it's perfectly safe. If you follow my instructions, nothing will happen to you.'

Of course I cannot do it. I feel dirty for even having the conversation, as if my relationship with the Office has already been contaminated. I'm still staggered that I find myself in such a situation. Looking back, I see now that I've been a target for some time. Zach was obviously primed and pointed at me. By whom? It can only be the Stasi* or

---

* The Ministerium für Staatssicherheit (Ministry for State Security), commonly known by the abbreviation 'Stasi', was, from April 1950 until it was disbanded in 1989, the secret police force of the Communist-controlled German Democratic Republic (East Germany). Its role included the collection of external intelligence,

KGB* – and someone who knows I like Brahms and African sculpture. They did a very professional job. Still, I should have known. The way it was done appeared to be so natural, sitting in the seat that should have been R's at the Albert Hall. How did they fix that? And R – what of him? Could those unworthy suspicions that I tried to suppress have had merit after all? Could that proffered umbrella in Barcelona have been part of a carefully choreographed approach? I don't even want to think this.

R knew about my childhood. No, I mustn't let myself follow this train – it makes a mockery of everything that I am, of my instincts, my desires, every day we shared. It cannot be. Yet what about the time I found him searching my desk, with the lower drawers open, as Q Branch had recommended? He knew where I worked. He'd been awake long after his usual turning-in time on the night of the burglary. It couldn't be. It must not be true. Who can I go to? Not to Helena, not to Bill – he would be horrified – and 007 is not in the right frame of mind. Oh Pa, this is all about you – oh that you were here now to help me find a way out of this terrible predicament.

under its head of foreign intelligence, the renowned spymaster Markus Wolf. Its key targets included the US, British and French occupational forces in Berlin.

* The Komitet Gosudarstvennoye Bezhopaznosti (Committee for State Security), the main Soviet security and intelligence agency and secret police force. Formed on 13 March 1954, its tasks were external espionage, counter-espionage, liquidation of anti-Soviet and counter-revolutionary formations within the USSR, border security and guarding the leaders of the party and state and critical state property.

Wednesday, 20th June

I'm surprisingly calm at the Office; it's only when I get home that I want to put a pillow over my head to blot out the voices shouting at me, pulling me this way and that. I'm meant to be making the drop on Friday. I know where the papers are, but I've made no move to call them in. I'm not going to do it. I can't. I wake up in the middle of the night in a state of panic and various options seem to shoot down from the sky and crowd around me. Could I compose a fake Berlin assessment? Play them along until I had some clue as to whether Pa is alive and, if so, where he is being held? Then dawn breaks and I realise that I'm being unrealistic, that they'd never fall for such a predictable substitution. What would they do if I just failed to make the drop? I'm in desperate need of advice – I want to tell Bill, but am scared of his reaction.

This lunchtime, I slipped into Records and made for the Zs. Nothing under David Zach. I've put through a routine enquiry to the FO asking for his visa details, but don't expect that to come to much. I even looked quickly through the photographs of known Redland operatives, but none looked anything like Zach. I stayed late tonight and went down to the Identicast room, to try to mock up his face. I didn't know the Records duty officer at the controls of the machine, which made it easier. I was fully prepared to pass it off as a routine request, but he never asked. I sat in a chair facing a huge screen. He asked me first for the main lines of the face and as he flashed up on the screen various head sizes and shapes, I was able to say yes or no. As soon as we'd found one I was happy with, he left it on the screen and we began to build on it. First the nose shape, haircut and colour, eye shape and size, chin, mouth, cheeks and ears. We slotted in his heavy eyebrows and perfect teeth. Although I thought I had a clear picture of Zach in my mind, it was still difficult to describe each feature individually. After about an hour we came up with a face that was, if not identical to Zach's, then a recognisable approximation. 'That's him,' I told the operator. He said he would make a photograph and send it up to the eighth floor. I turned away from the screen with a shudder, which made the man laugh. 'I must say I've seen worse. This one looks like a normal bloke, I'd say.' Rather too normal, from my point of view. If he'd had an eye-patch or a turned-up raincoat, maybe I would have been forewarned.

That's the problem. I find I'm constantly looking behind me these days, whether I'm in the bus queue or waiting for a sandwich at lunch. I've started to vary my route to and from work, and before even leaving the house I check the front windows time and again for any suspicious loiterers. I'm almost sure that I've seen a pale-eyed man twice, both times near the park, but I can't be certain, and even if it was the same man, he probably lives near here too. I know I'm being over-jumpy.

But no, I can't brush under the carpet the strong likelihood that I'm being followed, and have been for some time, maybe even years? He knew what I ate for breakfast. If I don't go along with this, would I put others into jeopardy? Helena? Up to now, they've made no threats, only promises. I've exactly forty-eight hours in which to decide what to do next.

Thursday, 21st June

Today I almost made a copy of the Berlin master plan. I could have done it easily – that's what is so frightening. Even if I had been overseen making the copy, no one would have thought anything of it. Miss Moneypenny, M's dependable personal secretary. There's no document that I cannot access, no signal that I don't have a right to read. My bag is never searched, my confidence never questioned. And I know much of consequence – as well as plenty that is not – that goes on within the walls of that building, in some cases more so even than Bill, who has no direct line into the Powder Vine. I would never be suspected. And this one thing they are asking for: it's information that, although top secret, is held in half a dozen different ministries and departments. You could make a good stab at it through a close reading of the PM's speeches and answers in the Commons. Would it be so very bad to divulge this one, non-specific piece of information? As Zach said, it would not jeopardise lives – it could even save some. And to me, to Helena, the reward would be priceless.

Friday, 22nd June

In half an hour's time, I am due to place this envelope behind the pillar in the Brompton Oratory. I made the copy at lunchtime. It was a way to postpone the decision that I must make in the next ten minutes. My options are still open. I've not yet burnt any of the proverbial bridges.

I think my rubbish is being searched. Rafi dropped his ball between the railings this evening, and when we went down to retrieve it, I could swear that someone had gone through the dustbins. I always put my rubbish in a bag tied up with string, then place it in the dustbin tie-first, yet there it was in the dustbin with the tie facing upwards. It's not that there's anything there to interest anyone, but still, the feeling that my intimate discards are being examined is discomforting in the extreme. I always knew that the possibility of surveillance came with the job, but this is a step beyond what we were warned to expect, and I don't like it one bit.

One minute until I should leave. I should be putting my coat on now – I could still get there in time if I ran.

Saturday, 23rd June

Loelia's wedding. A wonderful, happy day. Never had I seen so many of us secret people gathered together in such open conviviality. The entire surviving 00 section, past and present, over whom Lil had clucked and tutted, were there, oozing suave ruthlessness and a certain regret. Only 006 was missing, which I know was a source of great disappointment both to him and to Lil. She has loved every man she worked for, cared for them as if they were a son, brother, lover (though, to the best of my knowledge, she never succumbed to any of their obvious charms).

She looked radiant, a decade younger than she did on the day she left the Office. It's as if the responsibility she carried every day for her men had been lifted from her slender shoulders, leaving her carefree and buoyant about what the future might hold. I've never seen her more beautiful – her dress was made of heavy satin, with a low, swan's neckline and a narrow waist, flowing out gently into a long, down-trimmed train. She wore a diamond tiara, which matched the enormous, jewel-encrusted ring that had once belonged to Gerald's grandmother, and she carried a bouquet of rosebuds, just a faint blush off white.

There were eight tiny bridesmaids with wide blue satin sashes tied around their waists, and two page boys in miniature soldier uniforms. Gerald looked proud and handsome in his morning-suit. The whole tableau was perhaps only let down by the maid of honour, me, who felt ridiculous in her cream raw silk Jackie suit and pillbox hat – and who wept throughout the vows. I have seldom felt less in control of my emotions, and I'm not entirely sure why. I was so pleased for her, and yes, perhaps a little sad for myself, and relieved and worried all bundled up together.

M made a wonderful speech, praising Loelia's good humour and resourcefulness in a gruff manner that to me, anyway, was no mask for his inner emotion. He managed to recount a number of endearing anecdotes about her Office life without in any way revealing what it was that she had done for all those years. After all, there was a whole side of the church who believed that she had been a secretary in the Foreign Office. We must never let down our guard. In the absence of 006, Mary, who knows better than anyone what Lil's daily life consisted of, danced the afternoon away with 009, before performing a less than graceful dive to catch the bride's bouquet.

I danced with 007. Unsurprisingly, he is a wonderful dancer and managed to make me forget everything, even the suit, as he twirled me around the dance floor. I felt like a princess, if only for a few short minutes. At one point, he murmured into my ear, 'Penny, why do I bother with all these women when the most desirable one in the world is here under my nose the whole time? Come home with me now, Penny, please.' I looked up into those blue-grey eyes, but he was gazing over my shoulder with a far-away expression and I knew it wasn't really me that he wanted. 'Now, James, I wish I could, but I don't think it would do either of us any good.' He looked down at me then, with a tenderness I'd rarely seen in his face. 'You're probably right. It wouldn't be fair on you, dearest Pen. You know, I've been going to see all these quacks around Harley Street, a hypnotist, some blasted man who stuck needles into my toes, even a head doctor, but none of them have helped. The hypnotist told me I needed a woman, but for the first time I don't really want one. I thought, perhaps, if it was a friend . . . I'm sorry.'

'Don't be,' I took his arm. 'Come on, let's get you a drink and forget we had this conversation.' I led him back into the throng, where he was soon joking with Mary.

Despite what he thinks he is feeling, he's looking a lot better than he did at the beginning of the year and his spirits appear to be lifting. The mission to Casablanca must have done him some good. 'I think I'd better stick around here a bit longer,' he whispered to me with a meaningful glance at 009 when I went to say goodbye. 'Someone's got to keep an eye on Goodnight, otherwise when 006 gets back all hell is going to break loose.'

It's rare that we get to see the wives, I reflected as I went to get my coat, though of course so many are familiar to me from their days in the Office. Few, like Loelia, find their partner outside the Firm, and when they do they inevitably leave to marry them. None of the women officers are married – except, of course, to the Firm. I wonder how many of them watched Loelia look into Gerald's eyes, as they exchanged vows, without even a touch of what might have been.

But today was mainly about joy, laughter, too much champagne and the giddy feeling of being on the outside, for a time, at least. For me, it was also about relief.

So I went to the Brompton Oratory last night. I ran all the way, I found the right altar and deposited an envelope behind the right pillar. But it was not what they'd been expecting. I couldn't do it. If this was a test, I failed – or perhaps I passed, depending on who set the questions. Instead of containing a Top Secret, For Your Eyes Only analysis of the British position regarding the Berlin crisis, whoever it was who went to retrieve the envelope from the dead drop found only a note from me. It was polite and respectful, and said only that, while I was grateful for the help that I'd been offered in tracing my father, I found that I was not in a position to fulfil my side of the bargain. With respect, I asked not to be approached again – I would, in any case, be filing a full report to my superiors.

Now I just have to hope they'll leave me alone.

July

I found my aunt's description of her friend's wedding particularly moving. She was an extraordinarily generous person, and I don't believe that envy was an emotion that she would have recognised. Yet she never married and she had no children, although she often said that she regarded me as her child, as much as my mother's. Indeed, in many ways I am more similar to her. As I have learned from her diaries, she had relationships – a few of them significant, but none so much as with her work, and with the man whose office door she guarded. M.

She first met him at the cocktail party held on the last night of her training course at the same terraced house in Victoria where she had gone for her initial interview. M – then deputy chief of the SIS and not yet known by his single initial – had been persuaded by the redoubtable head of personnel, Miss Stega, to preside over the minigraduation ceremony. Jane Moneypenny had come top of her class, and in her diary she describes M's firm handshake and cold grey eyes. 'He was an intimidating presence,' she wrote. 'He looked as if he didn't know what the hell he was doing shaking the hands of all these young girls, and he duly disappeared the second the ceremony was over. I doubt our paths will cross again.'

The next morning she was called into Miss Stega's office to talk about positions. She expressed an interest in Signals. She was duly assigned to the Communications division, and only after that was she given the address of the large grey building overlooking St James's Park that she would come to know as intimately as she had the old farm in Maguga.

Her work was at first fairly routine. As a junior clerk, she was not privy to the cipher keys. She would arrive at the large double front doors at nine – an hour before the official starting time – and after announcing her name and the two-word code for the week (her first was 'yellow retriever') she would press the button for the lift. Comms, as it was known, shared the top floor with the chief's suite. The current incumbent – known, like his predecessors, as 'C' – was an elderly, slim man, a career spook who had moved across from MI5 to inherit the top mantle shortly after a successful war masterminding, among other things, the Double-Cross System (a highly effective system of strategic deception, in which false information was fed back to the enemy through German intelligence agents who had been turned by MI5 and MI6 officers).

Miss Moneypenny's path rarely crossed C's – only once did she find herself using the lift at the same time, and then she kept her eyes firmly trained on her shoes. She enjoyed her work, and was constantly stimulated by the buzz and air of quiet urgency that infused every corner of the building. She earned a reputation for quick thinking, accuracy and good sense. Within months, she was being trusted to send and translate signals. Before the end of her first year she had risen to the position of signals operator.

It was one night in early November 1956, during the

Suez Crisis, with the Comms room in a state of heightened activity, that she found herself working for fourteen straight hours with the Deputy Chief, in place of his personal assistant, who was ill. As she recorded in her journal, she was impressed by his apparent total recall and by his ability to make instant decisions with confidence and to dictate word-perfect signals to agents scattered across the world. He gave no indication that he regarded her as anything more than a machine for fulfilling his orders.

However, two weeks later, when the immediate crisis had abated, she was called to his office. She was ushered into a large room, dominated by a leather-topped desk. The Deputy Chief was half obscured behind a shaft of light, smoking a pipe. His eyes showed no sign of recognition. He looked up from his files. 'Miss Moneypenny? Yes, you've worked here for three years now. Too short theoretically, but I should be able to see to that.'

'Yes, sir,' she replied.

'Like it here?'

'Very much.'

He questioned her minutely about aspects of her work, and her previous life. As she recorded that evening, 'I had a strong feeling that he knew more about me than he revealed.' Then he started testing her, setting up hoops for her to jump through. What would she do in this or that situation? If an agent sent through a Red Foxtrot when the top brass was away, how would she react? He gave no clue as to whether her answers pleased him, just shifted his gaze periodically from a painting of an orchid, which was hanging over the chimney piece, to stare piercingly at her.

'Any languages?' he asked.

'I speak Swahili,' she replied, 'but I'm a bit rusty. And schoolgirl French. No more, I'm afraid.'

'Excellent. Don't trust linguists. Report to this office at 08.45 hours on Monday. I don't like high heels, too much make-up or jewellery.'

'Yes, sir. Thank you,' she replied, aware she had acquired a new position, though unsure as to how.

'And you may call me Sir, but never when off duty.'

She had no choice in the matter. Nor did she know, until a few weeks later, that her new boss was to ascend to the chief's chair in a matter of months. The current C had been rumoured to be close to retirement, and the débâcle of Suez persuaded him to go earlier than he had planned. As his deputy – and the personal choice of the recently retired Winston Churchill – Admiral Sir Miles Messervy stepped unopposed into the top spot, bringing with him a new initial, M, and his new personal secretary, my aunt, Miss Jane Moneypenny.

Friday, 6th July

007 leaves for the Caribbean today. M returned from lunch on Monday at the American Ambassador's residence, called for Bill and issued a flurry of commands. 'Send up the recent signals file from Station A [America], please, Miss Moneypenny . . . Get Head of Section C [Caribbean] up here . . . Arrange a meeting with the armourer first thing tomorrow . . . And summon 007 immediately.'

This time, he was there to answer his phone when I called.

He was in with M for an hour and came back through the

baize door looking almost excited. 'It seems I'm off to see a man about a snake. Got to go home to pack my swimmers, Penny. Wish I could fit you and your bikini in my suitcase,' he said, with a ghost of his old humour. But he failed to invite me for a post-mission dinner. The one that never seems to happen.

It was apparent, after the Cuba Group meeting on Tuesday, that the situation over there had become more complex. Reading over the minutes, I had a feeling we would get involved somehow. Scott had reported that two CIA agents on the inside had died last week, apparently in a car accident, though the details are vague. They were the Cousins' main assets in place – on whose assessment of the situation they placed much of the weight of their current strategy. The agents, in turn, were running a Cuban double agent, code-named Caballo.

As Bill explained that evening, 'The Cousins are convinced this Caballo is the real thing, but M is not too sure. We believe they're putting too much faith in him. It's a risky business. They don't even know his real identity, but he's definitely close to the head man. At first he sent over some cracking stuff, but there have been a couple of strange incidents recently, culminating in this fishy car accident. The Cousins are still insisting Caballo is rock solid, but that could be because he's all they've got left, and they can't bear to admit it. Now the Attorney-General's* turned to us for independent help. He wants us to check out Caballo. Is he still with us, or was he a plant all along? It's a stiff task, but M's decided 007 is up to it. I hope to God he's right. Book him a ticket to Jamaica on Saturday, please.'

---

* Robert Kennedy, younger brother of JFK.

News of his mission had already hit the Powder Vine. I ran into Mary as I was leaving, who said he'd ordered the Operation Mongoose files up from Records and booked a session of unarmed combat, as well as target practice following his meeting with the armourer.

Now he's got his long-range sniper's rifle in the spine of his suitcase, along with the portable Triple X and full scuba gear that Ross at Station J signalled for him to bring. Mary's given him the Benzedrine and sleeping draughts he asked for and he's been fully briefed by a man who flew over from Washington specially. But I've never seen him appear so unexcited by an assignment like this.

Monday, 9th July

I'm sure I saw the pale-eyed man again, this time on the bus home from work. I don't know where he got on, but he was sitting several rows behind me when we reached my stop. He was reading a paper and I wouldn't have noticed him had the bus not given a sudden lurch, which threw me sideways, practically on to his paper. He appeared to give a start when he saw me, but it might have been shock at the sudden invasion of his seat. It could be a coincidence, but after all that has happened, I can't help but be suspicious. There's something about his face that makes me uneasy. I checked that no one was following me as I reached the house, and double-locked my door. I still feel as if I'm being watched as I retrieve this journal from the safe.

It is now over two weeks since I failed to make the drop, and I haven't heard from Zach. Every day I expect a phone call or a letter, but so far, nothing. Perhaps he believed me when I said I was going to tell my employers. I should have; they would have put him on the Watch List* and filed his description under suspected Soviet or Stasi agents. Perhaps they would then have had to investigate the truth about Pa – if indeed they didn't already know? I didn't think of that at the time; I was too ashamed at having been lured in so easily. And now, I fear, it's too late.

I've been dreaming about Pa. Does the fact I was trapped mean that everything Zach said was untrue? If so, how did he know all those things?

Wednesday, 11th July

There appears to be an increased urgency to the Cuba Group meetings. I have to admit I find them exciting, as though I have a front-row seat at the circus. Head of C [Caribbean]† is convinced that something major is brewing over there. He's a funny little man: dark, intense, with the barely contained energy of a bedspring that's been pushing against its cloth for too long. He's been in the trade since Oxford and relies strongly on what he calls his 'hunches'. You give him a piece of research and he'll say, 'Something smells wrong about it. My hunch is that what's actually going on is . . .' More often than not he's right.

In this case, his hunch is that Cuba is going to become the theatre for a major Cold War tugging match, and to date it

---

* An ongoing file of suspected enemy agents, distributed to all section and station heads, as well as to the Watchers.
† Peregrine 'Perry' Warhol, fellow of All Souls and former Professor of Political Thought.

looks as if Redland is winning. On 2nd July, Raúl Castro* paid a high-profile visit to Moscow.† According to *Pravda*, he returned to Havana with the promise of Russian technical equipment and advisers, as well as greatly beneficial trade agreements. 'That means weapons, mark my words,' he said. 'We should keep a very close watching brief on what's happening over there. The sooner 007 gets there the better.'

Saturday, 14th July

A letter from R this morning. I recognised his writing, of course, and opened it with a pounding heart. 'My dearest Jane, will you ever find it in your heart to forgive me?' it began. I'm not sure what I expected – confusion, recrimination, a demand to bring me to account, perhaps? But what followed was one of the most heartfelt declarations of longing that I have ever read. He wrote of the wonderful times we had shared; he treasured the memories and regretted everything he had done to contribute to the demise of our relationship:

> It could have been so different – I confess, I had hopes that it would lead to a happier denouement. You are an extraordinary woman. I have never met anyone with your inde-

---

* Younger brother of Cuban president Fidel Castro, and Cuban military supremo. A committed ideological Communist and long-serving member of the Cuban Communist Party. Small in stature, unlike his elder brother, and not known to be a womaniser.
† Raúl met Khrushchev, among others. The unstated aim of his visit was to negotiate the mutual defence agreement that would establish the legal structure for the deployment of Soviet forces in Cuba.

pendence and integrity and I doubt I ever will. I just wish I could have matched up to you. I was a fool to try to unwrap the layers of your character in one clumsy wrench. I shouldn't have been in such a hurry and then, perhaps, I would have had the time to savour each one? I know it's too late, but please forgive me and remember me with affection. Take care. I hope one day our paths will meet again.

I shed tears when I read that. I miss him more than I can admit, even to myself. It was I who had been unworthy. Integrity? If only he knew. I'd repaid his trust with evasion, initially, and towards the end with suspicion. But even now, when I replay my conversations with Zach over and over in my head, I still cannot expunge the thought – such a treacherous thought – that R was one of the few who knew about my childhood in Africa. I'd told him about Evie and Winnie, and the lower branches of the acacia-tree where I would sit, swinging my legs, writing my diary and waiting for Pa never to return. But it doesn't take the emptiness away.

Monday, 16th July

007 is en route to Cuba. He sent a long signal to M from Jamaica yesterday. It was reassuringly positive; a week in the sun, getting fit and planning his trip, appears to have done him good. He's decided that his best method of entry is by small boat, landing just west of Santiago de Cuba, making the final approach underwater. The original plan was to go in via the American base at Guantanamo Bay,* but

---

* The US naval base, known colloquially as 'Gitmo', was first established in 1898, when the US obtained control of Cuba from Spain at

this had to be abandoned after Castro declared the surrounding area a militarised zone and evacuated the local inhabitants. The base is now under virtual siege – it's a peculiar situation, to have battling countries living side by side, with the aggressor paying rent to his prey. Guantanamo, in any case, is thought to be riddled with Castro's spies.

He was most adamant that we do not disclose details of his trip to anyone. According to his sources, the Cuban military are screening the airports, pulling aside suspect visitors for what, from all reports, amounts to intense interrogation. Key landing beaches are ringed by heavy artillery, on the watch for another Bay of Pigs-type invasion. Castro apparently does not believe, however, that the Americans would try anything near his home town and power base of Santiago de Cuba. Consequently, there's less security in the east, leaving the coast clear – literally – for a discreet landing by 007.

Once in Cuba, 007 will take the cover of Arlen von Kaseberg, an employee of Universal Exports,* based in

---

the end of the Spanish–American War. In February 1903 the US and Cuba (by then independent) signed a lease giving the US occupation rights in perpetuity, or until a mutually agreed breaking point. Under the terms of the 1903 lease – and a subsequent 1934 treaty – the US has 'complete jurisdiction and control' of the area, for which it pays a yearly rent of 2,000 gold coins (a little over $4,000 in today's money). Up to the present day, it is the only US base in operation on Communist soil.

* A long-established cover organisation for British secret-service agents. Universal Exports, from the outside, was a functioning enterprise with offices around the world and a corresponding list of telephone numbers that were answered by efficient receptionists, able to

Zurich. Q Branch has ensured that the legend is intact; his passport has regular stamps from Cuba over the past decade and the Swiss have been briefed to give him collateral support. He plans to make his way overland to Havana, as inconspicuously as possible, and when there, to try to establish the identity of this Caballo. He'll be operating entirely without back-up. We have a skeleton diplomatic presence in Havana only. Until last year we had a small station there, acting under the aegis of an oil company. However, when Castro nationalised the refineries, our men were sent home, leaving us completely blind. We've had a certain amount of help from the French and Italians as well as the Swiss, but 007 has insisted that no one be alerted to his presence.

I do not have a good feeling about this mission. 007 sounds confident enough, and it's well within his capabilities, but there's something I can't put my finger on that makes me uneasy. Perhaps, for once, I know too much?

Friday, 20th July

Well, one of them has made it back safely, thank God. 006 came in from Novaya Zemlya just a few days later than we'd anticipated. He'd been travelling non-stop for five days and was completely exhausted; he'd lost weight and his usually ruddy face was gaunt and grey, but he insisted on submitting his report to M and Head of S before he went to sleep.

---

verify the identity of any supposed employee. In 1964 its use was discontinued – its cover assumed to have been penetrated by opposing secret agencies.

He almost stumbled out of the office and I called Mary up to make sure he got home safely. Transcribing his report later, it sounded as if he was truly lucky to have made it.

He went in from the west disguised as a Siberian fisherman. 006 probably speaks just enough idiomatic Russian to pass as a taciturn local, especially after a week or so away from a bath and a razor. Novaya Zemlya sounds like a God-forsaken place, cold and barren,* which of course makes it an ideal location for the most important Russian nuclear testing-ground.

We'd heard reports last year of an enormous explosion up there, at the end of October, which the Ministry was keen to confirm. They also wanted any information about the new generation of Soviet intercontinental ballistic missiles [ICBMs]. Both of the great powers have been spreading rhetoric and disinformation about their relative strengths and weaknesses on this front.† While spy-plane photo-

---

* The entire northern area of Novaya Zemlya is covered with a great ice sheet, while, further south, snowfields feed glaciers at the higher altitudes. The wind blows down from the Arctic and up from the Siberian steppes, making midsummer feel like an Alpine winter. The coast comprises fjord-like inlets, with sharp cliffs and rocky promontories, while the interior is mountainous, uninhabited and virtually unexplored. There is practically no vegetation, and virtually no animal or insect life save the odd vagrant bird, an ice fox, a brown or polar bear, and a few lemmings.
† In November 1960 a GRU officer named Oleg Penkovsky offered himself to the West as an agent-in-place. For the eighteen months that he was run by MI6 – under the code name Source Ironbark – he passed on innumerable top-secret documents, the most important of which spelled out the relative weakness of the Soviet nuclear capability. This contradicted the view of US hawks, who had long argued that the Soviets possessed superior nuclear power. However, from the

graphs* reveal a certain amount about surface appearance, they don't tell us about actual effectiveness and range. In any case, the Powers incident† has put paid to much activity in that sphere. So oo6 was sent to the boffins for a crash course on nuclear weaponry, before being catapulted into icy hell.

His mission was remarkably successful. By a stroke of luck, he ran into a cold and bored Russian technician, keen for company and an opportunity to complain about his boss. Presumably he didn't believe that an uneducated fisherman could be much of a security threat. When he mentioned that they were desperately short of manual labour, oo6 leapt at the

---

beginning, Penkovsky was treated with scepticism: the CIA in particular regarded him as a plant, a channel for the information that Khrushchev wanted the West to know. On 22 October 1962 Penkovsky was arrested in Moscow. He confessed, and was tried, found guilty and apparently executed.

* From the mid-1950s the USA had been using the U-2 single-engine, single-seat, high-altitude reconnaissance plane, developed by Lockheed Martin for the CIA, to capture accurate photographic images of the Soviet Union.

† On 1 May 1960 CIA pilot Gary Powers was shot down over Sverdlovsk in the western USSR while on a top-secret reconnaissance mission to photograph military installations and other intelligence targets. By virtue of its high cruising altitude, the U-2 had been previously thought to be invulnerable to either enemy fighter planes or ground-to-air missiles. Powers ejected and was captured on landing, tried and convicted of espionage. He was sentenced to three years' imprisonment and seven years' hard labour, but was freed twenty-one months later in exchange for a Soviet spy. On his return to the US, Powers was criticised by some for having failed to activate his aircraft's self-destruct charge to destroy the camera, photographic film and related classified parts of his aircraft before capture – and by others for not using an optional CIA-issued suicide pin.

opening. Two days later, he was working in the store-room attached to the central laboratory. In between carrying heavy boxes and crates from Zone A, where much of the testing up to this point has taken place, to the new scientific and administrative centre in Zone B, 006 overheard several significant conversations. Eventually, though, he was caught poking around the offices and had to make a rapid escape, through northern Russia to Norway. No wonder he's exhausted.

Extracted from 006's report, dated the day of his return, copied for the Joint Intelligence Committee (JIC) and currently filed in the National Archives (CAB 179):

```
I was able to ascertain that on October 30,
1961, a 50 megaton bomb, known as Tsar Bomba,
was detonated at what is known as Site C
(73.7N 54.0E). The bomb measured 26 feet by
6.6 feet and weighed 27 tons. A special
parachute was designed enabling it to be
dropped from a TU-95 bomber at a height of
33,000 feet over Novaya Zemlya. The fireball
reached from the ground almost to the height
of the release plane and light from the
explosion was visible 600 miles away. The
mushroom cloud was estimated to have risen as
high as 40 miles into the atmosphere. The test
was declared a success and work has started on
the construction of a template, this one
designed with a yield of up to 200 megatons.
```

After four weeks of working at the plant, 006 managed to infiltrate the laboratory late one night. There he found

papers relating to the recent test firing of the R-7 intercontinental ballistic missiles:

The R-7* has demonstrated significant degrees
of variance in aim and range. The scientists
are concerned — they cannot rely on the
missiles landing within 100 miles of their
target at a range of 5000 miles (Russia to
the East coast of the United States). They
are more confident about the R-12† and R-14‡
Medium and Intermediate Range Ballistic
Missiles, which are consistently
outperforming the ICBMs in accuracy over
shorter distances. The technicians had begun
a programme of stripping and recalibrating
all the missiles in batches of 50 at a time,
when an urgent directive from Moscow ordered
them to transport a large number of R-12s and
R-14s, along with nuclear warheads and

---

* The R-7/SS-6, with a maximum operational range of 5,000 miles,
was the first Soviet intercontinental ballistic missile (ICBM) developed and programmed for operational deployment in the USSR. In
October 1957 the R-7 launched the world's first artificial satellite,
Sputnik, into orbit, thus revealing its power – far in excess of anything the United States could produce at the time.
† Also known as the SS-4 – a Medium Range Ballistic Missile
(MRBM) with a maximum range of 1,400 miles – designed to be
fitted with warheads with explosive yields of 200–700 kilotons
(10–35 times the power of the Hiroshima bomb).
‡ Intermediate Range Ballistic Missile (IRBM), known in the West as
the SS-6. Has a range of 2,800 miles with a payload yield of 200–800
kilotons.

trained technicians, down to Severomorsk* and Leningrad [. . .]

I was trying to find papers to confirm whether the consignments had left when I was caught looking through top secret files. I was forced to take aggressive action, resulting in the certain death of two security guards, with another injured. I escaped under the security fence and, with a team of guards and dogs in pursuit, made my way to my vessel. I landed four days later at Murmansk. Unable to get a signal through to HQ, I decided to make the short journey to Severomorsk, in an attempt at confirming the missile movements. Security at the port was tight - the eastern side had been sealed and was patrolled by heavily armed Russian special forces wearing green epaulettes. I spoke to various local inhabitants, who said that there was an unusual number of cargo ships currently at dock. A long convoy of heavy transporter vehicles had arrived several days previously, but to date, the ships had not left port. Judging that I had little chance of infiltrating the loading area, I made my way instead across the border to northern Norway, arriving in Oslo one week later, on July 18.

---

* A major port on the Barents Sea, headquarters of the Soviet Northern Fleet.

Sunday, 29th July

It is as I'd feared. The nightmare is not over. I was taking our normal route across the park on Saturday when Rafi sniffed the air, bounded ahead towards the Serpentine and started barking at something the other side of the bushes. There were hundreds of people about, strolling, sunbathing on the lawns, playing tennis and badminton, and I couldn't see what it was that had excited him. I called him, but he just looked at me and continued to bark. It was more of a summons than an aggressive call. I walked briskly over towards him and crouching at the foot of the statue of Peter Pan, looking a little sheepish as he fondled Rafi's ears, was Zach. 'Hush, Rafi,' he said, looking at me. 'Now you've given me away and I'm going to get into trouble.' Then he stood up and smiled. I'd forgotten how handsome he is and was annoyed to feel myself blushing.

'I don't want to talk to you. Come on, Rafi,' I said, turning away.

'Jane, I'm sorry. I didn't want to put pressure on you. My aim was to help you. I know how much you want to track down your father. I thought I'd found out something that would make you happy. I'm afraid we both just got caught up in something that turned out to be rather more than we'd anticipated.'

'You mean you didn't . . . No, I'm not talking to you. This is ridiculous. I'll have to report seeing you, of course.'

As I turned to go, he reached out and grabbed my shoulder. 'Listen. You've got to believe me. I'm as much a pawn in this as you are. They just told me what to say and do.'

'Who are "they", and what have "they" got on you then? Why are you doing this?'

He turned his hands palms up and spread his fingers. 'We all have our private reasons.'

'Yes, but you know mine and I don't know yours. Who are you? Was anything you told me about yourself true?'

'Come on, let's go and have a cup of tea.' He'd started to lead me back across the park, when I recovered my senses.

'No,' I said. 'I don't want anything to do with you.'

'Please, Jane. I have a lot riding on this too. I need your help. I *really* need your help.'

I started to walk away.

'I'll call you this evening. Please listen to what I have to say.'

I didn't intend to answer the telephone. I should have called Bill instead and told him everything and asked for his help in dealing with it. But I didn't. Stubbornness and pride as well as shame, I suppose – the need to preserve the image of the irreproachable Miss Moneypenny. I should have gone out, far from the phone, but I was suddenly a little scared – scared that I would be followed, that my every move was being watched and recorded.

At 6 p.m. it rang. I left it and went into the bathroom. When I came out again it had stopped. A few minutes later, it started up again, ringing insistently, incessantly. It would stop and start again. I took it off the hook and switched on the wireless. But the ringing continued in my head and after about fifteen minutes I could bear it no longer and put the receiver back on. It immediately started to ring. I picked it up, intending to tell Zach to leave me alone, but it was Helena.

'Jane, thank God you're in.'

'Have you been trying all evening?' I asked.

'Of course not. Listen. I've just had a call from the hospital. They've been trying to get hold of you. Aunt Frieda's been taken in with pneumonia. I'm getting on the next train. Will you come to meet me, please? We can go to the hospital together . . . I'll phone you as soon as I've found out when my train gets in.'

I was so shaken by the news that I picked up the phone automatically when it rang again. 'When you were six, you were bitten by a snake in Samburu. You were far from a doctor. Your father made an incision in your foot with his hunting-knife and sucked out the poison. Then he bandaged it in his handkerchief and stayed talking to you all night until the fever had passed.'

This was family legend, an event I remembered with a clarity that is only conferred by a thousand retellings. But, as far as I could remember, I had never spoken of it to anyone outside the family except, possibly, R.

'Who is this?' The voice had a heavy accent, harsh. It was not Zach.

'A friend. I am sorry to disturb you when your aunt is ill.'

My knees gave way and I sat down suddenly. 'How did you know that?'

'Never mind. Can you get the information we asked for?'

I told him that I wasn't prepared to do it, that I'd informed my colleagues of Zach's approaches. 'We will trace you and then you'll have to face the consequences. You can't make me do anything,' I said, almost convincing myself.

'We have reason to disbelieve what you say. You have not placed any complaint on record with your organisation. If they discovered now that you have kept this quiet, you would be in significant trouble.'

I slammed the phone down. What he said was true: every rule in the book clearly states that any suspected approach by foreign agents should be reported immediately. I should have said something the minute I suspected that Z was not all he professed to be.

The phone rang again. I nearly left it, then remembering Helena, I picked it up. I nearly crumpled when I heard her voice, so calm and familiar. We spent the rest of the evening sitting next to our aunt's bed listening to her laboured breathing as she slept. Every now and then one of us would remember one of the nuggets of advice she had occasionally served up to us, as if it was some particularly tempting canapé. 'Now don't go marrying the first young man who asks,' she would say. 'Marriage is terribly over-rated. I had many proposals in my time, as you know. I may have some more before I finally fall off my perch, but the idea of spending the rest of my life with a man, sharing a bed with him . . . oh no.' She would shake her head. 'Men are at their best in the kitchen. What you want is a good career. And for that you need a degree.'

Dear Aunt Frieda, the original blue-stocking. When we first came to London, she treated us as the children she never had. I pray she gets through this. I would miss her desperately, those sporadic Sunday suppers of chicken soup and rice. The doctor says she has a good chance. She was awake when we went this morning and seemed to be breathing more easily.

I told Helena everything last night. It had got to the stage where I couldn't go on alone. It was surprisingly easy in the end. She'd long suspected, of course, what it was I did, though she had no idea of the details. I begged her to tell no one, not even Lionel.

'Of course I won't,' she gave me a hug. 'Don't worry.'

We were sitting on my bed. It all poured out – R, Zach, the phone call. Helena sat quietly facing me at the other end of the bed, hugging her knees to her chest in the position I knew so well. When at last I came to the end, the first thing she asked was, 'How does he know that you haven't reported it? Who could have told him?'

It was the question that had been lurking at the edge of my consciousness, that I hadn't dared to confront. The implications were terrifying: this was no longer about me, but the possibility – the probability – of a leak, and it couldn't have been Clive Mostyn, poor old CNE. I could no longer pretend that I could make it go away on my own; I would have to make a full report.

August

From the beginning – that cool Cambridge afternoon when I opened the first of my aunt's diaries and began to read – I knew that verification was going to be neither easy nor straightforward. Secret organisations are notoriously wary of declassifying one word more than they can possibly help, and the SIS is the champion of caution. When MI5, under its first woman chief, Stella Rimington, inched open its doors and archives to public scrutiny, its sister organisation did not follow. Today, the National Archives in Kew hold several shelves of declassified MI5 files – but few emanating from MI6. To be able to authenticate *The Moneypenny Diaries* to a level that I knew – once I was on the route to publication – I would need to achieve in order to dispel the assumption that they are works of fiction, I would have to find alternative sources.

The first step towards verification was simple: many of the events that my aunt wrote of are well documented. From books and journals I was quickly able to match her dates with, for example, the known launch date of Tsar Bomba from Novaya Zemlya, or Raúl Castro's visit to Moscow. Contemporary newspaper reports confirmed the death of Tracy Bond in a car accident on 1 January 1962. Sir James Molony was a well-known and eminent neurologist, a member of the Royal Society – although his connection to SIS was never formally documented. The Bay of Pigs happened, of course, as did the Suez Crisis and numerous other events of international importance that my aunt recorded, if only in passing.

My first few visits to the National Archives were more frustrating than productive. I spent hours spinning through their indexes, but found little of immediate relevance. My approaches for permission to search the archives of the Secret Intelligence Service met with a polite – and I suspect amused – refusal. I realised I would have to take another tack. Looking through the 1962 diary, it appeared that much of what I was seeking to confirm had a second-party element: there was a CIA presence, for instance, at most of the Cuba Group meetings, and, since Bond's mission to the Caribbean was at the behest of the US Attorney-General, it was possible that a copy of the relevant files had been sent to Washington. I decided to refocus my enquiries to the other side of the Atlantic.

A week after the end of the university year, I booked a flight to Washington, DC. I caught a taxi directly to the Gelman Library, George Washington University. The semester had not yet finished, and I walked into a collective daze of exam-weary students sheltering from the humidity outside. I found what I was looking for on the seventh floor, behind glass doors: the National Security Archive, a non-aligned and non-profit institution dedicated to the expansion of public access to government information. Since the passing of the Freedom of Information Act in the 1980s, the NSA has amassed an enormous volume of information of the sort that is not available in the UK. It was as a result of energetic NSA lobbying that many of the documents relating to US activities in Cuba in the early 1960s had recently been released to public scrutiny.

I had already been in email contact with a G. L. Chong, Senior Archivist, Cuba Section, and when I announced my name at the door I was told he would be right with me. I had just sat down on a faux-leather chair and started flicking through one of the catalogues on display when I heard my name being called: 'Dr Westbrook?' A young man with an unruly halo of spiky black hair was blinking in my direction through green-rimmed spectacles. He looked like a young badger emerging into his first spring. 'Hi. Gordy Chong. Great to meet you. Come into my cubbyhole. Apologies for the mess.' He led me through a burrow of small rooms, each occupied by a researcher buried under a sea of paper or typing furiously into a computer.

His office was no more ordered. 'I must tell you that I did my masters at Cambridge. Emmanuel College, 1998. It was an unforgettable experience, a most wonderful place. And the libraries . . .' He proceeded to extol the delights of the University Library, a utilitarian monstrosity whose possibilities I had nevertheless found exciting for rather different reasons to those of Mr G. L. Chong. I let him continue – it was preferable to explaining that I wasn't here on university business, that I needed his help on a private investigation. When he eventually ran dry of superlatives, I specified the papers I needed: the Operation Mongoose files and anything relating to British secret-service activity in Cuba, or the Cuban agent known as Caballo.

He looked momentarily puzzled. 'Caballo? I don't recall having read anything about him – not in the recent declassifications anyway. But for the rest, you've come to the right place. If it exists, we'll have it. I'll show you how to work the computer terminals, then you're on your own.'

Over the next week, I delved deep into the once-secret files of American intelligence. Gordy was right: it was a trove of incalculable value. Within days I had found Agent Scott's minutes of the Cuba Group meetings – my aunt's name even appeared on the list of attendees – as well as contemporary reports on the deaths of the two CIA agents near San Cristóbal in June 1962. I read detailed plans for the annihilation of Castro by a range of means including Mafia-fired bullets, analyses of the strength of the Cuban forces, and financial estimations of the damage caused to the Cuban economy by covert activities carried out under the name of Operation Mongoose. But no mention of Caballo – or of British involvement.

It was in early 2005, shortly after the British Freedom of Information Act was passed, that I revisited the National Archives. I was getting desperate; there were holes in my aunt's story that I needed to fill. I wasn't sure what I would do if I could not find the confirmation I was looking for. I submitted yet more requests for files which I knew I had little chance of viewing. I was probably looking somewhat frustrated, as an archivist took pity on me and suggested I look in the files of the Joint Intelligence Committee. 'We've just had several box-loads delivered – we haven't had time to go through them all yet, but they cover the dates you're interested in,' he said. 'You could come back in a few weeks to view them.' I smiled. I told him how helpful he had been, that I wished I could, but once term began I would be too busy. And I needed them very urgently. 'If I wear gloves and don't tell your supervisor, please could I look through them?' I begged.

It worked. I was shut in a room with five boxes of virgin files, and when I came out I had found my personal Holy Grail. Tucked inside routine JIC minutes, secretariat files and weekly reviews,* I came across a slim file of SIS agent reports, including those sent by Bond from Cuba and referred to in my aunt's diaries. They concurred in every respect with what she had written. There was no more cause for doubt.

Wednesday, 1st August

Lunch with Bill. As soon as I got in on Monday, I went to see him and told him I needed his advice, badly.

'Of course, Penny. What is it?' he asked.

'It's rather delicate, I'm afraid. It may take some time.'

'Lunch Wednesday. A steak at Bully's?'

While Bill tucked into his entrecôte, making apprecia-tive noises, I chewed on a piece of bread and wondered how to broach the subject.

'Come on, Penny, it can't be so bad. What have you been up to? Selling secrets to the Russians?' He laughed, but when I didn't join in, he reached across and took my hand. 'Come on, old girl, spit it out.'

So I told him about meeting Zach at the concert, about his offers of help in uncovering what had happened to my father, then his requests for secret documents. He stayed silent throughout, listening carefully. He's an extraordin-

---

* Stored at the National Archives in CAB 159 (JIC minutes, 1947–68), CAB 163 (JIC secretariat files, 1939–77) and CAB 179 (JIC weekly reviews, 1956–63).

ary man, Bill. He carries the weight of the Office on his shoulders; he is M's filter, his sounding-board and factotum all mixed into one. Whatever M sees, Bill has seen first. When M makes a decision, Bill ensures it is carried out to his exacting standards. Throughout the whole building, only M and Bill have access to every file, every report, every signal. And through all this he manages to remain a good friend, to me, to 007, and even to M, if he knows the meaning of such things.

When I'd brought him up to date, he thought for a minute longer, then smiled gently. 'I'm so glad you told me, Penny; I only wish you'd come to me sooner, then I could have helped you through it. You must have been through hell. Don't worry any more. Leave it with me for a bit; I need to think. We'll try to fix it involving the fewest people possible. Our first priority is to identify whoever it is that's been after you, and to get them off your back. Then we need to trace this leak.'

He was silent for a while, appearing to make his mind up about something. 'I'm sure I'm not telling you anything you didn't guess when I say that we learnt in February that we had a mole in the Office. Kingfisher* said it was a section head. It came as a complete shock to the Old Man. He set Dorothy Fields to work on finding out who it was. She'd whittled the list down to two; one was CNE. At first, we assumed that his suicide was an admission of guilt, but Dorothy had always favoured the other man. We decided to act as though the investigation was over, in order to smoke him out, and

---

* The former Stasi officer who defected to the British in West Berlin on 1 February 1962, and was subsequently flown to Stockholm for interrogation.

indeed a couple of things have come up recently which suggest that her instincts were sound. What you're telling me now appears to confirm it. I'm going to brief Dorothy on this straight away. She's spent so much time exploring the back channels of this sorry affair; perhaps she'll have some ideas. At this point, I don't think we need to take it any further. But don't worry. If they contact you again, make some excuse to get back to them. Then we can devise a plan to try to discover who they are.'

The relief is extraordinary. I feel as if I could sleep for weeks. It's only now that I realise how much it had been affecting me, making me creep around furtively with one eye always over my shoulder. Every time I get this journal out, I feel a stab of fear – but I still can't stop writing. It's the one time when I feel in control of what's happening. I keep wondering whether I should move the hiding-place. But then it hasn't been discovered yet, so perhaps I shouldn't tempt fate?

Monday, 6th August

I went into the powder room this morning, to find general sadness at the death of Marilyn Monroe. Raine was kneading her pearls with what looked like repressed fury. 'They killed her. I'm sure of it,' she said. We all told her to stop being ridiculous, but she wouldn't let go of her outlandish theories. 'No one who saw her singing happy birthday to the President in that bead dress could ignore the force-field of attraction between them. It was only a matter of time.' Poor Raine hasn't recovered from CNE's suicide. She refuses to believe that he was guilty of anything and insists he was being framed and couldn't take the pressure. I imagine Marilyn's overdose brought it all back again.

Tuesday, 7th August

A detailed report from 007, at last. I was beginning to worry. I always do when they fail to check in as planned. If we hadn't received something today, the emergency wheels would have been given a greasing, at least, if not nudged into action. Thank goodness, though, I arrived to a long signal on my desk, 'PERSONAL TO M EX007', three pages, still encoded into five-letter groups. I alerted M as soon as he got in, and once I'd sorted the rest of the signals for him, I got out my Triple X and started to work on 007's.

I particularly enjoy his reports. They read more like adventure stories than terse explications of a mission, which I am sure is as much for my benefit as for 007's; he relies on me to edit out some of his more vivid descriptions before submitting them to M. I still derive immense satisfaction from the process of ciphering and deciphering. Setting the dials, keying in accurately what looks like a jumble of nonsense, then the moment of revelation as it's transformed into plain text. The thought that these ugly black boxes, so mechanically basic on the one hand, but so fantastically sophisticated on the other, tipped the balance of both wars in our favour – it's wonderful. The three years that I spent in Comms were never boring; we all worked hard, in an extraordinary atmosphere of camaraderie. I never lost the sense that we were the central pivot of the Firm – with the stations around the world and throughout the building forming the spinning spokes. So now, when a confidential signal is directed to M's eyes only, I attack it with relish.

For the time I am working on them, I am transported into the events they describe; it's probably the closest I will ever get to the thrusting tip of this business, active service.

Over the months that follow in this journal, relevant extracts from the papers discovered at the National Archives in Kew have been inserted as close to their correct chronological position as it is possible to put them. In several cases the long reports, filed by 007 on his return to headquarters, served to expand on and elucidate his often cryptic signals from the field; for the sake of clarity, these have been merged into single narratives. The following report by 007 was directed to M, dated 2 August 1962, and deciphered by JM:

Beached safely at Postino Bay 10 miles west of Santiago. The coast was floodlit so I scuttled the boat and made the final approach underwater. At daybreak, I approached the city, where I acquired a vehicle from a private vendor. Santiago is riddled with armed Barbudos – Castro loyalists with untrimmed beards and automatic combat weapons. Security is tight. My papers were checked four times between arriving and leaving the city limits, but although it was transmitted back to their HQ, my identity did not appear to set off alarm bells.

The report proceeded to describe his journey west towards Havana. Across the entire country, he found evidence of strong support and enthusiasm for the revolution and for Castro personally. Nowhere did he detect significant opposition, although how much of that was a result of active suppression and fear he could not tell. Once in the capital, he settled into the Hotel Riviera and started to build a reputation for himself as a hard-living, corruptible businessman with contacts in the Middle-European arms trade:

```
Havana is still overrun with Mafia types, who
can only be inches away from confrontation
with the Barbudos. At night, the hotels are
full of finely dressed men and women gambling
and dancing as though there is no tomorrow,
which for them there may not be. The rooms at
the Riviera have thickened walls, reputedly
to mask the sound of gunfire. The beards
strut about in fatigues and heavy boots.
While they are happy to accept free drinks,
they eye the money passing across the baize
in a proprietary fashion. It can only be a
matter of time before the Mafiosi find their
hotels nationalised.
```

When he dropped the name Caballo into a late-night drinking session with a pair of policemen whose uniforms bore the insignia of Castro's feared inner guard, he detected crossed glances:

```
I feel that Caballo must be part of the
security forces and am getting closer to him.
But these men are wary, of Westerners
particularly, and I need to secure their
```

trust. They now believe I have something that they want. I am insisting that I must deal with their commander. A meeting has been set up for next week, but time in Havana is an elastic concept.

Please note that I have been unable to locate a reliable radio transmitter. All embassies are under close surveillance and are thus unsuitable. This message is being delivered by the agency of a friend from Rome in a safe concealing device, but the routing is probably secure for one use only. I will endeavour to find a reliable channel of communication over the next week. Until I do please do not respond via this route. Signed 007.

Friday, 10th August

007's latest report arrived last night in the diplomatic bag from Washington, just as I was leaving to meet the girls in Bully's for a birthday drink. I'd not been much looking forward to it; these past few months have been so full of turmoil that I don't feel I deserve a celebration. So 007's report arrived at an opportune moment – in any case, thirty-one is hardly an important milestone to mark. This report had been smuggled out by a Swiss diplomatic attaché, coiled into the handle of his razor, and was on M's desk by the time he arrived this morning. As soon as he'd read it, he called for an emergency meeting of the Cuba Group, including Head of S, but without Cousin Scott. It seems as if Head of C's hunches were correct; certainly there are strange happenings in Havana. 007 reported the arrival of scores of Russians, purporting to be agronomists and specialists in farming techniques and animal husbandry, but he's convinced that some, at least, are soldiers – top brass at that. He saw a couple being driven around in a jeep with Castro's army chief.

He'd heard rumours that Russian ships had been spotted docking in the major ports close to Havana. He determined to try to verify whether this was true, and if so, the nature of their loads . . .

In JM's diary there follows a summary of 007's report, but for the sake of completeness the relevant paragraphs of the original report have been inserted here, again merged with his final, debriefing, report:

```
I hired a local driver to take me to Mariel,
a major port 30 miles west of Havana. He
responded favourably to monetary persuasion
after initial hesitation; there has been an
edict forbidding foreigners from leaving the
city boundaries. Fortunately, when we were
stopped at the road-block, the soldier did
not look too carefully.
```

They drove along the coastal road, through semi-industrial flatland. On several occasions they passed army jeeps, and tractors pulling covered trailers, driven by clean-shaven, pale-skinned young men in identical checked cotton shirts rolled up at the sleeves. Once they crossed a long transport caravan heading towards Havana, but the trailers were tightly covered and 007 had no way of determining their load. After an hour they started ascending into the hills:

We saw Mariel first from above: a well-
protected bay, the port to the north-east of
the town itself, a cluster of small colonial
buildings and painted shacks filling the
deepest point of a valley heading inland. I
disembarked in the centre of town and sat in
a café overlooking the main road back to
Havana. A steady stream of army vehicles
headed to and from the port area - otherwise
the streets were noticeably empty of
civilians.
    An old man approached. He had served in the
Navy after the war and spent a year in
Liverpool, before returning to his home town
of Mariel, where he had worked in the port
until his retirement. He accompanied me to
the port gates. As we walked, he described
recent strange activity in the port area. A
month ago, several foreign soldiers had been
to visit. A week later, a passenger ship had
docked in Mariel and many hundreds of young
men had disembarked. All wore civilian
clothes - fawn trousers, checked cotton
shirts and heavy boots - but marched like
soldiers. The ship had strange writing on its
sides, possibly Russian or Polish. Two weeks
ago, the order was given for everybody living
within a half-mile radius of the port area to

evacuate their homes. The same men had taken over port security, barring any Cubans without special papers from entering and leaving.

As we approached a road-block half a mile from the port gates, a jeep passed and I recognised one of my Havana security contacts in the passenger seat. His driver stopped at the tall iron gates to the port and two guards ran out of the sentry house. They wore uniforms of black with green epaulettes. I walked the perimeter of the port fence; there were guard stations at regular intervals and security appeared to be tight.

Walking back into town, my Cuban contact said he had heard that all major deep-water ports in Cuba have been taken over by these men. The local people are scared. They do not know what is happening and fear another American invasion.

'It certainly appears that the Russians are moving into Cuba,' said Head of S after reading 007's report. 'They're transporting goods and personnel that require high levels of *maskirovka*.' He looked across at M: 'That's deception, sir. There's a possibility that the cargos could be missiles – perhaps, given the evidence of the epaulettes, the same missiles that 006 surmised were being loaded on to ships in Severomorsk?'

'Thank you, CS,' said M. 'If your analysis is correct, the situation is serious. We need to get a message to 007 to try to find out the exact nature of the cargo. It's extremely irritating that we cannot contact him. Let's try to get a message through that Frenchman again. Meanwhile, keep quiet about this. We need not tell the Cousins; we don't want to alert them to 007's movements.'

Wednesday, 15th August

An urgent cable from 007 arrived this morning, addressed to 'M, Eyes Only'. It was in plain text, but brief:

```
BUSINESS HERE SUSPENDED BY UNEXPECTED
REVELATIONS CONCERNING EXPORT PROVENANCE
STOP IMPERATIVE EYE DEPART ON BUSINESS
TRIP TO COASTAL AGENTS WHO REPORT ARRIVAL
OF NEW CONSIGNMENTS ON PASSENGER LINERS
STOP THE HORSE IS TROJAN REPEAT TROJAN
STOP WILL REPORT WHEN POSSIBLE SIGNED VON
KASEBERG
```

'Is M on his way?' asked Bill as soon as he'd seen the cable. 'Make sure the Cuba Group is standing by. We're going to have to act on this immediately.'

They were all assembled by 10.30. 'I have here a cable from 007,' said M. 'It's pretty self-explanatory. His cover's blown and he's had to go underground. Gone back to the ports to check out what's on these passenger ships – do we have logs of their movements? Can you check their port of origin, please? This Caballo is definitely a double – he's probably been working against the Cousins from the beginning. We can assume that means Castro knows all about Mongoose and that Caballo arranged the deaths of those two agents. Is it possible that 007's presence in Cuba was leaked somehow? Well, let's check and recheck. Either way he's in danger.

'We must tell the Americans. I'm going to have to do it personally, directly to the top. Can't trust the London channel any more. In the meantime, we need to work out the implications. S Section – you find out what's been happening at your end. Let's get any information we can from Cuba – satellite pictures, intercepts from the listeners, anything. Chief of Staff, you're in charge of collation. I want twice-daily reports while I'm away. Triple X through the Embassy. We've also got to establish a secure channel to 007. Someone ask Q Branch what they've got up their sleeves. We need to be able to communicate with him.'

As the others left, he motioned for me to stay. 'Your passport's up to date, Miss Moneypenny.' It was not a question.

'You're coming with me. I'll need secretarial assistance. Make arrangements for a girl to come up to help Chief of Staff while we're away. You'll make sure she runs a tight ship. Book us on the first flight to Washington on Saturday morning. Send cables to the White House and McCone* to let them know we're on our way and will need to see them first thing on Monday morning on a matter of the utmost importance and urgency. That will be all. For now.' As I turned to leave, I saw him reaching for his hot-line to Downing Street.

---

* On 29 November 1961, John McCone – a staunch Republican, successful businessman and former chairman of the Atomic Energy Commission – had replaced the long-serving Allen Dulles as director of the CIA. McCone's hawk-like instincts eventually brought him into conflict with the Kennedy White House.

M hates travelling by plane and does so only when it's unavoidable. He's been to America once in the six years I've been working for him and that time he managed to go by ship. I can tell that he's not looking forward to this trip. He'll be gruff and difficult for the next few days and I'll have to keep my head down and ensure everything is done before he's even asked for it.

I have to admit, I'm excited about it. What a way to see America – first stop the White House. Not to mention escaping my mess here. M has made no indication of how long we can expect to stay over there and he's not the sort of person one can ask things like that. I shall just have to pack enough for a week, and then if we stay longer, I can recycle. He's staying with the Ambassador; I'm to be billeted with the Ambassador's personal assistant in Georgetown. Helena is coming down to see Frieda again on Friday evening and she'll take Rafi back with her – he'll enjoy the break. Mary is moving up to my desk while Joanna Comely takes over her duties; she'll be more than happy with the opportunity to exchange pleasantries with the oos.

Thursday, 16th August

Drinks with Bill. He grabbed me as I was on my way out. 'A word, please, Penny.' We went to a small bar on Ebury Street. 'It's no bad time for you to be going away,' he said. 'I haven't told the Old Man yet about our little problem. I'm trying to keep it as tight as possible. At present, it's confined to Dorothy and myself – and our mole, of course. She's fairly sure she's got him in her sights, but in any case, she's going through the list of people who could be privy to security information about employees. It's not long, but long enough. She's been cross-referencing it with what we learnt from Kingfisher and there are some overlaps. We're looking into it, but of course we don't know whether it's the same chap we're after. To be honest, I don't think we're going to get to the bottom of it until you have another contact. I imagine it will happen, so long as he doesn't get wind that we're after him. That's why it's best to be quiet about it.'

'I'm so grateful, Bill. I can't begin to tell you . . .'

'Well, don't then,' he replied. 'I know you'd do the same for me, if it came to it. Now have a good time over there and forget about all this. Nothing can happen while you're away. If we don't hear from him when you get back, we'll have to put our thinking caps on and try to devise some way to lure him in. We need to get to the bottom of this. Over the last few years this office has come to look like a colander. It's downright embarrassing.'

Friday, 17th August

It's midnight and I've just come back from dinner with Helena. A delight, as always. She manages to remind me that there's a world out there beyond our secret one. She's as excited about my trip as I am. From childhood, we've dreamt of visiting America together, getting a big American car and driving from coast to coast. I told her that we would, some day. I'm just going ahead to get a feel for the lie of the land. Now I must pack. It's hot enough over here; apparently it will be stifling there, over 100 and humid. I hope the OM doesn't melt under his spotted bow-tie.

Sunday, 19th August, Washington, DC (transcribed on 8th September)

I left my journal behind and am writing this up from a small notepad I bought at the airport. The flight was unexpectedly enjoyable. I didn't realise how tense I'd become about the possibility that I was under constant surveillance; for the first time in months, I couldn't feel the watching eyes on my back. The BOAC double-decker Stratocruiser was half empty and M insisted on a row to himself upstairs. I think he was half terrified at the thought of having to make conversation with me for the entire night. He told me to 'relax, enjoy yourself' while he went over the Cuba file. We stopped at Shannon for dinner and when he made no move to invite me to join him I sat at my own table and gazed out of the window at the planes arriving and departing. How much travelling has changed. Nine years ago, Helena and I left Kenya by boat and it took ten days to sail to Southampton. Today, we could fly in a day and a night.

I've never flown so far before and I enjoyed every second of it – sitting in my own capsule far from the fears that have engulfed me over the past months. I felt suddenly affectionate towards M, upstairs with his files, chewing his pipe; I have spent more time alone with him than with anyone else over the past eight years, and yet in many ways he's a mystery to me. I sometimes wonder whether he would notice if I left, or whether he would continue to call my successor Miss Moneypenny?

Monday, 20th August, Washington

An audience at the White House with the Attorney-General* – 'Call me Bobby': an invitation which, needless to say, M did not hasten to take up – and Secretary of State 'Bob' McNamara.† I found it thrilling from the minute the Embassy Rolls swept us through the heavily policed iron gates leading to the building in which more power is concentrated than any other in the world. We followed bespectacled young men down thickly carpeted corridors, past statues of presidents past, and finally to the huge book-lined office of the Attorney-General. I was treated with charm and respect and given my own chair at a small desk across the room from the A-G's personal assistant, who was taking notes on their behalf. The Americans' youth was immediately striking; they are both full of energy, handsome and highly motivated. I found them most impressive.

I was interested to note that M acted no differently towards them than he does to any of the ministers in London who frequently cross his threshold. He was polite, formal, but entirely in command. Once and

---

* Robert F. Kennedy (1925–68), US Attorney-General from 1961 to 1964, when he resigned to stand for the US Senate. He was elected senator for New York and served until his assassination in Los Angeles on 6 June 1968, while campaigning for the Democratic presidential nomination.
† A former academic, decorated Second World War pilot and president of the Ford Motor Company, Robert McNamara (b. 1916) served as Secretary of Defense from January 1961 until 1968, when he resigned over policy disagreements with President Lyndon Johnson on the Vietnam War.

always a Rear Admiral. He kept his suit coat on throughout, even when the others took theirs off and rolled up their sleeves. He lit his pipe without first asking leave, and didn't hesitate to grunt and disagree when something they said displeased him. As far as M is concerned, while we have much to thank the Americans for, we are still the senior country, particularly in intelligence concerns.

'Mr Attorney-General. Thank you for seeing me at this short notice,' he began. 'I took the unusual step of coming here myself to relate to you the intelligence that we have gathered, as well as my team's possible interpretations of it, as I believe it has the potential to escalate into a serious problem.'

Kennedy thanked him and nodded for him to continue.

'As you know, we have been keeping abreast of the situation in Cuba, thanks in great part to the co-operation of one of your men in London, Agent Scott.'

Again Kennedy nodded. 'It was our wish to inform you of our operations in that theatre,' he replied.

'Thank you. We have recently gained access to certain intelligence which I felt you should know about straight away. It concerns Caballo.'

'The CIA's high-placed source?'

'The man they believe to be their source,' replied M. 'Not to put too fine a point on it, we have reason to believe that Caballo is a plant – his loyalties are with Castro.'

The Americans looked at each other. 'The Agency gave us their assurance that he was clear. There was some initial doubt, I understand, but they checked him out as thoroughly as was possible, given the difficult circumstances – he refused to reveal his true identity. But all the information he gave us, initially at least, was bang on target, and we've sent men into Cuba as a result of it,' said McNamara. 'Could I ask on what basis you make that assertion?'

'I'm afraid I am not at liberty to tell you, but I can assure you that our source is entirely trustworthy.'

'You're sure about this Caballo?'

'Nothing is certain in this business, as you gentlemen well know. But I did not travel halfway across the world to divulge idle speculation.'

Kennedy turned to McNamara. 'You remember, there was concern after those two men died over there a couple of months ago. I asked the Agency then whether this source of theirs was bona fide. When they insisted, I was still a little uneasy, and turned to our friends over the pond for assistance in doublechecking. I didn't tell you at the time. It was the President's personal wish.' He turned back to M. 'Thank you, sir. We're grateful to you for coming all this way to tell us this and we would welcome any further intelligence on this matter. The ramifications, as you no doubt have realised, could be serious indeed. Castro is a loose cannon and I'm sure the Russians find him irresistible. I will apprise the President of this development. I'm sure he will want to discuss it further. You're staying in town a bit longer?'

'Yes, at the Embassy. I've prepared a full briefing on our latest Cuba intelligence for you. I have also brought one for the Director of the CIA.'

The Americans exchanged glances. 'Admiral, sir. I would be grateful if you could hold off giving it to them for the moment, please,' said Kennedy. 'Let us talk to the President first. He's in Chicago until tomorrow, and I don't want to trust the information over the telephone. You will hear from us within the next day or two.'

Wednesday, 22nd August, Washington

I have met the President. I had a high opinion of him before, but he still managed to surpass those expectations. I'm not sure I have ever been in the same room as someone who exudes such charisma; you can almost touch it. He managed to make me feel like the only woman in the world for the two seconds or so in which he held my hand in his and looked me up and down. Even the oo agents could learn something from JFK about how to treat women.

M was only slightly slower to be bowled over. At first, I saw him eyeing the President's youth with a degree of scepticism, but within minutes it was clear that Kennedy was on top of the situation – he knew every detail of the events and operations in Cuba and had thought through the implications of Caballo's treachery. 'Look, we have some kind of mess to clear up with our friends at the Agency. Lansdale's* busy planning Course B of Operation Mongoose and who knows how much is dependent on compromised information? I had an uneasy feeling about this Caballo guy all along – that's why I asked Bobby to get you guys in to help. I had this feeling that perhaps we shouldn't have trusted him. But that's in the past. Presumably you have a man in Cuba that you can trust?'

M nodded his assent.

'I don't need details of who or where he is, but I would like to be kept up to speed with what he discovers as soon as you know yourself. Is that a deal?'

---

* Brigadier Edward Lansdale (1908–87), acknowledged guerrilla expert and veteran of campaigns in the Philippines and Vietnam. Brought in by the Kennedys in November 1961 to spearhead the Cuba operation, he drew up plans for Operation Mongoose.

'Yes, sir.'

'I want to know what the hell Castro's up to now and how the Russians are involved. I don't trust Khrushchev.* He's denying any aggressive intentions, but that doesn't mean anything. Meanwhile, he's dangling Berlin over our heads.

'Now, Admiral. I'm in a somewhat difficult position. I didn't tell the Agency about our double-checking operation on Caballo and I don't think they would be best pleased to learn about it now. Obviously, we have to let them know right away that Caballo is a dud. I'm afraid that's just going to make them and the service chiefs even more hungry for battle, but we must be cautious. Less than two weeks ago, McCone warned that the continued Soviet aid and assistance in Cuba would present what he called "a more formidable problem in the future".†

---

* After the death of Stalin in 1953, Nikita Khrushchev became First Secretary of the Communist Party and ruler of the USSR. A former miner who had joined the Bolsheviks in 1918, he owed his education to the October Revolution and was a firm believer in the benefits of a workers' state. He became a member of the Central Committee in 1934 and of the ruling Politburo in 1939. In 1956 he stunned delegates at the Party's Twentieth Congress when he denounced Stalin and the excesses of his era. He was certainly the most colourful of the Soviet leaders, fond of dramatic gestures designed to achieve propaganda gains. He reigned over the launch of the first satellite, *Sputnik*, as well as the first dog, man and woman in space, leading the West to believe, for a while, that the USSR was ahead in the arms race. He was forced out of his position by opponents in the Politburo in 1964, and lived quietly in retirement until his death on 11 September 1971, aged seventy-seven.

† On 10 August, at a meeting of Kennedy's security advisers – the Special Group (Augmented) – to discuss the latest developments in Operation Mongoose, McCone for the first time raised the possibility

'I'm only telling you this so that you're aware of the sensitivity of the situation we are now in. I hope you will honour me by keeping our discussions today entirely confidential.'

'Of course, Mr President,' M replied.

'I would very much like your continued help in this matter. What I am about to propose will keep you away from your organisation for a few days longer. I know you're a very busy man, but you also understand that the implications of this for the whole world could be potentially catastrophic?'

M inclined his head and pulled his pipe out of his breast pocket and started to fill it. The President's Chief of Staff and personal assistant exchanged looks of horror, but the President merely smiled.

'You would be doing me a tremendous personal service if you would agree to go down to Miami to the JM/WAVE HQ to meet Brigadier Lansdale and his team. He needs to be briefed about Caballo. If you wouldn't mind, it would be much the best if he thought the impetus behind the collection of this information emanated from you. In addition, I would sure appreciate your input on the whole operation. Can you do that?'

'I'll have to consult my minister of course, but I can't foresee any opposition,' said M.

'Great news. I look forward to hearing your man's reports. Thank you again, Admiral, and good afternoon.'

---

that the Soviets might have been in the process of deploying nuclear weapons in Cuba.

Sunday, 26th August, Miami, Florida

A day off in Miami and I've been to the beach. It's extraordinary, miles of white sand on the fringe of a big city. We flew down on Friday. M had spent the previous day at CIA HQ,* but he said that I wasn't required, so instead I walked around Georgetown. What a beautiful place. The streets are lined with perfect brick houses, each with primped lawn and painted shutters. I stayed in a pretty cottage on S Street with Gloria Goschen,† who, naturally, was keen for news of London. She took me out for dinner one night, to a hamburger restaurant. It was like a rabbit warren – a series of underground caverns, full of diners and people slotting money into juke-boxes. It seemed very relaxed – most of the men wore blue jeans, and the women casual cotton dresses. 'Is this where the students come?' I asked Gloria. She laughed. 'No, this is a Georgetown power-dining centre. Look over there,' she pointed at a man with razor-short hair and heavy-rimmed glasses. 'He's a White House counsel, very close to the Kennedys, while he,' she pointed at another table across the room, 'is the President's chief speech-writer.' In England, these same people would be smoking cigars in leather armchairs at Blades.

Miami is similarly informal. It's easy to forget that people actually work here. We're staying at a grand hotel called the National on South Beach. The lobby has a marble

---

* A large complex designed to feel like a college campus, located in Langley, Virginia.
† Formerly personal assistant to Head of Section A in London; moved with him to Washington, before transferring on to the ambassador's personal staff.

floor and mosaic ceiling. You walk straight through the bar to glass doors opening on to the garden, which in turn backs on to the beach. I love palm-trees, their trunks so straight, their fronds so animated. I think M was rather shocked by its glamour when we arrived; it had been recommended to us by the Ambassador as his favourite in the city.

We spent most of yesterday in Coral Gables, at the JM/WAVE HQ. It's a mini-complex within the university campus, dressed up to be a technical company – at least that's what the nameplate says. But it's surrounded by a huge fence, patrolled by men wearing sunglasses and ostentatious weapons. Even on a Saturday, there was a hubbub, busy-looking people carrying clipboards and sticking pins into wall charts of Cuba, talking rapidly in Spanish. M spent much of the day cloistered in Lansdale's office. Again, I was not required and instead I went for a walk through the woods to the main university campus – more sprinkled lawns and palm-trees. When I returned, I sat under a tree outside the building reading my book. As I stood up to go back in, I realised that I hadn't thought about Zach for over a week. I feel miraculously liberated. For now, anyway.

Monday, 27th August, Miami

At last, a message from 007, smuggled out with an escaping Cuban émigré and dated a week ago. I know M had been anxious about having had no contact with him. At least he is alive, albeit in a precarious situation with the local security forces. He requested as a matter of urgency that we send him a radio transmitter.

The captain of a small fishing vessel, the *Mohito*, is en route to Miami Bay Marina to collect it. His name is Alain Rodriguez and he expects to arrive, all being well, before dawn on 29th August. He will greet the welcoming party with the phrase 'The sea is calm this morning,' to which the reply should be 'Yes, it is good fishing weather.' I have promised him $250 as the assignment carries some risk. I believe him to be trustworthy, but the sea around Cuba is full of sharks, not all of the fishy variety.

M spun into order mode. 'Excellent, at last we'll be able to contact him. Find out what Q Branch recommends. It's too late for them to get any of our equipment over here, but perhaps our hosts can help. Q Branch can liaise. Then contact the Embassy and see if they have an operative available in Miami to meet the ship. I'm going to have to go back to London tomorrow morning – but perhaps you could stay an extra day to make sure everything goes off smoothly.' It was more of an order than a request, but one which I was more than happy to fulfil. An Embassy chap is due down here tomorrow afternoon. Until then, I'm going to enjoy holding the fort.

Wednesday, 29th August, Miami

The agent from Washington never arrived. At six in the evening, I received an urgent message at the hotel to say that he had been involved in a motor accident. There was no one available to take his place, no one anywhere near Florida. 'What about the transceiver?' I asked.

'We made independent arrangements for it. The CIA are sending it to Miami under guard in one of their planes. It's their latest model,* top secret, lent to us only under duress and after promises that we would keep it safe. It should arrive in Miami within the hour. They're due to deliver it to the hotel. The paperwork has been cabled ahead. Look, how can we help? Shall we ask the Agency for assistance?'

'Negative, thank you,' I replied. 'I'll contact London and ask for orders.'

As luck would have it, 006 was the duty officer that night. When I explained the situation, he just said blithely, 'Then Penny, you'll have to step in yourself.'

'Me?'

'Of course. Come on, it'll be a piece of cake. You just have to turn up, say the code and give him the box. It couldn't be easier.'

'Don't you think you should get authorisation for this?'

'From whom? The Old Man's not back yet and Bill's been up for the last three nights working on some hush-hush crisis and said only to disturb him in a situation of national urgency. This isn't exactly a Russian plot to kill the PM.

---

* Developed by Delco in conjunction with NASA and the CIA and brought into operational use in 1962, the 5300 was a solid-state, high-frequency transceiver, resembling a lunch box with a hinged lid. Smaller and thus more portable than its predecessors, it both transmitted and received on four (separate) crystal-controlled channels. It had additional features which made it well adapted to clandestine use: a switch that turned off the power automatically if the lid was closed, and a 'whisper function' to increase microphone sensitivity.

You'll be fine. Take a torch and a flask of tea, or whatever the Americans drink instead, and enjoy the night sky.'

'Well, if it's an order, I'm more than happy to obey.'

'It's an order.'

I waited in my room for the transceiver to arrive, which it duly did, along with a full guard of hefty men. Once they'd left, I thought I might as well get to the port ahead of time. I picked up a cushion and walked out through the garden, turning right along the beach until I reached the small park on the southern point of the peninsula. There was a long wooden jetty, from where I could clearly see the boats rounding the point into the port area. At this time of night, there were very few, maybe one every hour, and the moonlight was strong enough for me to be able to make out their names. The marina was only about fifty yards into the bay to my right. I wandered around it for a while, peering into the berthed yachts bobbing in the gentle sway, feeling a little self-conscious at carrying my heavy lunch box with the transceiver inside. It was a beautiful, cloudless evening, mercifully cooler than the day had been. There was nothing that resembled a Cuban fishing vessel moored in the marina, so I took my book back to the jetty and sat down to wait.

The night slipped past slowly. Every hour or so, I got up to stretch my legs and to walk along to the marina to check that the Mohito hadn't slipped in unobserved. It was only when the darkness started to lift that I became anxious. Something had gone wrong.

September

For some years now, Cuba had been the proverbial thorn in America's side. Just ninety miles south of the tip of Florida, and with an educated population and a large army, it was close enough to be threatening if not 'onside'. Its previous leader, Fulgencio Batista, although nominally an ally of his powerful northern neighbour, had become increasingly corrupt and despotic, to the point where the United States was not unhappy to see him deposed. However, it was less than enthusiastic about his successor.

Fidel Castro Ruz, a lawyer, scion of wealthy landowners from the south and leader of a group of revolutionaries known as the 26 July Movement, seized power at the stroke of midnight on 1 January 1959. He was greeted with rapture by the majority of Cubans. There were reports of wholesale executions of former Batista officials. Over the next few years Castro set about systematically cutting the close ties – economic and, by extension, political – between Cuba and the United States. While it was not until several years later that he declared himself openly to be a committed ideological Communist, his actions – and those of his circle of 'Barbudos', the bearded ones – had already begun to strike fear into the heart of Washington. The number of Cubans under arms swelled, along with the bureaucracy. A network of informers was set up to report on anyone who was '*gusano*' – wormlike – in spirit (not in favour of the revolution). In the three years following the revolution, tens of thousands were imprisoned. Foreign-owned companies were nationalised, and private beaches were opened to all. Before the end of 1959, diplomatic and trade relations had been forged with the Soviet Union. In April 1960 Khrushchev elected to send Cuba a gift of weapons.

Towards the end of his term of office President Dwight D. Eisenhower drew up plans for a US-led invasion of Cuba. The Republicans lost the election before he could see them enacted, and the baton was passed to the new Democratic presidency. In January 1961, days before Kennedy's inauguration, diplomatic ties between the two nations were severed. Three months later, on 17 April, the attempted coup met with failure on the beaches of the Bay of Pigs. Over a thousand men were taken prisoner. The same day, the Cuban secret police found a cache of eight tons of weapons belonging to the CIA in Havana, and for the first time Castro revealed to his people his vision for a socialist Cuba. The mistrust between the two nations had hardened into active enmity.

In the United States, the Kennedy administration set Operation Mongoose into action, intending to hasten Castro's downfall by a more covert route. Castro cemented relations with the Soviets. One by one, the glittering lights of Havana were dimmed and the casino doors closed for the last time. Instead of chandeliers there were cannon; instead of masked balls there was drill practice. Another invasion by the US was regarded as inevitable. It was a matter of when, and how best to beat it off. For

Castro, the only hope for his small nation – and for his presidency – was to harness the full military might of the opposing superpower.

Sunday, 2nd September, Miami

An extraordinary few days. I don't know quite how to describe what I've just done; I'm not sure I believe I did it. I was worried when James's boat failed to arrive for the transceiver. Instead of waiting for another night, I started canvassing the fishing-boats as they came in with their dawn haul. I was eventually directed to a scruffy craft, captained by a large man with an expansive moustache and a gold front tooth. His name, he told me, was José Piñero and he had just returned from a tuna-fishing expedition round Cuba.

I asked him if he knew a fellow Cuban captain named Alain Rodriguez. 'Of course, I know him well. I see his boat in Mariel before I leave, but I no see him. There were soldiers on it. I not know why.'

I must have looked upset, because he invited me aboard his boat and made me a cup of gritty black coffee. 'Now why you want Alain Rodriguez?'

'He was coming to collect something for a friend who is in Cuba now,' I told him.

José looked concerned. 'Your friend – he is Cubano, or Ingles?'

'No. He is European,' I said. 'A Swiss businessman.'

'I am glad he is not Ingles or Americano.'

When I asked why, he told me that three nights previously, he'd stopped at the port of Mariel to visit his family.

The harbour area had been closed, so he'd moored along the coast and made his way into town by foot. There he heard that a man had been seen being marched on to a Russian cargo ship by soldiers in black uniforms. 'They say he mebbe Ingles, mebbe Americano. He was shouting, he not want to go with the men,' José told me.

I asked if he knew what this man looked like.

'They say big man, dark hair, pale skin.'

It was enough. Without thinking, I told José I would give him $250 if he took me to Mariel.

'OK, mebbe tomorrow,' he said.

'No,' I insisted. 'I must go now.'

It took a few hours to unload the tuna and refuel the boat and then we were off. Seventeen hours on a rolling, bucketing ocean, clutching the transceiver, in an unsteady boat stinking of engine oil and old fish. I had time then to think about the consequences. I would face disciplinary action for sure, probably lose my job. I know I should have signalled HQ before I left, but they would only have told me to stand down and wait for an agent to arrive and that could have been too late. I acted on instinct, and even then I didn't regret it.

I managed eventually to fall asleep for a few hours, wedged between coiled ropes and fish-tanks, and when I woke we were approaching the lights of a small port. 'Mariel,' José informed me. 'Soon it will be light. We have breakfast, then I take you to my mother's. You can rest there.'

We docked quietly. I could smell the tropics; wet heat mingling with palm-trees, thickly scented flowers and rotting rubbish. As we walked into town, José pointed to a ghostly silhouette, which dwarfed the flotilla of fishing-boats and tugs bobbing in the harbour. '*Omsk*.* Ship your friend was taken on.'

In the half-light, I could just make out her name, painted on the hulk of her stern below a string of Cyrillic letters. We walked along the esplanade to a small café, already open and serving the fishermen thick dark coffee and spicy fish stew. There was a constant soup of Spanish chatter and no one paid me much attention. José lent me his binoculars and as we ate I watched the buzz surrounding the *Omsk*. I could soon make out the bosses – four men, dressed in black military-style uniforms with green epaulettes, issuing commands. A host of scurrying workers – large, fair-haired men in civilian clothes – were offloading huge crates. Ten of them walked beside a vast trolley as it rolled slowly down the stern ramp. Strapped to it was a metal tube, at least sixty feet long. This they carefully loaded on to a string of attached trailers, pulled by a truck with tracked wheels. As I watched, five more of these tubes were unloaded, installed on to trolleys and driven away. By the time dawn had broken, the dockside was quiet.

Then the soldier-types vanished into the bowels of the ship. Just as we were about to leave, they reappeared, march-

---

* Newly built in Osa, Japan, and registered in Vladivostok, the *Omsk* was a large-hatched ship over 500 feet in length and as tall as a ten-storey building. She had a reinforced bow for ploughing through icy Baltic waters and, inside her hull, eight giant compartments, each over sixty feet from side to side and as high as a house. When she set sail from the USSR she was equipped with every modern device, from radar and gyrocompasses to echo-sounding instruments; on her decks were all the weapons of modern warfare, including guided-missile launchers to keep other ships at bay.

ing a tall man between them. I stopped and strained my eyes. I felt my heart leap. The man's head was bowed and he was stumbling a little, but it looked like James. As they approached the wheel-house, he suddenly turned and struck out at one of his captors, kicking another at the same time. It was a token attempt and he was quickly overpowered, but it was enough to convince me it was him.

The reality of my situation hit home – it was as if, up until that point, I'd been riding the wave of a fantasy, pulled along by the need to rescue James. Now, all at once, I felt scared and alone and far out of my depth.

Somehow, I needed to find a way to get him off the ship.

On his return, Bond later filed a detailed report* describing the events leading up to his capture:

I was at the Floridiana waiting for my
contacts to arrive when I overheard two men,
clearly Cuban security police, laughing about
the deaths of the two CIA agents. 'They were
dead meat from the minute they stepped into
the country,' they sneered. 'GG was playing
them like puppets.' I managed to make their
acquaintance through some judicious
generosity at the bar. Over the course of
several nights of drinking together, I
ascertained that the GG they had mentioned
was their chief, Geraldo Gil, the head of
Castro's secret intelligence unit.

---

* Among the treasury of documents found in the National Archives, the relevant passages of which have been reproduced here.

I asked them to arrange a meeting with GG, hinting that I had some military hardware for sale at basement prices. 'Amigo, he would like to meet you too,' one of them replied. 'He always likes to meet foreigners.' They both laughed. 'Particularly capitalist ones. He went to school in London. He speaks very good English. You speak English, Swiss man?' I nodded and bought them another drink.

I was sure I was on to Caballo. Even his initials, GG – horse; *caballo* in Spanish – pointed towards it. It all added up. I needed to meet him to confirm it. This wasn't as easy as I had hoped. Over the next ten days, several meetings were set up and then cancelled. I was taken to a cock-fight outside Havana, which disintegrated into a brawl. I managed to prevent one of my hosts from being wounded – I wouldn't be surprised to learn that my loyalty was being tested. Shortly after, I received a message from Gil in my hotel room, setting up a meet for midnight in the night-club of the Havana Libre hotel. I arrived early and waited, but he didn't show. At two, as I was preparing to leave, one of his henchmen came in and beckoned me to a side-room. 'Our boss will be along in a minute. He said to offer you one of these.' He passed across a fat cigar, which I refused. 'My boss says you are to smoke a cigar.' His voice was threatening. I refused again, pleading a dislike of cigar

smoke. But he smiled and said, 'This time, my
friend, you will. They were a gift from your
capitalist imperialist friend America.'

I protested that I was from Switzerland, a
neutral country, and that my only interest
lay in finding a good buyer for my products.
He laughed. 'We do not believe you are who
you say you are, Mr von Kaseberg, and soon we
will discover your true identity. If you want
a chance to get out of here, you will light
this cigar.'

I remembered the Operation Mongoose memo
about the exploding cigars. I took the one he
offered and got out my lighter, but at the
point of contact I threw them both across the
room at one of the guards by the door. It
made a tremendous bang. After another minor
scrap, I managed to make my excuses and
leave.

Still without proof that Gil was Caballo, Bond followed
the security men back to a tall concrete office block near the
Plaza Cívica and waited until they came back out of the
building, this time with a large, red-bearded man whom
they treated with some deference. They got into a jeep and
headed off on the western road out of Havana, Bond following them at a safe distance:

I had to drive much of the way with my
headlights off. There were few cars on the road
and I couldn't risk being seen. They drove fast
— it was only when we left the highway and took

215

a small road north to the coast that we were
forced to slow down, to make way for a long
convoy of army trucks and tractors pulling
trailers laden with goods covered in
tarpaulin, heading away from the coast. There
was a large accompanying guard and I pulled off
down a side-track just in time.

I kept the Cubans in view, and before long
they drew up at a small coastal town,
dominated by the belching chimneys of a
cement factory. When the clouds parted, I
could see from a sign on the factory gate
that we were back in the town of Mariel. The
jeep approached an iron gate, set into a tall
wire-mesh fence. It was waved through with a
salute. I hid my car off a track leading into
the hills behind the town and went down on
foot to investigate the port. I found a gap
in the perimeter fence and a good vantage
point, from where I observed the Cubans
approach a large freighter named the *Omsk*. I
could read a sign on the fore gangway, which
said it was bringing grain from Siberia. But
there were also rocket launchers on the deck
– which seemed superfluous for the load it was
meant to be carrying. A reception committee
of uniformed soldiers trotted down the
gangplank and saluted Red Beard, before
leading him aboard. I made a careful approach
to get a better look. When the coast was
clear, I climbed a ladder at the bow and
attempted to secrete myself in one of the

lifeboats. Unfortunately, I came face to whiskers with a napping Russian sailor, who let out a loud shout before I was able to silence him. Despite some energetic resistance, I was soon subdued by a phalanx of armed Russians.

I was led to the bridge, where Red Beard was talking to one of the men in black. 'Who are you?' he demanded in Spanish. When I didn't reply, he asked again in English, Russian and French. 'My name is von Kaseberg. I am a Swiss businessman,' I told him. 'And I would appreciate it if you could call off your men, otherwise I will be forced to report you.'

'To who? The United Nations?' He let out a deep-bellied laugh. 'You are not in Switzerland now. Tell me what you are doing here. This is a restricted site.'

'I was looking for General Gil. I was told he would be in Mariel and I have a proposition to make to him.'

'What is it then? Spit it out,' he said.

'Are you General Gil?'

'Whether I am or not is nothing to you. Tell me your proposition.'

I told him about the early-stage American Hawk missiles* that I had to offer and he

---

* Developed in the 1950s, and originally named after the bird, these surface-to-air missiles were saddled with the acronym 'Homing All the Way Killer', soon after they came online in 1960.

just laughed. 'I am not interested in such chicken-feed,' he spat. 'And now you must prove your credentials.'

'If you would just release me, I could return to my hotel and bring you all my papers, as well as specifications of my wares,' I said. 'Then perhaps we could have a civilised meeting.'

Red Beard — who I now know was indeed Gil[*] — grunted and showed his teeth again. He said he was going to do independent research into my identity and in the meantime I should think of myself as his guest. He told his men to take me down to a small cabin on the upper deck and lock the door. Some hours later, I was summoned back up to the bridge, where Gil was waiting with the side-kicks I had last seen at the end of my fist in the Havana hotel. 'Do you know what we do with spies?' he asked. 'Yes, I know who you are, Agent 007 of the British secret service. Sadly I am not going to have the opportunity to show you how spies are generally greeted in Cuba, as I have to go back to Havana on a matter of urgency. So I am going to leave you instead in the custody of my friends from the KGB. I have every confidence that they will take very good care of you.' With a last flash of

---

[*] Also known as Barbaroja, or Red Beard, Major-General Geraldo Gil was chief of the Cuban Directorate General of Intelligence (DGI) from 1959 to 1994. He died, of cirrhosis of the liver, in 2002.

his teeth he was gone. The KGB were less
vocal. They gave me a bottle of vodka and
said they were going to execute me as soon as
they had received authorisation from Moscow.

Monday, 3rd September, Miami

I woke early this morning and as I was walking along the
beach I saw a pod of dolphins gambolling through the
ocean, and was seized with the glorious, tangible feeling
of being alive. In spite of everything, I loved Cuba – it had
a vibrancy and colour that I've seen nowhere else. Had I
not been insanely worried about 007, terrified that I
wouldn't be able to rescue him, that his life might have
been resting in my hands, I would have been strangely
happy in that little room at José's mother's house.

For most of the day, I sat on a stool by the window, the
transceiver at my feet, binoculars trained on the Omsk,
anchored just down the hill from where I sat watching.
Once, when I got up to stretch my legs, I caught sight of
myself in a small mirror and my first thought was of horror
at my dishevelled hair and smudged cheeks. I was about to
set to work with a comb and hanky, when something
stopped me. I realised to my surprise that I was looking at
an image of myself as a child, a person I thought I'd left far
behind, and that I didn't want her to go away. Maybe it was
that person – the child who had felt at ease sleeping alone
under canvas with the roar of nearby lions as a lullaby –
who gave me the courage to see the day through, to put
myself in danger to save another?

If I knew nothing else, I knew I would try to rescue

James, whatever the danger. There was no question about it: I was going to do everything I could. I didn't allow myself to consider the possibility of failure and I'm not sure I gave much thought to my own peril, just to James's. For a second the thought flashed across my mind that I must care for him deeply, to be prepared to sacrifice everything for him, but I pushed it straight back into my unconscious – it would do me no good to think of 007 like that. Perhaps it was an unconscious effort to purge my latent guilt over the Z affair? I suppose, with hindsight, I should have signalled for help, but I knew there was no chance of instant back-up and every bone in my body sensed that he was in immediate danger; I couldn't have stood down, whatever my orders. It seemed easier to stay out of contact.

I watched throughout the day, as they loaded crates and sacks full of sugar. Deck-hands scrubbed and polished. One of the officers drove off in a vast, pistachio-green American car and reappeared an hour later with a crate of bottles, which he held above his head to cheers from the crew. I didn't see James again, but there was always one man left standing outside a door on the upper deck, as if on sentry duty.

At dusk, José's mother knocked gently on my door and beckoned me down to eat, and when I shook my head she brought some fried rice and a bowl of spicy beans up to the room. I was not yet ready to leave my look-out post. I had seen a car full of women in bright skirts arriving at the ship and could hear the strains of jazz music from somewhere in its bowels. It sounded as if they were preparing to give themselves a handsome send-off.

Over the next few hours, I slipped out a couple of times and managed to find a small gap in the perimeter fence, through which I squeezed to get closer to the ship. The gangway had been pulled up, but I saw a ladder near the stern, leading up to the lifeboats. I went back to the house and waited a few hours – to give whatever had been in those bottles a chance to take hold.

It must have been nearing midnight when I slipped downstairs again and let myself out – I had to try, at least, to get James off the ship. My heart was literally pounding – I could feel the beats echoing in the back of my throat.

As I crept up to the boat, I wondered whether I should have brought the transceiver with me. Although it would have been a great hindrance, I hated leaving it out of my sight. Perhaps I could have hidden it in a dustbin on the esplanade and hoped to be able to rescue it before the stray cats decided to investigate? They wouldn't have had much luck with a radio transmitter, but I'd be in even greater trouble if I were to return without it. Looking back now, from the safety of this hotel room, I wished I had.

Climbing aboard presented no problem. There was the noise of a party coming from inside, but the deck appeared deserted. I crept around to the room where I guessed James was being held. I couldn't see the sentry and was just about to approach the door when I heard soft footsteps and a man came round the corner carrying a plate of food and a glass full of what I guessed to be rum. I slunk back into the shadow. He sat down, took his gun out of his waist-band and put it down by his chair and began to eat. I could feel the blood pounding round my head, but I knew I couldn't afford to let my fear take hold. I grabbed a handful of sand from a bucket near my feet and flung it at his face, and as he got up, startled, I jumped behind him and pulled my scarf around his neck.

It was a move I'd practised many times in the gymnasium on that self-defence course that M had insisted we all go on, and it worked exactly as the instructor had demonstrated. 'Move, and I'll throttle you,' I hissed and although he couldn't understand my words, my intention was clear. I locked his arm behind him and kicked his gun out of the way. He struggled, but his eyes were still streaming from the sand, and I managed to restrain him. Keeping a tight hold of his arm, I loosened the scarf and pushed him back down on his chair then tied his hands with the scarf behind the chair and stuffed my handkerchief in his mouth. Then I retrieved the gun. My hands were shaking as I felt around for his keys. I eventually fitted one into the lock and pushed open the door. And then a large black weight leapt on me.

The next thing I heard was James's voice: 'Moneypenny, what the hell are you doing here? Go home at once.'

'I came to bring you the radio,' I replied.

'Penny, this is no joke. The guys out there are KGB. They're waiting for confirmation of orders to kill me. They could be back any minute. Go now while you can.'

I told him I wasn't going anywhere without him.

Outside, I could hear my captive rocking forwards and backwards on his chair.

'Come on, quick,' I urged James. But he sat down on the bunk with his head in his hands. It was as though he was deciding whether to come. I grabbed him by the arm and pulled him towards the door. As I did, I heard a loud crash. The guard had managed to topple his chair and, still tied to it, was rolling down the gangway towards the main deck.

James seemed to click into action. He grabbed the gun

from me and pushed me against the wall. 'Keep behind me. They must have heard that.'

We slithered along the wall. I kept my eyes glued on James's back. I saw him tense, raise his gun arm and fire. A volley of shots came back at us. 'Keep your head down and run in the other direction. I'll catch up,' he shouted. I did as I was told, sprinting towards the front of the ship, where I'd earlier seen a lifeboat on a hoist. I was climbing in when I sensed a hand by my shoulder. I spun around and lashed out at my attacker with an elbow. He grunted and jumped on top of me. I struggled as best I could while he tried to smother me with his hand. I bit hard on his finger and he jumped back momentarily. As he was lunging towards me again, a single shot rang out and he collapsed as James jumped into the boat beside me. 'Another form for you to fill in. Come on, Penny, we're on our way. Grab that rope there.' I pulled and the lifeboat plummeted down and landed on the water with a tremendous splash. I was thrown forwards against the bow.

'James, the radio. Back on the shore.' I felt another shot race past my cheek and embed itself in the wood beside my face. James pushed me over the side into the water and when I surfaced I could hear him shooting. I started swimming for land and he was soon beside me. We clambered out and I started running towards the town. He grabbed me by the back of my shirt. 'Don't be stupid, Moneypenny! Do you want to get us killed? Forget the radio.' As I started to protest, he gripped my hand and pulled me in the direction of the small marina where I'd landed that morning. James was ahead of me, looking at the boats for a likely escape route. He'd just jumped into one and was fiddling with the ignition when I heard a motorbike come up behind us. As I was about to shout a warning, James shot. He must have caught the petrol tank as it instantly burst into flames. He pulled me sideways into the motor boat and within seconds the engine was up and we were speeding away.

My last sight of Cuba was of a man in flames running screaming along the dock.

Sunday, 9th September

Back home and I'm up to date with this diary, at last. Transcribing the scribbles I made on the road, I've relived the adventure: Miami, Cuba, the boat, James, our escape and eventual return to London to face the music. I think I was more nervous about explaining my actions to M than I'd been at any point in Cuba.

I can remember little about our speedboat journey back to Miami. Within minutes, I started shaking and collapsed on the back seat. I slept most of the way. I don't know how James got back on his own, navigating by the stars in an unfamiliar boat. I remember at one point I woke up to see him sitting tall at the stern, his hand on the tiller. 'Go back to sleep, my guardian angel,' he said when I groggily offered to help. 'We should be there soon after sunrise.'

The two days in Miami were essential recuperation time. I slept a lot and tried not to think about the rock-fall of worries that have been piling up inside my head over the past few months. James was wonderful throughout – I got to know a different side of him, one that had been trying to worm its way out since Tracy's death, but which, I suspect, he finds hard to embrace. He's a kind, thoughtful, generous man, as well as strong and extraordinarily attractive. I may have to reconsider my previous opinion about Kennedy. I'm certainly happy to spend plenty of time in the considering.

He came into my room on our first evening, while I was writing, and it was only sleight of hand that prevented him from catching me in the act. He was in better spirits and whisked me off to a wonderful restaurant called Joe's Stone Crab* on Southern Point, just across the road from the small park where I'd waited for his boat not to arrive. I showed him the jetty. 'I was so worried about you,' I told him. 'I thought your ship was never going to come in.' 'Well, it has now, my Penny,' he replied.

We sat for hours wearing plastic bibs, eating stone crabs with the melted butter dribbling down our chins, while he told me about his last visit here, the night before his first encounter with Goldfinger.† For a time I could forget what had come before and what I had still to face on our return to London. I couldn't bear to think about the radio; the consequences of having left it behind were too enormous to consider. I think he sensed my anxiety, as at one point he

---

* A South Beach landmark, first established in 1913, and as popular today. Appeared in Fleming's *Goldfinger*, loosely disguised, as 'Bill's on the Beach'.

† A cancelled flight in 1958 led to a chance meeting with Junius Du Pont, whom Bond had first met six years earlier, at the casino in Royale. In Miami, Du Pont was being beaten heavily at cards by gold trader Auric Goldfinger, one of the world's wealthiest men, whom he suspected of cheating. He offered Bond $10,000 to discover how it was being done. Bond watched their game and soon discovered that the contents of Du Pont's hands were being transmitted to Goldfinger through his 'hearing aid' by his secretary, who was sitting in the window of Goldfinger's suite with a telescope trained on the game.

put his hand on my arm and said, 'Don't worry, Penny. I'll see to the Old Man.' And at that time, in that place, I would have believed anything he told me.

As I caught the lift up to the eighth floor on Tuesday morning, my stomach was scrunched into a knot of terror and guilt. I was convinced that my chair had already been filled; even old Fletcher seemed to have a sympathetic look on his gnarled face. I prayed I hadn't lost my job – yet I couldn't see how they could keep me: I had flagrantly broken so many rules. To my surprise, as I was walking into my office, I saw James leaving M's room. He gave me a wink as he passed. 'You can come in now, Miss Moneypenny,' M said. 'Sit down.' I sat facing him on the straight-backed chair that had almost moulded to my contours over the course of the last five and a half years. 'What you did was beyond the scope of your experience and orders,' he began. 'You could have been badly hurt, not to mention compromised an operation and risked the life of an undercover agent. On top of that, you left behind a top-secret radio transceiver. If that falls into enemy hands, we'll be in deep trouble with the Americans – and that's the last thing we need now,' he added, almost in an aside. 'They've not asked for it back yet, and with luck we'll be able to stall them for a while. This kind of headstrong behaviour cannot be tolerated by untrained operatives in this service.' I just looked at him; I knew what was to come.

'So I suppose we're just going to have to send you on a series of training courses.' I didn't know what to say; that wasn't what I'd been expecting. ''007 has given me a full report of what happened. He assures me that had it not been for your bravery and willingness to take the initiative, he would have certainly been executed by the KGB. In addition, I understand that you and he have gathered information about Russian activities in Cuba that could turn out to be of extreme international importance. He told me that you had no option but to leave the transceiver in what he assures me is a safe place. We'll have to find some way to retrieve it. In the meantime, this afternoon both of you are to meet with the American Ambassador* and Agent Scott, as well as the Minister. I want you to describe everything you saw during your time in Cuba. Make the necessary arrangements, then bring in the morning signals.'

The next three days seemed like an endless, exhausting string of meetings between here and Grosvenor Square. James and I described and drew the tubes we had seen being loaded on to the transporter vehicles, as well as the insignia on the epaulettes of the officers. A changing guard of Americans listened, asked the same questions again and again, but made no comments on our actions. Fortunately, they didn't mention the radio. I was usually dismissed at this point, while James had to undergo further interrogation about his dealings with Caballo. The CIA, in particular, were still reluctant to admit they'd been duped.

Saturday, 15th September

It's extraordinary how news spreads around the Office. My Cuban escapade was meant to be top secret, but somehow by Monday night everyone seemed to have heard about it – when I went to powder my nose before leaving, the entire room burst into applause. I had to fight back the emotion.

---

* David K. E. Bruce, America's envoy to London from 1961 to 1969.

Since our return, I keep almost crumpling in tears. Shock, I suppose, a delayed realisation of what might have been – that we might so easily have not made it back to this familiar building.

'I look forward to your demotion to the seventh floor,' said Mary with a wicked glint in her eyes. 'It'll be a privilege to serve oo-Moneypenny.' Everyone laughed.

'Don't be ridiculous,' I said. 'I just found myself caught up in a series of circumstances that I couldn't control. Now that I'm back, it's business as usual.' But they carried on ribbing me and eventually insisted on taking me off to Bully's, where they tried very hard to extract details of what it had been like to work alongside 007. I'm not sure if it was the work aspect that they were interested in, but I managed to keep my counsel.

Tuesday, 18th September

It's taken me the best part of ten days to catch up. M disappeared on the Monday after we got back, for what remained of his regular two-week fishing holiday on the Test. Once the Americans had finished with him, James took ten days of leave. Bill told me that he'd gone to France, on his yearly pilgrimage to Royale-les-Eaux to visit Vesper's grave.* 'This time, he'll have Tracy to weep over too. I just hope he doesn't put all his pennies on red; the way his luck's been going this year, black will come up every time.'

---

* Each year following Vesper Lynd's suicide in 1952, Bond returned to the casino at Royale for the last weekend of the season.

Last night, Bill took me for supper to a cheerful French bistro near his flat in Earl's Court. 'I wanted to bring you up to date,' he told me. ''Fraid we've had no luck confirming our suspicions. We just don't have enough to go on. Have they tried to make any contact with you? . . . Thought not. They'd know you've been away, of course. But that wasn't exactly a secret in the Office. We've tried to track down your friend Zach. Either he's disappeared into thin air, or he's not living under that name. I think we can confidently assume it's a false identity and that he's changed it again. We ran all the information you gave us about his past through our records and checked with CID and immigration, but they've no record of any David Zach entering or leaving the country in the time periods in question. Certainly no mention of any trouble he might have got into in the past. The photo-fit you gave us rang no bells with the Watchers either. So we've come to a dead end on that particular alleyway.'

He stopped talking and looked at me. 'Anything wrong?' he asked. I attempted a smile and shook my head.

'It's been a hell of a few months,' I admitted. 'There were times when I honestly thought I was going to crack. What with 007 and Zach and my father, and then Cuba and the radio. I feel so guilty about that . . .' I felt the tears trying to slip out and blinked them back as he squeezed my shoulder.

'Penny, you've been magnificent, a real trouper. Just hang on in there a bit longer. But I'm afraid there is something else. While you were away, I was contacted by that bloody Troop.' I noticed that the adjective appeared to have become permanently affixed to his name. 'He was going on about some man he'd seen in your company outside the

Office, a Richard Hamilton.' I raised my eyebrows and told him that it was irrelevant now – R had gone away and I doubted I'd ever see him again.

'Well, if Troop's right – and I've no reason to doubt him on this one – it might have some bearing on what we're dealing with here.' I sighed. I didn't want to hear this. 'It seems he's popped up in Berlin.'

I said I knew that – he was working out there for a firm of architects.

'Maybe, but he's been photographed on a number of occasions meeting some men, a couple of whom, at least, we have reason to believe are top Stasi agents.' He paused. 'Another fits the general description of Zach.'

I was temporarily rendered speechless.

'Did you know Hamilton speaks fluent, accent-less German?'

'No,' I admitted, 'I didn't. But then I never asked.'

'We don't know what they were talking about, of course. It could have been an unlucky coincidence. After all, there must be a few million blond-haired Aryans in Berlin alone, but Troop's put him on the Watch List and I'm afraid we're going to have to regard his association with you as potentially suspicious.'

I put my head into my hands. 'Oh, Bill, I can't believe it. I'm so sorry. Perhaps I'm not cut out for this line of work after all. Do you think I should resign?'

'Don't be an ass, Penny. After what you achieved in Cuba? You're one of our best men.' He reached over to touch my hands. 'Don't worry. It's probably innocent and we'll have it cleared up in no time. I just thought I should warn you before that bloody Troop gets his mitts on you.'

Wednesday, 26th September

This is truly extraordinary. My life is being turned in so many directions I'm not sure exactly who I am any more. Not just Miss Moneypenny, M's dependable private secretary, that's for sure. On Monday, M received a telephone call from the PM, shortly followed by one from Washington. I don't know exactly what was said, but as soon as he'd put his telephone down, he asked me to summon 007.

It was James's first day at work after his trip to France and I was concerned to see the sadness back in his eyes. However, he smiled when he saw me. 'Hello, Penny. I've missed you. Have you missed me?' I was about to reply when M came out and, by the look on his face, not in the best of tempers. 'Come in here, both of you. Quick quick.' He put his head around Bill's door. 'Chief of Staff, we're expecting some chaps from Grosvenor Square. Send them straight in when they arrive, please.'

When we got into his office, M sat down in his chair, then made a big fuss about filling and lighting his pipe, tamping down the burning tobacco into the bowl, before replacing the matchbox in his pocket and tilting his chair back. Despite his air of calm, I could see a small pulse of tension beating high up on his right temple. 'We're about to receive a visit from our American friends,' he said rather unnecessarily. 'Yesterday, despite some sterling avoidance tactics by Head of Q, it became apparent to the Cousins that we had mislaid their new Delco radio. It transpires that it is one of a new range, developed by NASA for the US space programme. As you know, they are very touchy about their rockets and suchlike, and as you can imagine, they were not best pleased to learn that it had been mislaid in Cuba. Then, this morning, I received a request from President Kennedy himself, which I had been persuaded to accede to by the PM – very much against my better judgement, you understand. But I'm afraid the radio issue has put me in an impossible situation. Your Cuban escapade, as I have made clear to you both, was a mess of unauthorised action exacerbated by inadequate communication, which was only mitigated by its unexpectedly fruitful consequences. You were damn lucky, both of you, to get out alive.'

A knock on the door interrupted the lecture. At M's bark, Bill showed two tall men into the room. One I recognised as Ambassador Bruce, who greeted us both warmly. 'Commander, Miss Moneypenny, I'd like to introduce you to Calvin Petersham. He arrived this morning from Washington, as the President's personal envoy.' His part in the meeting clearly over, the Ambassador sat down and transferred his attention to Petersham.

'We'd like to thank you once more for the excellent job you guys did over in Cuba, the small matter of the radio aside,' he began. I was surprised. I hadn't been led to believe that it was a small issue. But then, the pay-off began. 'We were very interested in your description of the cargo being unloaded from the Russian vessel in Mariel.' (He pronounced it Mary-L.) 'We've spent the last two weeks attempting to identify its content, both through high-altitude photography from our U-2 surveillance planes and from a human mission. Unfortunately, adverse weather conditions have so far prevented the success of the former, while the task group we sent over from Miami was picked up on arrival and sadly, we have reason to believe, executed that same day. We have to conclude that security at our operations base has been compromised.' He stood up and started pacing up and down the room.

'It's imperative that we find out whether the Russians have sent attack missiles to Cuba. At present, all we have to go on are your descriptions and a whole lot of rumour and conjecture. To this end, President Kennedy has commanded me to ask you whether you would be prepared to return to Cuba to track down that Russian cargo and bring back photographic evidence to determine what exactly it is. I cannot sufficiently stress how imperative this operation is, not only to the future security of both of our countries, but to that of the world. It's only with knowledge that we can decide what steps, if any, we need to take. Perhaps it'll prove to be the agricultural machinery and short-range weaponry that Secretary Khrushchev has maintained. But if it's the nuclear missiles that Chief McCone has been warning us about, then we're all in deep shit – if you'll excuse the expression.' M nodded, still looking grim, as Petersham continued.

'I realise that this mission is not without its dangers, but you've proved yourselves before to be the only people capable of penetrating the Cuban defences, and the President would sure be grateful if you'd try again. It would also give you an opportunity to retrieve the radio,' he almost leered in his unctuousness. 'This, I must stress, is an earnest request, not an order. Your Chief here has already told us that he's not happy about it.' He turned to M, who impaled me on his gaze while addressing the American.

'I consider sending an untrained woman into the field as lunacy. Plus 007 has only just returned from Cuba, where his cover was compromised. It goes against every rule of espionage. But the Prime Minister is urging me to accede to your President's wishes, and I've told him only that I will ask them; I will not order them to go.'

He looked at us through the pipe smoke. I wish I could have read his wishes, but his grey sailor's eyes remained impenetrable. James was the first to speak. 'I would be prepared to go,' he said. 'But I don't think it would be a good idea for Miss Moneypenny. As you said, sir, she is not trained for this type of mission.'

I shook my head. 'No, sir, if you will allow me, I must go. I am the only one who knows where the radio is hidden and I couldn't live with myself if it were to be found by the Russians.'

Petersham seemed to take that as settled, as he gave us a broad grin, held out his hand and wished us good luck. 'I'll be taking the first plane back to Washington and will convey your answer personally to the President. I know he'll be very grateful.' After they left, M returned to his chair and picked up his files. It seemed we were being dismissed.

'Penny, we need to talk about this,' said 007 as we got back into my office. 'Don't be foolhardy, I beg you. You can tell me where the radio is. I'll be better off out there without you to nanny. It's not too late to change your mind.'

'Me to nanny! Have you already forgotten the position you were in when I rescued you from the KGB? In any case, I don't know if I could describe how to get to José's mother's house, and even if I could, I doubt she would let you in.'

He shook his head again. 'It was very fortunate for me that you came. But you shouldn't have and now I'm urging you to stay behind. In fact, it's an order.'

'Under whose authority, may I ask? Do you think you've more power over me than the President of the United States? You're an old-fashioned chauvinist, 007, and I'm coming to Cuba whether you like it or not.'

When I got home that night and the indignation had faded, I was forced to face up to my decision. Was I running away again from the situation at home? Probably. In doing so, was I putting the Office at additional risk? Possibly. But the thought of the radio kept haunting me, and I couldn't banish the memory of the state 007 was in when I found him locked in that sweltering cabin on the *Omsk*. He seemed resigned to death, almost to be choosing it. Yes, he kicked into gear when he was forced to, but it was as though he was on automatic pilot, driven by the need to get me home safely. Perhaps I could protect him again? I fear he's lost the taste for adventure and the overriding belief in the justness of the fight. 'I just want to lie on a beach and swim in the ocean with a good woman beside me, Penny,' he said when we were in Miami. 'I could have done that with Tracy, and with Vesper, maybe even with Tiffany. Now I can't face the tedium of that cycle of flirtation, capitulation and retreat. Oh, Penny, what I need is a woman like you.'

I wish he wouldn't say things like that.

Saturday, 29th September

We fly to Miami this afternoon. It seems as if no one thinks I have made the right decision. Bill tried to remonstrate with me and M has been positively icy, even for him. When he gave us our last orders, he addressed every word to 007. In an instant, what I had regarded as bravery crumpled into foolishness. Perhaps, if I can recover the radio, he will forgive me? It was only when he shook my hand that I detected a slight softening in his eyes. Could it be that the OM is feeling some sort of inexpressible concern? About me?

October

I wonder now whether M would have allowed my aunt to return to Cuba had he known the true strength of the Soviet military force out there. From the end of spring 1962, when Khrushchev conceived his plan to 'throw a hedgehog at Uncle Sam's pants', until Aunt Jane and Bond's return in October, a total of 41,902 Soviet troops were shipped to Cuba. They were accompanied by an extraordinary arsenal of weapons – missiles, guns, tanks and fighter planes – as well as the services necessary to support them. In September alone, 66 Russian cargo ships made the 7,000-mile crossing to dock in ports less than 100 miles from the Florida coast.

That Uncle Sam failed to detect the spines advancing on his nether regions was testament to the successful employment of *maskirovka* (deception). Operation Anadyr, as it was named, was conducted under conditions of absolute secrecy. The Soviet troops were told that they were going on strategic exercises. Many believed they were headed to the Arctic and packed accordingly; to support this myth, trains carried loads of sheepskin coats, boots and fur hats to the loading docks. All Party and Communist Youth League cards were confiscated on embarkation, and contact with the outside world was prohibited. On their first evening on board, each soldier was issued with civilian clothes – a lightweight suit, a checked shirt and a hat. For most of the 18–20-day journey, the several thousand men were confined below deck; at night, groups of 20–25 men at a time were allowed out for air. The more fortunate soldiers were billeted on a luxury liner, the *Admiral Nakhimov*, which, according to a Georgian newspaper report, was inaugurating a new tourist cruise line to Cuba.

Even the ship's captain had no prior knowledge of his destination. Minutes before casting off, he was handed a large sealed envelope, tied with brown ribbon. Inside, there were smaller envelopes, with instructions that they should be opened in sequence at particular co-ordinates. Only in the last one was he told to proceed to a designated port in Cuba – after burning the contents of the envelopes.

On arrival in port, the ships were greeted by officials from the Cuban Ministry of Agriculture. It generally took two to three days to unload one ship; military equipment was unloaded by night, then stored in sheds or moved directly to the military bases via back roads, accompanied by a Cuban guard detachment and Russians dressed as Cubans. Only Spanish was meant to be spoken. There was total radio silence; all communication between field units and Havana headquarters was oral, and Soviet troops were not permitted to address their commanding officers by rank.

But, still, it is impossible to conceal that number of foreign soldiers. Eyewitness reports described phalanxes of identically dressed blond men goose-stepping along the waterfront, while the centre of Havana ground to a halt as hundreds of Soviet military vehicles sat bumper to bumper, unable to move. It was essential to the success of

Operation Anadyr that information of this kind did not leak out to the West. Any spies that were identified were imprisoned or executed. Cuba was theoretically sealed from the outside world.

Sunday, 14th October

Looking back over the last two weeks is almost like trying to replay a dream; so real at the time, it crumbles into dust when you try to pick out individual events. We made it: that is the punch-line, the part where fantasy and reality converge. On several occasions I feared we might not.

We got to Cuba without incident. After a night in Miami on the way, we set off in a US Coastguard motor launch just before midnight on 3rd October. About ten miles from the Cuban coast, the engines were cut. 007 went to the back of the boat, unlocked the huge crate that had been sitting on the aft deck and swung open its doors. I'd no idea what he was doing; since trying to prevent me from returning to Cuba, he'd virtually ignored me, as much as that is possible when sharing the same space of about eight square feet on a plane. Frankly, I found it childish. When I tried to ask him to brief me on the mission, he waved me away as if I were a mildly irritating insect. It was only on the boat, with the lights of Cuba almost in sight, that he addressed his first words directly to me as he beckoned from the boat's stern.

'Time to go, Miss Moneypenny. You're ready?' I nodded.

'How are we going to land?' I asked. 'I thought the coast was heavily patrolled.'

'That's why we brought Bugsy,' he said, pointing to the

open back of the crate. 'Meet Q Branch's latest toy.' I walked into the crate and gasped. In front of me was what looked like a giant mechanical beetle, with a 'body' of spherical metal, rounded wing-like ballasts to either side and two thick portholes, one at the front and one on top. 'Isn't she a doll?' said 007 wryly.

I must have looked a little puzzled, as his voice soon developed a tone of exasperation, not dissimilar to the one I have heard Head of Q using on him when trying to explain the workings of a new gadget. 'It's a miniature two-man submersible. It was developed by a crazy Czech, who had some idea of searching for the wreck of the *Titanic*. But then he ran into a spot of trouble with our navy and we got custody of little Bugsy. Q Branch has been having fun adapting her. This is her maiden mission under a new flag. I spent the day before our departure in Portsmouth learning how to operate her. Hurry and strip off into your swimmers, then hop in, if you're really coming along. We need to make Mariel before dawn.'

Bugsy wasn't exactly spacious inside; comfort had been sacrificed to miniaturisation in accord with Q Branch's latest mania, but I managed to slide into a bucket seat behind 007. At one point, his proximity would have been thrilling, but in his current mood I was more afraid of catching frost-bite. Once we'd been lowered into the sea and descended to our cruising depth of a hundred feet, though, I forgot his churlishness and began to enjoy myself. Bugsy was fitted with an infra-red spotlight and shoals of fish swam frequently through its beam. We were approached by a school of hammerhead sharks, their bizarre, widely spaced eyes peering through the porthole as they passed. Apart from the dull hum of the engine it was so quiet: the calm before the storm.

After an hour, 007 switched off the spotlight and cut the engine. 'We're about a mile east of Mariel, 500 yards from shore. I'm going to anchor, then surface her. We'll have to swim in from here and should land near the beach you described. Are you ready?' I unbuckled my seat harness and grabbing the watertight container which held my clothes and equipment – a hairbrush camera, strangely incongruous in our current situation, a lipstick torch and a Triple X encoder – I slithered up to the exit hole. It was a dark night, cloud covering the stars and moon, but mercifully warm. 'Get into the water and wait for me,' hissed 007, 'then follow me to shore.' As we swam, I tried not to think of the sharks.

By the time we reached land, my eyes had become accustomed to the dark and I easily found the path out to the road. 'We need to get that radio and find somewhere with a good view of the port,' said 007.

I told him that José's mother's house was on the hill just outside the militarised zone – with binoculars you could see everything from there. We walked in silence, 007 half a step behind me on the roadside. At one point, we heard a car approaching and he pushed me into the undergrowth until it had passed.

We arrived at the house just as the sky was beginning to pale. José's mother opened the door warily to our knock, but appeared delighted when she saw me and quickly pulled us both inside. Through sign language, I managed to ask her if we could use the small upstairs room again, and when she disappeared into the kitchen, I rushed upstairs and went straight to the bed. The relief was extraordinary: there it was, the Delco radio, wedged into the corner under the bed where I'd left it. I went back downstairs with a lighter heart. José's mother emerged from the kitchen a few minutes later with the inevitable bowls of fish stew, beans and rice. We ate them watching dawn break over the port. I felt the excitement flood back into my veins. It was the 4th of October.

Since I'd been there last, security had been tightened. There were guard posts every fifty yards along the perimeter fence and even at dawn the docks were a hive of activity. Cranes were lined up near the point where the *Omsk* had been moored and a queue of transporter trucks and trailers was parked just outside the gates. It looked as if they were expecting an arrival imminently.

A few hours later James pointed at the horizon, where a large cargo ship was materialising out of the heat haze. She docked shortly before four and within minutes the waiting ground crew were swarming all over her. I passed the binoculars back to James, to read the name at the stern, written in Russian. 'The *Indigirka*, home port Vladivostok,' he told me. 'But she could have come from anywhere.'* We watched as the men, in what was by now clearly a well-

---

* The Russian freighter in fact set off from Severomorsk, on the morning of 17 September 1962, under conditions of the utmost secrecy. Of the Kremlin leaders, only Khrushchev and Praesidium member Frol Sozlov were briefed. Neither captain nor crew knew their eventual destination. Carefully tucked inside the *Indigirka*'s hold was the first consignment of forty-five one-megaton nuclear warheads for R-12 MRBMs, as well as smaller warheads and bombs for tactical weapons and air-force bombers. In total, the ship carried the equivalent of over twenty times the explosive power that was dropped by Allied bombers on Germany throughout the entire Second World War. Until a conference in Havana in 1992, to mark the thirtieth anniversary of the Cuban Missile Crisis, it was widely believed by the West that the Soviets had not managed to deliver any warheads to Cuba.

rehearsed routine, started to unload the cargo. They were careful but efficient and worked steadily into the night. 'They're going to be a while. You had better grab some sleep while you can,' he told me.

It was still pitch black when he shook me awake. He was dressed in a checked cotton shirt. 'Borrowed it,' he said when I raised my eyebrows. 'I've been down to the dock area and managed to get a look at the cargo. I didn't see any of those sixty-foot tubes you described, but they were taking especial care over two dozen large crates plastered with warning signs. They were being guarded by green epaulettes – more KGB. They seem to be in a hurry to get this first load going before it's light. We're going to follow them. I've got a vehicle – the driver's feeling a bit sleepy now, but he should wake up by lunchtime. For God's sake don't forget that blasted radio again.'

He'd hidden the Cuban army jeep down a small track. He pushed me into the back and threw me a blanket, telling me to lie down and under no circumstances to move or make a noise. Even in the middle of the night, it was stifling. Within minutes of starting, we'd stopped again, with the engine still running. I heard the jeep door slam, then the rasp and click of a lighter. Gradually, I began to identify the background noises; beyond the steady metallic rattle of cicadas, I could make out a low-pitched whine, followed by a click and a foot stamp, an accelerating engine and then the whine again: the gate opening, a car being waved through with a clicked-heel salute, the gate closing again. It was not far away, and I soon realised that ours was not the only idling engine sound. We must have joined a convoy waiting to set off. There was a low murmur of voices – I think they were talking in Spanish. Footsteps approached and I held my breath. A voice said something to 007, who replied with a grunt, followed by the rasp and click of his lighter again. I breathed out. Then there was a shout, more car doors slamming and a chorus of gunning engines. We were on the move.

Once we had been going for about twenty minutes, I felt a hand on my back. 007 had turned around. 'You can take the blanket off and lie on the back seat,' he said. 'They won't be able to see you as long as you don't sit up.' I unfolded myself and stretched out. I could just see through the side window and in the jiggering light of the following vehicle's dimmed headlamps could make out small wooden shacks and painted matchbox houses. We were on a small winding road and once, when the convoy slowed to a stop and inched towards a sharp bend, I glimpsed piles of rubble set back from the roadside, where buildings had been rapidly disassembled, presumably in order to allow long vehicles to get around the corner.

After about two hours of slow progress, 007 tapped me and told me to get back under the blanket. He slowed and opened his window. I felt rather than saw a torch light being swung around the jeep's interior, then 007 was jabbering away in what sounded like Russian and I heard another voice, this time Spanish, raised in reply, before we suddenly accelerated away at top speed. Ten minutes later, he swung to the right and cut the engine. 'That was close. You can come out now, Moneypenny. We were stopped by the Cuban guard, on the look out for their missing jeep. I managed to persuade them I was Russian, but we'd better be careful.' He'd switched on his penlight and was studying a large-scale map of Cuba. 'I think we're somewhere near here,' he said, pointing at a town called San Cristobal. 'We were heading south-west pretty steadily. The rest of the convoy turned right on to what looked like a new road. There was a tall, heavy mesh fence and armed guards at the gate. I just saluted and they waved me on. My guess is that we can't be too far from the town, though God knows it looks as if we're in the middle of nowhere.'

Dawn had just broken and already I could feel the damp heat smothering us, as heavy as the blanket I had just put aside. We were parked on a rocky track in scrubby brush-land, interspersed by the occasional palm-tree. To each side, I could see shadowy round-topped hills, but no sign of any-thing that looked like a missile site. 'It's a good spot as far as camouflage goes,' said 007, as he got out and stood on the bonnet of the jeep, sweeping his binoculars steadily from east to west. 'But it must be hellishly hot working outside all day. Come on, let's try to find the town and get settled somewhere, then I can take a look at the base this evening.'

San Cristobal was little more than a cluster of painted one-storey houses around a pretty central square. As we drove in, I immediately recognised the maraca rattle of the dried pods of the flamboyant tree, as they waved in the early-morning breeze. I got a flash of Kenya, where the blooming of the flame-trees marked the end of the wet season. Cuba too must look spectacular in the spring when they are in flower. We drove slowly around the plaza – past a handful of shops bordering the main road on the eastern side, a church on the west, a large ceiba-tree* in the centre.

---

* Considered a magical and holy tree in Cuba. Legend has it that the first mass after Columbus's landing in Cuba was said under a ceiba-tree in what is now central Havana, but, since Columbus never made it that far and had no priest on board his ship, this is unlikely.

I was conscious of being watched by a hundred pairs of eyes – old men sitting like statues on benches outside their houses and in the square, nothing moving except the suspicion in their eyes.

007 waved merrily at them, then took the southern road out of town, over a metal bridge spanning a wide river; along its banks I caught sight of clusters of shacks beneath mango- and avocado-trees. He turned sharply down a track and pulled to a stop by a mid-sized house, painted pea green, with two rocking-chairs on the porch. 'This looks a likely spot,' he said. We got out and knocked on the door, and through a combination of sign language and proffered dollars, were shown to a room at the back, dominated by a large brass bed. 'Don't worry, Moneypenny, I'll take the floor,' James said drily. 'Just don't let the lady of the house know that we're not married. They still tend to be rather religious once you're out of Havana.' Once I'd persuaded him that I was perfectly capable of sharing a bed without taking advantage of him – and that I wasn't tired anyway – he lay down, put his gun under his pillow, still attached to his hand, and promptly fell asleep.

I spent the rest of the morning wandering around the town. The suspicious eyes soon lost interest when I smiled but didn't bother them. I found a small café, serving excellent coffee and the creamiest ice-cream I have ever tasted – a welcome respite from the stifling heat. It was a quiet, peaceful town and I was relieved to be away from 007's – admittedly thawing – disregard. Despite the danger that I knew we were in, I was enjoying myself; given different circumstances, I could have been on holiday. It was a strange thought and I had almost to pinch myself to recall the very real and urgent nature of our mission. The first objective had been successful, but we were far from out of the woods. Only once did I see an army jeep speed in. It screamed to a halt in front of the bodega and a large blond man went into the shop, watched by the entire town, and emerged minutes later lighting a cigarette. It was clearly not a regular occurrence; they couldn't be using the town itself for provisioning.

I was sitting on the porch outside our house when James emerged, refreshed and back in his Russian civilian disguise. 'You wait here while I go and recce the base.' I refused.

'I'm coming along, James,' I said. 'I've come this far and I can recognise those missiles, if that's what they are.'

He shrugged and we were soon driving through the dusk. He stopped short of the gate and we crept around the fence for what felt like miles, until we found a stretch that didn't appear to be guarded. He quietly snipped a hole in the wire before turning to me. 'Now I must order you to stay here. I'm far safer on my own and I need you to raise the alarm if something goes wrong. If I find the tubes, then we can make plans to photograph them. But if I'm not back by midnight, drive into town, signal M with the co-ordinates of this place, then make your way to Havana as fast as you can and get on the first plane out of here.' This time, I put up no resistance. We synchronised our watches and I sat under a palm-tree to wait.

As the hands of my watch crept past eleven, I felt the first prickles of fear creeping up my arms; by half past, I had a hole the size of Kimberley in my stomach. I checked my watch incessantly, bargaining with myself for reasons to wait longer than midnight. At five minutes to twelve, I was lying by the fence, trying to catch sight of James through the hole. I watched as the hands of my watch crept towards midnight, looked once more through the hole, then closed my eyes tight, willing him to arrive before I had counted to a hundred.

I'd just girded myself to go back to the car when I heard the slightest rustling of grass. I opened my eyes to see a shadow slithering through the fence. I've never been so relieved to see anyone in my entire life. I put my arms around his neck and hugged him as hard as I could, tears coursing down my cheeks. 'Hush, Penny, it's all right. Come on, let's get out of here. We've got work to do.'

As we drove back, he told me what he'd seen – a construction site on a grand scale. There were multiple command and support buildings, lines and lines of two-man tents, even a laundry and a bakery, as well as a helicopter and rows of fuel trucks, bulldozers and armoured tanks. At the centre, he found huge concrete slabs, surrounded by earth embankments topped with rolls of barbed wire. 'I'm pretty certain there were missile-launchers anchored to the concrete,' he said, 'but everything's been well camouflaged – it's all covered with netting. I think I saw your tubes too, Penny, beside the launchers. I couldn't get too close though, the place was crawling with Russians. It looks as if they're working night and day to get this place ready. We've got to send a signal to M right away.'

Back at our lodgings, I had a makeshift shower (a bucket of water over my head) as he composed his report. Then I punched it into the Triple X, plugged the keyboard into the recovered Delco and prepared to transmit. 'Mark it "Most immediate – urgent response required",' James said. 'The Russians are bound to have sophisticated tracking equipment scanning the air waves – my guess is we've only got a day or so before they pick up our signal, realise it's not one of theirs and come looking for us.'

'But what about the photographs?' I asked.

'Impossible, from the ground anyway. I told M I couldn't do it – they'll just have to take our word for it. Come on, Penny. After you've sent this, you're going to bed. I'll keep an eye out for curious Russians and wake you when the reply arrives.'

It seemed only minutes later that I was being shaken awake. But the sun was streaming through the window and I was bathed in sweat. Another bucket of water over my head and I got to work on M's brief response:

```
EXMAILEDFIST MOST IMPERATIVE YOU GET
PHOTOGRAPHIC EVIDENCE REPEAT PHOTOGRAPHIC
EVIDENCE OF TUBES DESCRIBED STOP REPORT
DAILY STOP
```

I looked at James. 'I've got to get that helicopter. It's the only way,' he said. 'I'm going to have to do it in daylight. It's not going to be easy and I'll need your help. If they don't already know someone's out here, they will soon and they'll increase security. We need to go in today. Let me think.' He paced up and down the porch, while I sat in a rocking-chair trying not to think about what he was plotting. Then he looked at his watch. 'It's nearly midday. Come on, let's go.' We carefully wrapped the radio in my silk scarf and hid it in the garden under a hibiscus bush behind the house. I picked up my equipment bag and followed him to the jeep. We drove back through San Cristobal and this time the watching eyes appeared to regard us with something closer to welcome.

We parked in the same spot near the palm-tree. It was a sweltering day, with no clouds to shelter us from the beating sun. My thin cotton dress stuck to my back.

Mosquitoes circled our ankles and ears, landing softly when they thought we weren't paying attention. I felt drips of sweat running down my forehead and spine. I vowed never to complain about English winters again – if I was lucky enough to live until the next one. Once James had explained the plan, the thought of snow and clouds became even more attractive. 'You don't have to do it, you know. I can go alone.' I shook my head.

'No, James. I've got this far and I'm going to complete the mission.'

To my surprise, he grabbed me and kissed me hard. 'Good girl, Penny. Put on some lipstick and I'll see you on the other side. They're not going to harm you. Just stick to your story and keep that radio well away from them. Then make your way back to Havana and wait for me at the Hotel Sevilla.' I sat under the tree for an hour. Then I went back to the jeep, slowly drove on to the main road and turned left. I soon found the track leading to the compound gate, took a deep breath and turned down it. At the gate, I was immediately approached by the guards, who jabbered at me in Russian, then circled the jeep, looking closely at the number-plates. I talked straight back at them in English, relieved when their faces registered no comprehension. 'I'm delivering the vehicle,' I said. 'General Gil told me to bring it here.' There was no flicker of recognition even at the General's name, so I talked on, firmly, louder and louder, asking to be taken to their commander, and they continued to ask me questions to which I could not respond. Already, we were drawing quite an audience.

Eventually, they decided that they'd have to take me to their superiors. First they beckoned me out of the jeep, and searched both it and me. I silently gave thanks for James's insistence that I left the radio behind at our lodgings. When they found nothing, they ushered me back in, one of the guards jumped into the passenger seat and, with our growing escort trotting alongside, directed me across the camp, towards the northern boundary. As we passed, I caught sight of the helicopter, then quickly turned away, pointing at a building in the opposite direction. They started talking together, each eager to explain what it was. If these boys – for that is what they were, none of them long into their twenties, with sunburnt faces and sweat-drenched shirts – hadn't been Russian, they would have been almost appealing. Contrary to what I'd expected, they were friendly, like puppies desperate for someone to play with them.

We drew up in front of a small concrete building and the guard got out and knocked on the door, before entering. He was followed out minutes later by a well-built man with a small moustache, younger than I'd expected, wearing dark-grey trousers and the inevitable short-sleeved checked shirt, tucked into his belt. He looked at me intently with pale-grey eyes, then held out his hand and said in broken English, 'How do you do. My name is General Igor, agricultural adviser to the Cuban government.* Welcome to our experimental farm.' It was so preposterous that under other circumstances I might have laughed.

'My name is Jane Grey,' I told him, using the name on the passport that Q Branch had supplied. 'I'm a friend of General Gil's. He asked me to deliver this jeep to you.'

---

* Major-General Igor Stratsenko was in command of the missile-division headquarters outside San Cristóbal (A. L. Gribkov and W. Y. Smith, *Operation Anadyr* (Chicago, 1994)).

'But we did not request a jeep from the General – why would he be wanting to give one to us? We have been alerted by the Cuban military that one of their jeeps was stolen, while under the temporary use of my compatriots. The, er, farmer's clothes were taken by the thief.' I did my best to look innocent and as I was clearly not wearing men's clothing the Russian let it pass and started questioning me about my purpose there. He was still speaking when I heard the unmistakable pulsing whirr of a helicopter propeller building up speed. I grabbed his hand and started towards the inner door of his office. 'Please, General, I am feeling rather faint . . . The heat . . .' He followed me and closed the door behind us just as I heard a shout coming from the direction of the helicopter. I held on to his arm and made my knees buckle. He appeared unsure as to what to do with me. 'A glass of water, please.' I gave him my most beseeching smile, as the shouting outside continued. There was a sharp rap on the door and a young man burst in, clearly agitated, and spoke in rapid, breathless Russian. The General removed my hand from his arm. 'I am sorry. We have had an accident with some of our, er, farm machinery. I have to go. Please stay in my office and we can talk when I return.' Then he almost ran for the door.

I looked around. Laid out across his desk I saw what appeared to be blueprints of missiles, and maps. I smiled at his secretary and asked again for a glass of water, miming drinking it; then, as she turned to get it, I sat down on the chair opposite the General's desk. I put my bag on my lap and got out the hairbrush camera and, turning towards the secretary, started brushing my hair, talking loudly to cover up the soft click as I pushed the shutter down on each stroke of the brush. I put the hairbrush away with some satisfaction. Now I had to get away quickly, somehow.

I stood up and walked over to the window. There seemed to be hundreds of men running in every direction and pointing at the sky. I watched as several of them started tearing back camouflage nets to reveal small surface-to-air missiles. 'Hurry up, James,' I said to myself, as I heard the first blast of machine-gun fire coming from the other side of the building. I decided to take my chance to escape; the decoy work had been done. I flashed a smile at the secretary and headed towards the door, muttering General Igor's name. She seemed unsure, but didn't know what to do as I slipped out.

There was no one near the building and, thankfully, the jeep was still where I'd left it. I walked across purposefully, trying to ignore the gunfire that was rattling out from all sides. As I got into the driver's seat, I glanced upward in time to see the helicopter swoop back around over the compound. He must be trying for more photographs. I drove towards the gate, miraculously ignored. The gate, however, was closed and I was approached by the guard. I smiled 'General Igor didn't want the jeep after all,' I said, and pointed towards the main road. The guard shook his head. 'Havana. General Igor said I should take the jeep to Havana,' I insisted, pointing and nodding furiously, but he refused again and, miming making a telephone call, he started walking back to his guard-post. I knew I had no option: they would never let me out easily. I slammed my foot hard on to the accelerator and ploughed through the still-closed gate, sending it flying back. Then I drove for my life towards San Cristobal, not once looking back.

I swung off the road, down the track towards our lodgings. They could only be minutes behind me. I ran around the back and grabbed the radio and the rest of James's stuff and, thrusting a handful of dollars into the startled hands of our landlady, jumped back into the jeep and headed down the track, deeper into the lush vegetation. When it petered into a single-lane path, I jammed the jeep into a thick bush. From the map, I remembered that the railway crossed just to the south of the town; if I was lucky, the path should take me there. I half walked, half ran along the path, the radio case knocking against my knees, startling a farmer driving a hump-backed bullock in front of him with a long whip.

After a short while, I emerged from the forest and found myself overlooking a vast plain. Just below me, I could see the railway tracks. Gambling that the station would be back towards the town, I turned right and continued walking until I could make it out in the distance. I felt suddenly weak, but I made myself keep going. It was mid-afternoon, but the heat was still punishing. I reached the station a minute before my legs finally gave way and I fell to the ground shaking all over.

The next thing I remember, I was sitting on a chair in the stationmaster's office, a fan turning overhead and my bags down by my feet. A kindly old man in a tattered uniform was offering me a glass of what looked like cloudy water. I took it and gulped – it was the most delicious coconut-water. I smiled weakly and collapsed back into tears. Here I was, sitting in the middle of nowhere, unable to speak the language, with no idea whether James was alive or not. 'Havana?' I asked the stationmaster. 'Train to Havana?' He nodded. 'Si, la Habana.' He pointed to the clock on the wall and put one hand straight into the air and another pointing down. Six o'clock. I had two hours to wait. I sat back and closed my eyes.

I must have drifted off to sleep, because I was woken by the noise of shouting in what I immediately recognised to be Russian. My heart started pounding as I looked around the bare room for a hiding-place. Behind the door would have to do. I heard more voices, this time spitting out words in broken Spanish. 'Hombre e mujer, Ingles?' My heart leapt. They were searching for both of us; they must have realised we were working together. And James too; he must have got away. I heard the stationmaster saying 'No, no hay hombre aquí.' The door opened. From where I was standing I could see the radio case, under the chair I'd been sitting on, and prayed they would not notice it. After what seemed like minutes, the door closed again, and I heard the sound of a car starting up. I sat down and put my head in my hands and wept. I don't know if it was fear or relief or exhaustion – probably a combination of the three – but at that time I would have done anything to be back at my familiar, solid desk, working through the daily signals, chatting with the girls in the powder room, exchanging the occasional banter with the oo agents. I don't know how they do it, how they live with this level of tension and fear on a daily basis. Yes, one hears about the addictive lure of adrenalin – and to a certain extent I had felt it on both my trips to Cuba – but I couldn't deal with it on an extended basis. No wonder 007 had been so destroyed by Tracy's death – his chance to escape from the unending precipice.

The train journey was long and hot, but otherwise mercifully uneventful. I wrapped my scarf around my head and neck like the Cuban women and slept. As we were approaching Havana, the train lurched to a stop and I heard doors opening and shouted questions in Spanish. Again, they were asking for an English woman and a man.

I kicked my bags under the seat. The lady opposite looked intently at me, then reached across to put her cage of two squawking chickens on to my lap. She smiled and looked away. It worked: when the soldiers came into our carriage, they looked no further than the chickens before moving on.

When we drew into the station, I picked up my cases and the chicken cage and followed their owner unchecked through the guards and out into the warm Havana night. Once relieved of my clucking companions, I hailed a taxi and sank back into the red leather seats for the journey into the town centre. Even in my shaken state, I couldn't fail to appreciate the beauty and drama of the Cuban capital – the grand colonial houses, painted in ice-cream pastels, lining the Malecon* on one side, with missile-launchers and huge cannon on the other, manned and pointing out to sea. We turned right, up a broad, tree-lined avenue, and stopped outside an impressive hotel, painted terracotta pink. 'La Sevilla,'† my taxi-driver announced as uniformed doormen flocked to greet me. Within an hour, I was between cotton sheets.

---

* Havana's dramatic seafront boulevard.
† Built in 1908 and inspired by the Alhambra Palace in Granada, the Sevilla quickly became – and remains to this day – one of Havana's grandest hotels. Guests over the decades have included the famous and the infamous: from singer and dancer Josephine Baker (who was refused entry to the rival Hotel Nacional because of her mixed racial origins), boxer Joe Louis and opera singer Enrico Caruso, to mob leader Al Capone, who took over the hotel's entire sixth floor for his entourage of bodyguards and thugs.

Monday, 15th October

I've been back for only two days, but the San Cristobal episode feels as if it happened to another person. Even the three nights at the Sevilla, waiting anxiously for James to arrive, and my relief when he eventually knocked on the door, grey with dirt and exhaustion after being hunted across the country by the KGB and the Cuban security forces, both baying for his blood. It was only when he was in the room, with the door locked, that I felt safe, for the first time in what seemed like weeks. Then the intricate plans to slip out of the country unobserved: the Cuban underground, new passports, disguises, decoy cars and the last-minute dash for the Air France Caravelle.

Smith met us at Heathrow and whisked us straight back to the Office on Saturday, where M was waiting, a wonderfully familiar sight with his pipe and spotted bow-tie. I wanted to hug him; I would have loved to have seen his face had I tried. I placed the radio transceiver on his desk. He seemed relieved to see us, even if he could not show it. 'There's a courier waiting from the American Embassy, ready to take the films straight to Washington,' he said. 'They plan to send a U-2 up tomorrow to take some more pictures at the co-ordinates you supplied. Q Branch is going to be disappointed about the photographs; I know they wanted to take a look first, but we can't keep the Cousins waiting – this is their show. And speaking of Q Branch – you have some explaining to do, 007. A small matter of an abandoned beetle named Bugsy.'

James groaned. 'Sir, with respect, it would have been impossible to retrieve the submersible. I had half the Cuban army after me, not to mention an entire Russian missile division.'

'I understand that you stole a Russian helicopter from a suspected nuclear missile base, 007,' said M, in an icy tone. 'Did you consider the potential consequences of their using nuclear weapons on you? Or the possibility of retaliation elsewhere – perhaps Berlin? At the least, your rash actions placed a substantial section of Cuba in jeopardy, as well as yourself and Miss Moneypenny.'

'Sir, you said the photographs were imperative.'

'You can explain everything in your final report. You were very lucky to escape and these photographs could prove to be important. But in the future, you have got to act less recklessly. You look dreadful. Go home now and report back on Monday morning.'

Once he'd left, M turned to me: 'Miss Moneypenny, good work. As you know I was not in favour of your participating in an active mission. But you got that confounded radio back here safely and acquitted yourself with credit. Now you go home too and on Monday I want to see you back where you belong.'

It's funny, but my desk didn't feel like where I belonged when I got to it, this morning. I had longed for it on numerous occasions in Cuba, when 007 was lost and in peril, when I felt the Cuban army breathing at my shoulders, but now it was here in front of me, familiar, solid, comforting even, it seemed so far removed from where I had just been and from the part of myself that I had discovered – or perhaps rediscovered – in Cuba. I'm sure that as time passes I will settle back into the rhythm of Office life. I just didn't expect to feel so disconnected.

M is acting as though I had never been away. I even had to hear from Bill that the film we had taken had arrived safely at the National Photographic Interpretation Center in

Washington,* where it has presumably already been developed and examined. Perhaps I'll never know exactly what it was we photographed?

Wednesday, 17th October

I am a heroine on the Powder Vine. It must be one of the most efficient news-gathering operations in the world. I haven't had time to tell anyone the complete story of my Cuban adventures, just a word here and there to Mary and Janet. But before the ink on my report had dried, every secretary in the building appeared to know that I'd shared a small submersible with 007, which seemed to excite them far more than being chased by Russians. Perhaps we all have a natural appetite for gossip, which, forced to suppress outside the Office, we explore with ravenous hunger within?

I can't plead exemption. Within hours of my return to work, I knew that Mary and 006 had spent a weekend

---

* The body responsible for analysing all photographs and images collected by the U-2 spy-planes and from other clandestine operations. In 1962 the director of the NPIC was Arthur Lundahl, who took personal responsibility for analysing the photographs taken by Bond and JM, as well as other images collected of Cuba at that time. On 16 October, the day after receiving the films from London, he advised the White House that there was now hard photographic evidence that the Russians had offensive nuclear missiles in Cuba. A meeting was immediately convened of the President's closest security advisers, a group referred to as the Executive Committee of the National Security Council, or EX-COMM. Over the next thirteen days, this group was in almost continuous session, debating and devising strategies to combat the nuclear threat.

together in the Peak District; that Raine had resigned to work as a nanny to poor Clive Mostyn's children – his wife, Amelia, has apparently had a nervous breakdown – and that the true mole had been unearthed. By the end of the day, I knew what only eleven people in the country, including the Prime Minister, were officially supposed to – that the traitor was Bobby Prenderghast [since 1958, Head of Southern Africa]. It has come as a tremendous shock – to everyone except Dorothy Fields, who apparently had him marked from the beginning.

Prenderghast's sexual proclivities were widely suspected – and often discussed in the privacy of the powder room. But his work had never been in doubt, at least not so far as I knew. After Burgess, checks on those suspected of having homosexual tendencies have been doubled, but I'm sure I would have heard had there been question marks about P. To be blunt, apart from the sex thing, he doesn't fit the normal profile. He wasn't at Cambridge for a start – King's, London, as far as I can remember – and, certainly superficially, he isn't in any way like them. He wears drab, mid-grey suits, plain ties and socks, and he sort of shambles down corridors as though intent on repelling attention. I'd have described him as a bit weak, particularly in the field of human relationships. Not at all a typical Firm employee. Yet he is said to be brilliant, with an elastic mind capable of analysing the potential effects of any given action, many steps down the line. I know M rated him highly; he was personally responsible for his elevation to Head of SA.

M was particularly shaken at the revelation, by all accounts; Dorothy told him the day he returned from our trip to Washington and apparently he spent the following days – while we were in Cuba the first time – closeted in this office. There was even a rumour that he'd offered his resignation, but the PM had turned him down.

The effects of P's treachery will be far-reaching. We'll probably spend the best part of the next year unravelling the mess – which agents have been blown, which codes compromised; whether he was working directly with anyone else. Then there'll be the knock-on effects to our reputation and the regard in which we are held, particularly by our allies.

At the moment P is in a suite at Claridge's,* with guards on the door, being interrogated for ten hours a day. Head of X is taking turns with various Africa specialists, with a chief inspector from the Special Branch sitting in. It can only be a matter of time before it leaks out.

No wonder M is not in the best of moods. It makes Cuba seem even further away.

Monday, 22nd October

M was summoned to Downing Street this afternoon. He returned in a state of uncharacteristic – but barely perceptible – excitement. He called me into his office. 'Moneypenny, we've done it,' he said. 'Those pictures you and 007 took in Cuba were indeed nuclear missiles, as we guessed – what the Russians call R-12s, Medium Range

---

* This grand old dame of a hotel on Brook Street was so frequently used by distinguished foreign visitors that all rooms were permanently bugged.

Ballistic Missiles.* The Americans have been sending their spy-planes up all week to try to confirm their exact placement, but there's been high-level cloud over the entire western sector of Cuba.† There appears to be a great deal of action around the sites, but they haven't yet managed to get a clear picture of the missiles themselves. Based on your and 007's pictures, however, they're convinced that Redland plans to attack the US.‡ The President told the PM that he couldn't wait much longer. They need to take action. He's making a speech tonight.'

I don't think M has ever talked to me like that before. Perhaps he'd momentarily forgotten my place in his scheme of things? I could see in his eyes that hard glitter of excitement of a man of war confronted with a challenging foe. I wish I could share it, but I can't help but feel afraid. Is the world on the brink of nuclear conflict? What if they unleash those missiles on America? Were they placed there for defence or attack? By finding them, have we hastened the world to war, or saved it?

---

* In total, 36 R-12 MRBMs – with 24 launchers divided between 3 regiments – and 24 R-14 IRBMs had been shipped from the USSR to Cuba before the US realised the gravity of the situation.

† Over the previous six weeks, a total of five planned U-2 missions had been forced to turn back empty-handed after encountering adverse weather conditions.

‡ Among the documents that the Soviet double agent Oleg Penkovsky gave to his British handler was a manual entitled *Protecting and Defending Strategic Rocket Sites*. This contained detailed descriptions of the 'footprints' made by MRBMs, which helped the CIA's photographic interpreters to confirm the existence, at the least, of sites in Cuba being readied for nuclear missiles.

Tuesday, 23rd October

I stayed up to listen to President Kennedy address the world last night. He announced that 'unmistakable evidence has established the fact that a series of offensive missile sites is now in preparation on that imprisoned island. The purpose of these bases can be none other than to provide a nuclear strike capability against the Western Hemisphere.' Unmistakable evidence? I do hope so.

Millions of people listened to his speech. It was a humbling thought. He announced a quarantine of military equipment being shipped to Cuba and went further, to declare, 'It shall be the policy of this nation to regard any nuclear missile launched from Cuba against any nation in the Western Hemisphere as an attack by the Soviet Union on the United States, requiring a full retaliatory response on the Soviet Union.'*

---

* Kennedy's seventeen-minute address was broadcast live on 22 October at 7 p.m. Eastern Standard Time. Earlier that day, envoys from the State Department had informed America's allies around the world of the President's decision. US Senate leaders were summoned to Washington for a special briefing. Most were taken by surprise by the situation, and many openly doubted the wisdom of a quarantine – or blockade – calling instead for a pre-emptive air strike. In this, they were echoing the advice of the US Chiefs of Staff, who had urged the President from the beginning of the benefits of aggressive military action.

In advance of the President's address, almost 300 US Navy ships had set sail for the Caribbean. In Guantánamo Bay, three marine battalions were brought in to reinforce the base, and military dependants were evacuated. Military alert was raised to DEFCON 3 (Defense Readiness Condition, summarising the state of US nuclear defence – with 5 being peacetime, and 1 imminent nuclear detonation), and

I cried when I heard it. I am terrified by our current situation, and I am terrified for Cuba.

Wednesday, 24th October

The blockade began today.* I called James on the inter-office phone, but there was no answer.

Thursday, 25th October

I've bought a television. I rush home from work to watch coverage of the Cuban Missile Crisis, as it has been dubbed. Today, at the United Nations, the American Ambassador

---

instructions were given to the generals to be ready to launch missiles within minutes of the President's speech. Twenty planes armed with nuclear bombs were also in the air in striking distance of the USSR.

A copy of Kennedy's speech had been sent to Khrushchev several hours before it was broadcast. The Soviet leader's reaction was swift: he regarded the 'quarantine' as an act of war, and gave instructions that Soviet ships on their way to Cuba should not stop. His reply to Kennedy was direct: 'I must say frankly that the measures indicated in your statement constitute a serious threat to peace and to the security of nations . . . We affirm that the armaments which are in Cuba . . . are intended solely for defensive purposes . . . I hope the United States Government will display wisdom and renounce the actions pursued by you, which may lead to catastrophic consequences for world peace.'

In Cuba, Castro mobilised all his military forces. The air force was scrambled, the army and navy placed on full alert. On the Malecón, the missile-launchers were primed and ready.

* At 10 a.m. EST. By the end of the day US ships had taken up position at regular intervals along the quarantine line, 800 miles from Cuba.

showed photographs of the missile sites purported to have been taken by US reconnaissance planes. I can't help but wonder . . .*

Sunday, 28th October

Escaped to Cambridge for the weekend. Helena, Lionel and I watched the television incessantly. We saw the announcement late on Saturday night that an American spy-plane had been hit by a surface-to-air missile and crashed into the jungle.† I hated coming back to London tonight. No one can think about anything else. People stop you in the street to talk about it. Sometimes they cry. Complete strangers.

---

* Since the situation had become public, American jets had been flying regular low-level reconnaissance missions over the missile sites. The photographs they brought back showed the Soviets readying the missiles for launch. Behind the scenes, there were frantic attempts at diplomacy. To give the Russians more time, Kennedy pulled the quarantine line back 500 miles, to a distance of 300 miles from Cuban shores. At the same time, he ordered the military alert status to be raised to DEFCON 2, the highest level in US history up to that point.

† On Friday 26 October the US stepped up the pressure by increasing the frequency of low-level flights over Cuba to one every two hours. The following day a U-2 piloted by Major Rudolph Anderson was shot down over eastern Cuba. The US interpreted the action as a clear escalation of pressure by the Kremlin. (It later turned out that the order had in fact come from a Soviet commander in Cuba – without Khrushchev's knowledge.) Both sides realised that they were teetering on the brink of nuclear war.

Monday, 29th October

The crisis is over, apparently. Khrushchev wrote to Kennedy last night announcing that he had ordered the dismantling and removal of all Soviet offensive weapons in Cuba.*

As soon as the news came through, I rushed down to James's office. But his desk was empty. 'Never came back from lunch,' said Mary. 'He's in the dumps again. Arrived late this morning still in his dinner-jacket. Drunk as a

---

* Behind the scenes, there had been an exchange of letters between Kennedy and Khrushchev, and a series of meetings between the Attorney-General and the Soviet ambassador to Washington. In addition, there had been a back-channel approach to a US TV reporter by a senior KGB official, in which the possibility of the US withdrawing from its new missile sites in Turkey had been brought to the negotiating table. Moscow proposed a straight swap: its missiles would come out of Cuba if the US removed theirs from Turkey. While Kennedy felt he could not agree publicly to these terms, privately he assured the Soviet ambassador that the US would be prepared to remove its missiles quietly a few months after the crisis. But, at the same time, he issued an ultimatum, threatening US military action if the USSR didn't dismantle its bases in Cuba immediately. In the phrase of the time, Kennedy and Khrushchev stood 'eyeball to eyeball' while the world stared down the gun barrel of nuclear war. In the end, the possible consequences proved too terrifying and Khrushchev quietly agreed to the terms of Kennedy's deal. He gave the order for the missiles to be dismantled and crated. On the Voice of America radio station, Kennedy welcomed his decision. Only Castro, who heard about the agreement over the radio, was furious. Four weeks later, on 21 November, Kennedy formally ended the quarantine and relaxed the Strategic Command's Defense Readiness Condition from DEFCON 2 to DEFCON 4. The US missiles were removed from Turkey in April 1963.

skunk. Said he'd lost half his savings at the baccarat table last night. He sat down at his desk, picked everything out of his In tray and slapped it straight into the Out tray without so much as a glance. He's going to get himself into trouble again.'

I sat down. 'What self-indulgent twaddle. I thought that Cuba had got him back on track. He really did a terrific job – but the OM still gave him a dressing-down about reckless behaviour when we got back. Maybe that's what's eating him? He hasn't even been to see me since then.'

'Do you think he's still mourning Tracy?'

'I imagine so. I don't know what else it can be. Unless he's really fallen out of love with this place. I certainly wouldn't want to live through another two weeks such as we've just had – knowing that our actions, in some way, could have tipped the world into war. But now that it's over . . . I can't describe the feeling – midway between relief and exhilaration, I suppose. It's certainly put the rest of my worries into perspective.'

'So what happens now?'

'I don't know. The OM's patience is running pretty thin. He's booked lunch with Molony again on Friday, perhaps to talk about 007? I just hope he snaps out of it. Otherwise I'm going to give him a piece of my mind.'

November

A conversation I once had with my aunt came back to me. It took place in 1987, the summer of my A-levels. I was staying with her in Scotland while waiting for my results. We were taking our usual dusk walk along the beach behind her cottage, discussing the options for my gap year. I had signed up with Voluntary Service Overseas (VSO), and was trying to decide between placements in Africa and Latin America. 'Where in Latin America?' she asked.

'Possibly Guatemala, Mexico, or Cuba,' I replied.

She stopped in her tracks. When I turned to see why, she was staring out to sea. I couldn't see her expression, but her voice, when she eventually spoke, was soft – with hindsight, possibly regretful. 'Cuba,' she said. 'You'd love Cuba.'

I asked if she had ever been. She half turned towards me. 'I always meant to take a holiday there. If you go, perhaps I'll visit.' Then she smiled. 'But then I'll visit you wherever you end up – if you want me to, of course.'

In the event I chose Ethiopia. My aunt came to see me towards the end of my stint, after which we travelled overland to Kenya, to her country. We never talked about Cuba again. When I read her 1962 journal – particularly the entries describing her adventures there – I was struck afresh by how little I knew of her life. That she had been to a country without my knowing, and also lied to me – or misled me – about it, was at first an unpalatable shock. It was a sensation that would become familiar to me as I read the rest of her diaries. In time the shock dimmed to mild surprise, mingled with amusement and not a little envy: she had been present at many of the turning points in recent history – events that I am constrained to study through other people's words.

As my research continued, the events about which she wrote and the characters she wrote of became more familiar to me. I felt I knew them – certainly I knew things about many of them that they would never suspect. I was filled with an urge to meet whomever I could. One weekend I unearthed the photographs that Mark had taken at Aunt Jane's memorial service and spread them across the floor. I looked at them carefully, one by one, but somewhat to my surprise there were few faces I could immediately identify. I had a list of names compiled from the signatures – those I could decipher – in the book of commemoration that most people had signed after the service. I wrote each name on a Post-it note, then spent the next hour sticking them on to the photographs, shuffling them around until I thought I had a name to match the face. It was like a game of Pelmanism. Only, without a key, I had no idea which matches were correct.

There was one photograph that I kept going back to. I was almost certain it was Bill Tanner. I remembered him squeezing my arms as he said goodbye, telling me that he remembered Aunt Jane's tears of joy when I was born. I remembered that he had given me a card and told me to keep in touch. But did I still have it? If I did, it would be in the file I kept while organising the service, which was probably in a box in the garage. The next weekend, I found it: Colonel Bill Tanner, The Old Rectory, Lattoe, Wiltshire. But would he still be there? The photograph showed a slim man in his mid-to-late sixties. Fourteen years had passed; he was probably eighty, if not older.

I kept the card by the telephone for a week. I don't know what was stopping me from dialling his number. If there was anyone I wanted to meet at that moment in time, it was Bill Tanner. I would have traded dinner with Shakespeare, Mandela and Sam Shepard for the chance. Tanner had worked alongside my aunt for more than twenty years; every document M saw was co-signed 'CoS', or Chief of Staff; he had been Bond's closest friend in the service. If anyone could unlock the remaining secrets in my aunt's diaries it would be him.

Finally, and with some trepidation, I called the number. A clear voice answered on the third ring: 'Tanner.' No sooner had I introduced myself than I had an invitation – perhaps it would be more accurate to say an exhortation – to tea on the coming Saturday, along with military-style directions to his house.

I was greeted with extraordinary warmth and ushered into a long room, decked with faded velvet furniture. Sun streamed through the French windows, highlighting the dust shimmying through the air. The coat of arms of 42 Company, Royal Engineers, was displayed with pride over the mantelpiece. A fat black Labrador lay dozing in front of the fire. Bill Tanner appeared younger than I had expected, spry, with clear blue eyes and an infectious laugh. 'You mean to say your aunt kept a diary the whole time she was with us?' he chuckled. 'She was always a dark horse. Penny Moneypenny – M would have cut off her hands had he known!' And he laughed some more. When I explained I was considering publishing the diaries, he looked a little more serious. 'I don't know what the Official Secrets Act would say about that,' he said. 'But, then again, they can't prosecute your aunt, and I shouldn't think they'd bother with you. Look at what's happening now – websites, autobiographies, official histories and the like. Go for it, girl. Show them what we did. It was a lot more fun then than it is now, I can assure you.'

Tanner's memory for detail was impressive, as I was to learn during subsequent visits to his Wiltshire rectory, when he revealed yet another perspective on the events described in my aunt's diaries. Over frequent lunches in the officers' canteen, Bond had apparently related his exploits in vibrant detail that Tanner was happy to relay to me – once he had taken that first step away from the world of secrets. But he did not forget himself completely; when I asked Bond's true name, he just smiled and winked. 'Couldn't possibly tell you,' he said. 'More than my life's worth.'

'Does that mean he's still alive?'

Tanner shook his head again. 'Mum to that too, I'm 'fraid. Wouldn't want you beating down too many doors.'

But he was happy to look through the memorial-service photographs, identifying his old colleagues and chuckling occasionally as he recalled some anecdote about them. 'Lost touch with most of them. Sad really.' He shook his head. 'We were held together by that place. When the bond was broken, we scattered.' He pointed to a tall, well-groomed woman with rows of pearls around her neck. 'That's Loelia, your aunt's old best friend.

Married an Hon and ended up a duchess when his cousin died. Frightfully grand. She died last year. Mary's still in Jamaica, I understand.' He picked up a picture of a smiling lady with faded blonde hair. 'Always get a card from her at Christmas. Boothroyd went soon after your aunt, I think. He always had a soft spot for her. Look at him there – he must have been close to a hundred. I do believe that's Melinda, the Old Man's niece. She was always going to be a looker. I wonder what's become of her. She can't be more than thirty-five now.' As I looked at the photograph, I remembered her asking me at the service whether my aunt had kept the fourteen-pounder shell in which her uncle used to keep his pipe and tobacco. She had of course, and it is on my desk now as I write this.

'Was Bond there?' I asked. He shook his head.

'As far as I can recall there was no one from the Double-O section. Certainly there are no photographs of them. 006 was in South Africa already – he started up a security company there. Don't know what's become of him. And 009 bought a farm on the Welsh border. I think he's still alive. Possibly lecturing at Hereford. Now, how else can I help you?'

I asked about Caballo. 'I've been able to find no confirmation of his existence,' I told him. 'There's nothing at all in the American files, and even in Bond's reports the name of the CIA source has been redacted.' Tanner responded without hesitation: 'Yes, I remember him. It was all top secret. Eyes Only, read-and-burn stuff. The Cousins insisted. He was their only source, and he was not going to be compromised. But then Penny and James came along and blew the whole thing sky high. What a fuss that caused. Meetings with the American ambassador, letters to and from the White House and Downing Street. Whoa, they caused a stink. But I hate to think what would have happened if they hadn't.

'Your aunt was a truly remarkable woman, you know.' For once, his face was serious, his eyes perhaps a little misted. 'I miss her every day.'

Friday, 2nd November

M returned from lunch with Molony, then called for Bill. They spent an hour together, and when Bill came out he asked if I knew where 007 was. 'M called him on the red phone, but Mary answered. If you see him, tell him to speak to the Old Man urgently.' I thought that when I did see him, I would tell him more than that.

An hour later, 007 walked into the room, looking as if he'd just mounted the steps to the gallows. 'You can go in,' I told him, making no effort to conceal my anger. I'm not sure he noticed. He squared his shoulders, looked at the padded baize door to M's office almost as if he thought it was going to bite him, then reached for the handle, walked through and closed the door behind him. Whatever he's done now, I hoped this wasn't the end of the road for him.

He was in there for nearly an hour, after which I heard M buzz through to Bill. 'Chief of Staff? What number have you allotted to 007?'

'7777, sir.'

'Right. He's coming to see you straight away.'

I was surprised. A four-figure number indicated promotion, but I didn't recognise the 7 prefix. I looked through the open door to Bill's desk, but he had his head down, busy shuffling papers.

Then M's door opened and James walked through with a smile on his face. He came straight over to my desk and bent down and kissed me on the cheek. I didn't know whether to kiss him back or slap him. I put my hand to my cheek as he said, 'Dinner tonight, Penny?'

'Sorry,' I told him. 'I'm going straight to Cambridge. It's my sister's birthday.'

'What a shame. Then be an angel and ring down to Mary and tell her she's got to get out of whatever she's doing tonight. I'm taking her out to dinner. Scott's. Tell her we'll have grouse and pink champagne. Celebration.'

'What of?' I asked, relieved and surprised that he was still with us; I'd been convinced that M had summoned him to strip him of his number, at the least.

'Oh I don't know.' He crossed the room to Bill's office and firmly closed the door.

I picked up the inter-office phone and called down to Mary. She was thrilled. 'I do think he's all right again, Mary,' I told her. 'Heaven knows what M's been saying to him. He had lunch with Molony today. Don't tell James that. But it may have had something to do with it. He's with the Chief of Staff now. And Bill said he wasn't to be disturbed. Sounds like some kind of job. Bill was very mysterious.'

Later that evening, I heard that 007 – as I will always think of him – had gone from Bill's to see Colonel Johnson at Section J.* James in Japan? On the surface it seems unlikely.

---

* Since the end of the Second World War, British involvement in Japan had dwindled to the point where, in 1950, it was no longer

274

Friday, 9th November

007 left today. He popped by my office to say goodbye, but when I asked where he was going, he just smiled and shook his head. And we shared a submersible together! I thought we had developed a kinship – if that's the appropriate word – beyond what we'd had before. A bond forged by shared peril. But then, I suppose, he has been through it all before, many times. For him, Cuba was just another on a long list of assignments in dangerous corners of the world. And now it's on to the next.

I suppose I'll find out what he's up to when his reports start coming in, and as long as his spirits are up, I'm happy. I wished him luck and a safe and speedy return.

Monday, 12th November

M called me into his office this morning. There was a tall man with him, dressed in an aggressively pin-striped three-piece suit with a carnation in his buttonhole and a bowler hat on the chair beside him. I had him pegged as an American before he even opened his mouth. 'Miss Jane Moneypenny, it is an honour to meet you, ma'am,' he said, his moustache ends twitching. 'May I, sir?' M nodded. 'On behalf of the American people, our President has commanded me to offer you the award of the Orange

---

deemed necessary to maintain a station officer there. The show – what there was of it – was run instead from London, based on whatever titbits were thrown from the rapacious CIA operation in the Pacific.

Star,* in recognition of your actions in Cuba which,' and he nodded his head importantly, 'made no small contribution to the successful resolution of the . . . er . . . situation over there.'

I didn't know what to say. That this cartoon character was offering me a medal for bravery seemed absurd. I turned to M for help. He gave me one of the rare smiles that lit up his face. 'On behalf of Miss Moneypenny, I would like to thank you for a great honour. Your country is our country's greatest friend and ally and it is a privilege to provide you with any small assistance. However, and with regret, I'm afraid we cannot accept this great distinction.† Please, however, convey thanks from myself, Miss Moneypenny and the Commander, who, as I said earlier, is out of the country at present.' I managed to stammer my thanks before, with an exaggerated salute, the American made his farewells and left.

I can't pretend that I was unmoved by the recognition, though what would I have done with an Orange Star? I think it came at a good time for M too – he had to brief the

---

* A rare American medal, awarded in the name of the President of the United States to a foreign national. The medal itself is suspended from an orange-and-white-striped ribbon and consists of a bronze star, $1\frac{1}{4}$ inches in diameter, with a $\frac{1}{16}$-inch-diameter silver star superimposed in the centre and the inscription 'FOR BRAVERY IN ACTION IN THE SERVICE OF THE UNITED STATES FLAG' engraved on the back.

† The SIS had a policy of accepting awards only under exceptional circumstances. After preventing rogue financier Hugo Drax from unleashing his Moonraker rocket on London, the Prime Minister had wanted to give Bond an award, which was politely refused on his behalf by M. Bond had similarly been offered – and declined – the American Award of Merit after foiling Goldfinger's attempt to raid Fort Knox.

CIA London station chief about Prenderghast last week. Bill said he was despairing at whether we'd ever be trusted by the Cousins again. McCone's already cut us off from the Pacific traffic.* Hopefully, he won't impose blanket radio silence, but that will depend, I suppose, on whether we manage to convince them that we've plugged all the leaks.

Tuesday, 13th November

James is in Japan – he cabled Mary via Melbourne giving his current address. I wonder what he's doing there? For once, the Powder Vine is in the dark; only M and Bill seem to know and they're not telling.

Friday, 16th November

007 sent a signal to M marked Eyes Only that Bill nabbed as soon as it came in. 'Don't worry about that one, Penny,' he said. 'My desk is fairly clear and the old fingers could do with the exercise.' Why all the secrecy?

Whatever the signal contained, it must have been explosive.† Bill rushed straight into M's office and within minutes

---

* Under the previous head of the CIA, Allen Dulles, London had received digests from the Americans of any sigint that concerned them. When McCone took up the position, however, he cracked down on the sharing of intelligence, apparently under the orders of the National Defense Council, out of fear of British security leaks.
† Bond had passed on the contents of a top-secret decoded message, sent by Moscow to its important stations abroad, and intercepted by the Japanese, detailing a Soviet plan to rid Europe of all American military bases and offensive weapons.

the OM was on the hot-line to Downing Street. Then, this afternoon, we were honoured with a visit from the Minister himself. M has cancelled his plans to go to Quarterdeck tonight and says he's staying in London 'to catch up on things'. When I asked if he needed my help, he said not.

Sunday, 18th November

The nightmare is returning, just when I'd begun to sleep easily again. Helena came up for the weekend and I took her to a gallery opening on Albemarle Street. It was an exhibition of photographs from Kenya – of painted people rather than animals, really quite good. We were going to the bar to get a glass of wine when I saw him. I grabbed Helena's arm and tried to turn around. But I wasn't quick enough. He'd seen us and started walking over. My first instinct was to run, but then I remembered Bill and his despair over the colander.

I just had time to nudge Helena before he reached us. 'Hello, Jane. I was hoping to run into you,' he said.

I didn't look at Helena when I introduced him – I didn't want to see her expression when she realised who he was. But I needn't have worried. She calmly shook his hand and smiled.

'It's good to meet you, David,' she said. 'I've heard a lot about you.' I dug my elbow into her ribs as she continued. 'You're a fellow Brahms-lover, I understand.'

They started chatting away about music and art and Africa, and I was left to gaze around the room. I could see Zach trying to catch my eye, but I wasn't going to make it easy for him.

Eventually, Helena ran out of steam. She drained her glass and held it out in front of her, expectantly. But Zach didn't take the hint, so I drained mine too. 'Thanks, Helena, I'd love another one.' She looked at me rather quizzically, but I smiled and nodded. As soon as she turned away, Zach took my arm. 'We've got to talk,' he said. 'I'll telephone next weekend.' I said I'd look forward to it. Then he asked me to say goodbye to Helena for him and slipped off through the crowd.

When she came back, she raised her eyebrows and I shook my head. 'Are all spies that attractive?' was all she had to say.

Monday, 19th November

I tried to talk to Bill today, but he was running back and forth between M's office and the Ministry. It transpires that the Russians staged another test explosion at Novaya Zemlya yesterday. The force of this one was felt almost 3,000 miles away, in Athens. Moscow confirmed later that it had been a 200-megaton bomb – four times the size of Tsar Bomba and tens of thousands of times the force of the bomb detonated at Hiroshima.

There was an immediate public uproar. By mid-afternoon, Trafalgar Square was thronged with peace campaigners, led by the CND.* On the news later, I heard that there had been similar spontaneous demonstrations of outrage around the Western world.

---

* The Campaign for Nuclear Disarmament was at that time regarded as a significant threat to the security of Britain.

For some reason, the explosion came as no surprise to M. As soon as the news came through, he ordered Bill to set 'Operation Redress' in action, before calling Downing Street and his opposite number in the Security Service. By the end of the day, reports were coming in to the effect that all Soviet personnel in the UK had been confined within a radius of twenty miles of their homes, while the Embassy, various consulates and trading offices were being visibly protected by armed police.

Before I left this evening, M asked me to send a cable to 007, care of Melbourne:

CONGRATULATIONS ON MAGIC PRODUCT* STOP GREATLY APPRECIATED THANKS DUE TO THE TIGER† STOP KEEP UP THE GOOD WORK SIGNED M

It was as close to a pat on the back as I have seen him give – particularly at a distance of 6,000 miles. It is too much of a coincidence that it came on the same day as the Russian bomb.‡ Well done, James – it sounds as if he is indeed back on form. I look forward to his return.

---

* For the preceding year the Japanese had managed to interpret much of the Soviet wireless traffic from Vladivostok and oriental Russia, using their new, state-of-the-art code-cracking machine, the MAGIC 44.

† Tiger Tanaka, Oxford-educated head of the Japanese secret service. A judo black belt, heavy drinker and enthusiastic womaniser, he spied for Japan in the UK before returning to his homeland to train as a kamikaze bomber.

‡ Tanaka had shown Bond an intercepted Soviet message, which contained details of a Soviet plan to disarm Europe – by pointing the USSR's new super-missiles at each of America's European allies in

Thursday, 22nd November

A chance, at last, to speak to Bill. I collared him as he was heading to the canteen and persuaded him to come for a sandwich with me instead. We squeezed behind the tiny table at the back of Franco's and I looked at my cheese and tomato on wholewheat bread (no more ham and strong mustard for me) and told him that I'd seen Zach again. 'He's going to call me this weekend. I didn't want to speak to him until I'd had a chance to consult you. What do I do?'

Bill took a bite of his sandwich and chewed it carefully before replying. 'It would be very helpful to us if we could get him. We'll need every shred of evidence to convict Prenderghast, and if this Zach can bring anything to the table, then it would be most useful. That's assuming, of course, that he was the contact in this case. It doesn't sound as if Zach himself is a seasoned operator, but it might be as well to get him off the scene now. I think the natural thing would be for you to organise a meet. Would you be prepared to do it at your place? Then we can get in beforehand to mike it up and be standing by to pick him up when he leaves.'

My first instinct was to refuse, but then I told myself not to be silly. Z knows where I live and he's probably already

---

turn, with the threat that it would unleash them unless the Americans removed all their weapons from the European sphere. The Soviet stations to be affected would be informed one week in advance, to allow them to evacuate all Soviet citizens working in the country and burn all archives. Once M had received Bond's signal, he devised a plan to round up all Soviet nationals immediately on hearing of the nuclear test.

told whomever he's reporting to, so it wouldn't make much of a difference. I made Bill promise there would be someone standing by, in case anything goes wrong. He seemed relieved. 'Atta girl! I'll get going on this and then we'll meet a couple of days beforehand to run through what you're going to say. I'll bring Dorothy up to speed, and have a talk to Q Branch about getting one of their gadget men on to it. All you have to do for the meantime is to answer the telephone.'

Friday, 23rd November

The Prenderghast story has finally broken. It made the headlines of yesterday's *Times* and as a result there were questions in the House. Today, every paper in the country, probably the world, has devoted at least a few pages to this latest treachery. It doesn't make us look very good.

As a consequence of the publicity, the trial is going to be rushed through and is due to take place at the Old Bailey in the new year. If all goes according to plan, we should have Zach firmly in the bag by then.

Sunday, 25th November

He telephoned last night. He said he really needed to talk to me – that he had new information proving that my father is still alive. I tried to suppress a gasp, and sat down. I thought I'd convinced myself that everything he'd ever said to me was an elaborate charade – and most of me still believes it was. But still, the mention of Pa's name brings me up short. It can't be true – it just can't. I told him that I'd meet him, but that I wasn't prepared to betray my work.

'Please trust me,' he said. 'I'm doing this for you. I'm not going to ask you to do anything. I feel dreadful about this whole thing. I went back to Berlin this summer and all I could think about was how I'd let you down. I never meant for it to turn out like this; I honestly just wanted to help.'

I told him I still didn't believe him, but that I was prepared to talk about it. 'Why don't you come round here on Friday, 14th December? Half past six?'

He agreed. The date is set, the trap is sprung.

As I went to bed last night, something he said was nagging at me, but I couldn't work out what it was. I replayed the conversation in my head. It was only this morning that I worked it out: Berlin. He said he had been to Berlin – R is in Berlin. *Was* Zach one of the men he had been spotted talking to? I don't want to carry through this chain of thought. It must be a coincidence. It's just that all my coincidences recently are transpiring to be far from accidental.

December

Much as I have searched for confirmation of the events succeeding Bond's arrival in Tokyo, I have found nothing outside Fleming's account in *You Only Live Twice* (London, 1964). There, apart from minor discrepancies in dates, the story tallies closely with that detailed in my aunt's diaries. At the beginning of the book, lunching with Sir James Molony at Blades, M complains that he has sent Bond on two tough assignments over the past few months. 'He bungled them both. On one he nearly got himself killed, and on the other he made a mistake that was dangerous for others.' This was partially – albeit arguably – true. What was missing was Miss Moneypenny's role in extricating Bond from his predicament. Or that Bond's 'mistake' could have saved the world from nuclear annihilation. My aunt, in fact, rarely figures in Fleming's accounts, and when she does it is invariably from behind a typewriter: Fleming would no more have envisaged a secretary saving the world than M was able to. Galling as this might seem to those of us looking in from the outside, I am sure that was how she wished it.

She never had a yearning for the limelight. In her position she could not afford to. But even after she retired, in 1983, after thirty years in the service, she kept to the shadows. She went to live in a white stone cottage in North Uist, where she was known to all as Jane Penny. She kept in touch with a few of her former colleagues – mostly by letter. She went abroad twice a year, sometimes for extended periods, and visited us in Cambridge, but for most of the time she was on her own on a remote Scottish island. She spent hours each day reading – she once told me that she had shelves of books that she had bought but had never had the time to read and that she was determined to finish every one of them. Her only companion was another standard poodle, Rafiki's successor, whom she had named Uhuru, and with whom she would climb the rocky hills and stride along the deserted white sand beaches. I can picture her now, wild hair streaming behind her and a look of exhilaration on her face.

She always told me that she went to live on a remote Scottish island because it reminded her of Africa and her childhood. At the time, I thought it was a strange choice for a woman on her own. She was only fifty-two when she retired. Now, having learned more of her life, I can appreciate that she had already lived enough to fill a hundred more humdrum existences.

Monday, 3rd December

There's something not quite right with the 007 situation. I have a funny feeling in the pit of my stomach. This morning, Bill came by my desk to ask whether we'd received any signals from him. When I said no, he asked me to let him know as soon as one arrived.

Then, this afternoon, a call came in for M from Tokyo on

the secure line. 'It's Dikko Henderson,'* an Australian voice announced. 'I'd like to talk to your Chief, on a matter concerning our mutual friend. It's quite urgent.' When I buzzed M on the intercom, he said he'd take the call immediately. I put it through, but managed to get distracted looking for something on the other side of the room before I noticed I'd failed to switch off the intercom. I heard Dikko tell M that he was concerned about 007. 'This morning, his clothes were transferred to my hotel by some Japanese secret service chaps. Tanaka sent with them instructions for me to tell you that he'd taken our Commander friend on a trip out of Tokyo to visit the HQ of the little asset [the MAGIC 44] you're interested in.'

'That seems positive,' M replied cautiously, but Dikko sounded unconvinced.

'You see, sir, I called Tanaka's office, and they told me that he was on a mission to Fukuoka. That's in the opposite direction from the establishment he told me he was taking our friend to. And I can't believe that the Commander would take off without giving me some sort of message to send to the Office. I'm sorry, sir, I don't want to scaremonger, but it smells a bit fishy. These guys out here are tricky little buggers, if you'll excuse the language. You can never quite trust their motives. However much Tanaka might like our Commander personally, he's never going to give up something for free, and I'm a bit worried about what he'll extract in return.'

---

* The Tokyo representative of the Australian Secret Intelligence Service (ASIS), Richard 'Dikko' Lovelace Henderson. Bond went to Japan on an Australian passport, superficially as Henderson's number two.

As I was waiting for M's reply, I heard a knock at my door. I rushed across the room and flicked off the intercom before the girl arrived with the afternoon signals.

Tuesday, 4th December

Mary has heard nothing from 007 and I'm beginning to feel concerned. He's presumably still in Japan; yesterday evening, Bill asked Section J to bring him a detailed map of the country, as well as an intelligence report on the Fukuoka region.* It's apparently on the south island, facing South Korea across the Korea Strait.

I pray he's not in trouble again. I couldn't bear it. Apart from everything else, M and Bill don't need another worry while we're in the midst of this Prenderghast business. Since the news was announced, the building has been infiltrated by 'special prosecutors', ministry men, the police, Americans, everyone, it seems. I can't believe that it's not making the security position even more precarious. There can't be a lowly clerk in this place who hasn't by now been deposed and told to be on stand-by, ready to be called to testify in the trial, if necessary. The whole building has practically ground to a halt. Fortunately, I think I should escape – I had few dealings with P – though I know M will be heavily involved.

---

* Fukuoka is the principal town of Kyūshū, Japan's south island. A remote and rather lawless region, it was known to be the last stronghold of the Black Dragon Society, formerly the most feared and powerful secret society in Japan, but by the early 1960s more of a loose collection of brutal low-lifes.

Friday, 7th December

Still no news from 007. Bill obviously forgot, for a moment, that I wasn't meant to know anything about it, as he came into my office this afternoon to ask again whether I'd heard from him. Deep worry lines creased his forehead and he looked pale and tired. When I said, 'Not a word,' he shook his head. 'It's damn strange, Penny. I came in early to telephone Tiger Tanaka in Tokyo. The clerk I spoke to said he'd just stepped out of the office and would be back within the hour. If he's back, then where is 007?' (I noticed that even Bill couldn't grasp the reality of James's new number.) 'When I tried again, I was told Mr Tanaka was busy and would return my call when he was able to. Well, it's midnight now in Tokyo and I haven't heard a squeak. I don't think he wants to speak to me. There's something odd going down out there.'

Then he seemed to recollect himself. 'I'm sure he's all right. 007's a big boy, well able to look after himself. I'm afraid though, Penny, that we're going to have to postpone our dinner tomorrow. The Old Man wants me to spend the weekend with him going over Prenderghast. Everything's ready for next Friday night. They'll go in that morning to set up. Let's discuss what you're going to say next week – we've still got time. Try not to think about it until then.'

Some forlorn hope. I go to bed thinking about it and wake up the next morning with hypothetical conversations buzzing inside my head like trapped bluebottles. Zach, R, my father all live in my dreams, however well I manage to banish them from my daily existence. I'm going to spend the weekend sorting out and cleaning the flat. Perhaps I'll repaint the study? Haircut? Sometimes, a weekend alone, with no plans to see anyone, seems like a long time. I wish it was next Saturday already.

Tuesday, 11th December

M has spent all day with the Minister, discussing the implications of the Prenderghast affair. There's an unseemly amount of press interest in the up-coming trial. The papers appear to be comfortable passing on speculation gleaned from so-called 'espionage experts'. No one who really knows anything about our world would ever stoop to talking to the press – that would be treachery in itself – leaving the outer fringes, the failures and might-have-beens, to grab the spotlight while they can.

I'm worried about M. He's aged visibly over the past few months. On occasions, I catch sight of him getting out of his car, or walking along the corridor, and he looks suddenly stiff and frail. He has such a powerful presence, it's too easy to overlook that he's becoming an old man. What if he insists on retiring despite the Minister's objections? I don't think I would stay if he went, even in the unlikely event that his successor wanted to keep me. I can't imagine this place without M at the prow, guiding us wisely through stormy waters. How lonely it must be for him, with the weight of so many lives on his shoulders.

We'll all be relieved when the whole circus is over. I suppose it's better to have a large show trial with all the attendant publicity than to harbour a mole, still buried deep underground? At least now we don't have to fear the enemy within.

Wednesday, 12th December

A rushed lunch with Bill, who's clearly under terrific strain. Although he doesn't voice it explicitly, I know he's also worrying about 007 – their friendship must make Bill's efforts to stay emotionally uninvolved with service activities difficult. Back at our little table at Franco's, he ran through the arrangements for Friday. 'I don't know quite how to tell you this,' he began. 'Q Branch went over your flat yesterday, to identify the best places for invisible listening devices, and they found a bug in your telephone. Russian-made. We don't know how long it's been there, but you can assume some time.'

I sighed. 'Well, I suppose that explains how they came by their information. How horrible.' Privately, I thanked the foresight that had led me to relocate the diaries to Maura's basement while the boffins came in.

'We've left it there for the time being,' he continued. 'No need to show our hand. It's only for another couple of days. Try to ignore it, and if you've got something private to say, pop a tea-cosy over the phone, turn the music up and you should be all right. We'll replace it with one of our own on the day – once activated, it'll be continuously live. You don't need to pick up the receiver or anything.* It should cover the drawing-room and kitchen, but in case he takes

---

* Known as SF (Special Facility), and first used in 1942, this mechanism converted a telephone into a bugging device. Normally, when a handset is replaced on the telephone it disconnects the mouthpiece microphone from the lines to the exchange. SF, however, stopped the disconnection of the line, leaving the microphone continuously active and able to pick up any conversation within range, which was then transmitted back to monitors in the exchange.

you into the study or bedroom, we'll have fixed additional devices into the light-fittings. All very predictable, but we didn't want to do any structural work and he's not going to come with sweeping equipment. One would hope not, anyway. They'll be installed on Friday morning – our men will come disguised as telephone engineers – and removed as soon as he's gone. Have you made plans for the weekend?'

I said I was going to stay with my sister in Cambridge. 'Good idea. You'll want to get away from the scene for a short while, give yourself a chance to get the immediate images out of your head. Now, as for the meet itself, you're to come home at your regular time – don't vary your routine in any way. You can call in on your lady downstairs, but don't collect the dog. It could cause unforeseen complications, and we don't want any surprises.

'When he arrives, let him in and offer him a drink. As I said, the drawing-room would be best. Engage in conversation as naturally as possible. He'll make all sorts of promises to you, dangle snippets of information about your father, try to make you so eager for more that you're prepared to commit to anything in exchange. But he won't try to push that side: he'll just drop it into the conversation, try to make it sound simple and insignificant when placed against what he's offering you. Your job is to ensure that he makes that offer clearly and intelligibly. Try to extract from him who he's working for, why, whether he's met them, their channel to us and so on. You know the form.'

I nodded, the reality of what was going to happen in two days bursting down on me like a summer storm. He looked at me with his kind eyes and smiled. 'Chin up, Penny. You're going to do a fine job. We'll be downstairs listening to every word.'

I admitted that I was afraid of that.

He laughed. 'Don't be silly. It'll just be me and a Technical with the earphones on. If you want to call a halt to it at any point, all you have to say is "I've had enough." That's it – "I've had enough" – and we'll be through your door like an encyclopaedia salesman.'

I attempted a smile. 'I'll be fine, don't worry. Thank you, Bill. Thank you for everything.' He leant across to squeeze my hand.

'Anything for you, Penny – you know that.'

As I was getting ready to leave this evening, I started to feel nervous and vulnerable, as though I'd coated myself in nectar and lain down in a lavender bed. However much I try to ignore it, the fact remains that I'm under surveillance and have been for some good time. The idea of going back alone to my flat and waiting for the bees to call seemed unappealing. From the window, I could see the early evening fog congealing into a pea-souper. But everyone had left the office for the day, except Bill, and I couldn't ask him to walk me home. I couldn't think of anyone else to contact. For a fleeting moment, I allowed myself to think of R, but that was no good as he was in Berlin.

If I couldn't find a bodyguard, I decided, I'd have to take steps to protect myself. On a whim, I buzzed down to the Armoury and when Major Boothroyd answered I asked if I could see him for a minute.

Descending in the lift, I was still unsure as to what he could do to help, or even what it was I thought he could do. I didn't want to place him in an awkward position. He seemed very welcoming when he showed me into his windowless office and offered me a glass of sherry, which I accepted. 'We've missed our star pupil down here,' he began, with a smile. 'But from what I hear, you've had plenty on your plate. Now, tell me what I can do for you.' Without going into detail, I explained the position I was going to find myself in two days later. 'I'm not quite sure why I'm telling you this, Major,' I said, 'and I don't know if there's any way in which you could help . . .' I didn't get any further before he jumped up and sprang across to the locked door to the arms store, muttering, 'Of course you need protection, my dear girl. Never go into combat if you're not fully prepared. Need to be a step ahead of the enemy and whatnot.'

When he emerged, he was carrying a tan-coloured book on the palms of his hands, as if he were serving from a silver platter. 'Just the ticket, one Baby Browning at your service. I've shown her to you before, haven't I?'

He rooted around for a box of bullets and when he came out again I asked whether this was breaking every rule in the book. 'Not breaking, my dear Miss Moneypenny, merely bending. You should have a licence, of course, and officially we should sign the weapon out, give you a job number and some such rubbish, but I don't think that's really necessary, do you?' He gave me a wink and patted me on the bottom when I got up to go.

The Baby Browning is now on my bedside table, still in its literary nest – which I discovered, to my amusement, was a hollowed out copy of *Paracelsus*.*

In two days' time, Zach will be here.

---

* One of writer and poet Robert Browning's earliest works, first published in 1835.

Tuesday, 18th December

I finally feel strong enough to write, though whether I'll be able to describe what happened last week is another matter. I don't want to think about it, let alone record it. But I can't avoid it; I just hope that by reliving it here I can expunge the nightmares.

After the meeting with Bill, I felt full of determination, ready to face Zach and do what I had to. I worked late the next day; M had returned from the Ministry and there was a backlog of signals and reports to get through. I took the bus home as usual, intending to pack my weekend suitcase, ready for a quick getaway once the episode was over the following night. I tried not to think about it; bizarrely, I felt not only nervous, but treacherous too. Don't be an idiot, I told myself as I stared unseeingly out of the window – you can't betray a man like Zach.

It was dark when the bus stopped, and as I walked along Prince's Gate and turned left into the Gardens, I was conscious of it being foggy again. I couldn't see the poles of even the closest street-lamps and their lights glowed weakly through the dense air. I picked up Rafiki and was chatting to him when I opened the door to my flat. He started to growl, but I was too preoccupied to take much notice; I assumed he'd picked up the lingering scent of the Q Branch men. It was a good idea of Bill's not to have him with me when Zach turned up the next day.

I took off my coat and walked into my bedroom, closed the door then turned to hang up my coat. As my hands were up-stretched, I heard the click of a light-switch and the room went dark. I spun around. A man was standing in the bathroom doorway, backlit by the bathroom light. I was terrified. His face was obscured by shadow, but I could see enough from the pale street-light seeping in through the windows to make out a shape clasped in his right hand. 'Don't move,' he said, in a strongly accented voice that I recognised but could not place. I did as I was told – I don't think I could have moved if I'd wanted to. Only my brain was churning feverishly. Who was it? What should I do? Could I open the door, jump out of the room and close it before he got to me? I decided to do what I was told.

'Turn around, open the door and walk down the passage and into the small room. Sit down at your desk,' he ordered. I complied. He tucked the gun into his waistband, turned on the desk-lamp and shone it at my face. 'Who are you?' I asked.

'You can call me Boris,' he replied. 'I am a friend of Herr "Zach".' I shouldn't have been surprised, but I was. 'You should not have planned a welcoming surprise for him. That was stupid.' He pronounced the first syllable with a strong 'ssh'. 'Bugs in the phone, in the light-fittings? Child's play.'

'How did you know?'

He gave what passed as a laugh. 'I know many things about you, Miss Moneypenny. Did you think it was a coincidence that our mutual friend was at that gallery opening?' He gave a short laugh. 'I see you did.'

'What do you want from me?' I asked.

'It is what you want from us that I am interested in right now. Your father – you want to know about your father. I can tell you all about your father.'

'Yes, I want to know,' I said. 'But not if it means being blackmailed by you.'

He gave a bitter laugh. 'You don't know what pressure is – yet.'

I saw Rafi appear at the door, still growling. As Boris turned around to see what was making the noise, I jumped up, throwing my inkpot at him. It hit the side of his head, ink splashing over his face and shoulder, but failed to stem his momentum as he flung himself over the desk at me. I managed to dodge out of the way and lunged for the door. His hand grabbed my ankle and I fell to the floor, lashing out with my fingernails. Then he yelled and his grip loosened for a second. I saw Rafi with his jaws clenched around his hand, shaking it. He kicked out and Rafi yelped. Boris kicked him again, as I tried to wrench my leg free. But he was too strong. In no time he had my arms in a vice-like grip and was marching me back into the bedroom, with Rafi shut into the study.

He forced me to strip down to my underclothes, then pushed me back on to the bed. With one knee on my stomach, he trussed up my hands and ankles and tied them to the bed legs. 'You are making a big mistake, Miss Moneypenny,' he said in a low, menacing voice.

I took a deep breath. 'I've had enough. Just tell me what you want from me and we can get this over. If it's Berlin, I can get the papers.'

'Berlin?' he sneered. 'We have come a long way from there. Everyone knows the British stance on Berlin is merely an extension of what the Americans want. You think your secret service is so marvellous, but still you can't move without your big protector.' He gave another of his mirthless laughs. 'No. You are going to tell me how you broke the Pacific cipher and intercepted our traffic last month. You knew our intentions and that is unacceptable to my superiors.' His pale eyes almost glowed in the half-light and I suddenly realised where I had seen him before: in the park and on the bus, coming home from work. He had been following me, and for months. His was the voice on the telephone the night Frieda was taken ill. I was filled with fury; nothing mattered other than denying this creeping extortionist what he wanted, whatever the cost.

'I don't know,' I said honestly. 'And even if I did, I wouldn't tell you.' I spat at him and he slapped me across the face, hard, and even while my cheek was stinging I felt a sense of satisfaction at denying his demands. He slapped me again, harder this time. My teeth must have rammed into my inner cheek, as I felt blood pooling in my mouth. I spat it out. His hand was also bleeding profusely, where Rafi had bitten him. He must have noticed as, clutching it with a sneer on his face, he turned to go into the bathroom. I heard water start to flow.

I pulled at my arms; the rope had a bit of give and I was only inches away from the Browning on the bedside table. I bent my head and started tugging on the knot with my teeth. The rope gave another inch and then slipped free from the bed leg. My hands were still bound tightly together, but I could now reach the book, flip it open and pick up the gun.

Suddenly, my ears picked up another sound – the soft scraping of a key being turned in a lock. I froze. Someone was coming in through the front door. I couldn't take on two of them. But no one else had my key.

For some reason, my mind flashed to R and the evening he had emerged from the kitchen along with the scent of cooking. He had borrowed my spare key, but had he ever returned it? I tried to swallow but couldn't: if it was R – and suddenly I was convinced it was him – that meant my suspicions had been correct; he was behind this whole horror. I couldn't bear it. His betrayal felt worse than any other.

I must have been thinking in dream-time, as everything came into my head in the instant I heard the key turn in the lock. Boris was still in the bathroom, the water flowing from the tap; I was still tied to the bed by my feet, my bound hands clasping the tiny gun.

Footsteps approached the bedroom. I pointed the Browning at the doorway, felt my fingers take the pressure on the trigger. I closed my eyes for a second and when I opened them, there he was: R, standing in the doorway. I was ready to shoot, my fingers squeezing tighter, when I looked into his face. His eyes registered genuine astonishment, rapidly replaced by concern. I knew in a flash that I could trust him. I folded my hands over the gun. He opened his mouth to say something, but I shook my head and looked furiously towards the bathroom door. The tap had been turned off. Boris appeared in the doorway and there was a flurry as R leapt on him, knocking him to the floor.

The next second, he was kneeling beside me, untying my hands and kissing my face. 'Jane, what happ–' he began, when there was a loud crack and the expression on his face turned to surprise, briefly, replaced by pain, as he sank to the floor. I looked down to see blood seeping through the side of his shirt, where his coat had fallen open. Boris was getting to his feet, moving towards us, his gun in his hand and a murderous look on his face. I didn't have time to think – I just squeezed the trigger and shot at him, once in the stomach and once in the chest. He lurched towards the bed and fell to his knees.

I tore at my leg ties, dragged Boris into the bathroom and locked him in, then hauled R on to the bed. He was unconscious and still bleeding. I tied a sheet around him and ran into the study to telephone the ambulance and the duty officer at the Office. As I waited for them to arrive, I stroked R's hair and kissed his forehead and told him I was sorry, over and over again. When the medics came, they lifted him on to a stretcher, before returning with another for Boris. I jumped into the ambulance between them and as I sat holding R's hand his eyes flickered open. 'Jane,' he croaked, 'I missed you, I came back to say . . .'

I put my hand over his mouth. 'There'll be time enough to say what you want to when you're better,' I said. 'Rest now. Conserve your strength. I'm not going anywhere.'

Thursday, 20th December

It's hard being at work when I want to stay at the hospital with R. The operation appears to have been a success. They found the bullet: miraculously, it had missed his vital organs. There was some internal bleeding, which the surgeon says has been staunched, and we should know by next week whether the wound has healed properly. R drifts in and out of consciousness, but his temperature is dropping, which can only be a good sign. I have no idea what my feelings for him are, beyond concern, fondness and, yes, guilt, but I pray with all my might that he will recover.

Bill has been marvellous about everything. He came straight to the hospital on Thursday night when I called and spent hours holding my hand, listening to me berate myself for mistrusting R and leading him into danger. 'It wasn't your fault,' he told me again and again. 'We also had our suspicions about him, which turn out to have been unfounded.' He looked away from me. 'We'll talk about that another time. But you had every reason to be unsure. You mustn't blame yourself.' He arranged for Boris to be put under guard and called the Soviet Embassy, which naturally denied all knowledge of him.

At dawn, he said he had to go. 'I'm needed at the Ministry today to go over the evidence against Prenderghast and I'd better put on a fresh shirt. Don't want to let the side down. I'll go via Ennismore Gardens and pick up your little poet friend and return it to Major Boothroyd. I think we need to find some way of avoiding the paperwork. Let me work on it.' Then he gave me the keys to his flat and insisted I go back there for a rest before heading up to Cambridge. Reluctantly, I followed his orders; the matron promised to call when R recovered consciousness and suddenly I felt very tired.

I have spent this week rushing between the Office and the hospital. M has said nothing, though I know Bill briefed him on Friday. He probably won't ever mention it. Zach was spotted boarding a plane to Istanbul the evening of the incident – he must have been listening in and took fright when everything departed from plan. Our doctors say that Boris will make a full recovery. His only visible scar will be on his hand; Rafiki deserves a medal.

Still no news from 007 – something terrible must have happened. I just wish we knew what.

Friday, 21st December

This evening, there was a piece about Prenderghast on the news. They interviewed his parents, who looked shell-shocked and defensive and terribly, terribly normal. They've been forced publicly to swallow their only son's treason and homosexuality – an unappetising concoction, I would imagine. Yet they're clearly proud of him still, despite what he did; I don't think it can have sunk in yet. I can't help but feel sorry for poor P. There's not much to separate what he did from what I was a cat's whisker from doing myself. I came so close – on the eve of Lil's wedding, I nearly gave them the documents they wanted. They tempted both of us with our deepest desires, and mine remain unsatisfied.

I can't help thinking about it, going over everything that Boris said on that awful evening. It took a few days to shake clear. How did he know about the reception we were planning for Zach? How did Zach know Helena and I were going to the gallery opening? I hadn't talked about either of these in my flat, so the bug couldn't have picked them up – and by this time Prenderghast was safely tucked away in his suite at Claridge's, so he couldn't have seen the invitation on my desk at work.

I told Bill, who raised his eyebrows. 'We've been afraid of that,' he said. 'Both Dorothy and X say it doesn't add up; Prenderghast must have had a comrade on the inside. But he's not admitting to anything. We'll have to hope for better luck with Boris, once he's well enough for interrogation. We're going to have a hell of a time of it in the new year.'

Sunday, 23rd December

R is going to be all right. The hospital telephoned yesterday to say that he'd regained full consciousness. I rushed there to find him sitting up in bed eating scrambled eggs and bacon and looking attractively rumpled. He greeted me with a broad smile. 'Hello, Jane. I came back from Berlin to ask you to spend Christmas with me on a Scottish island. But now . . .' he shrugged his shoulders. 'They say I was lucky – as far as luck has any bearing on being shot by some ugly thug one's never seen before in one's life. I can't remember a thing about it – about anything much, in fact. It's a blessed relief, in many ways. Can we turn the clock back a year, please?'

I started laughing. He was back to being R, and at that moment I didn't want him to be anyone else. 'I'm so sorry,' I started to say, when he told me to be quiet.

'Any time you want a human shield, just call me. This bullet thing's really not as bad as it's cracked up to be. And who was that mug who shot me? Now, can we talk about Scotland, please? I know this magical island called North Uist. I think you'd love it there – it's a little like Africa, except for the weather, of course.'

I leant over to squeeze his hand. 'I'm not a fool,' I told him. 'You can't expect me to believe it was pure coincidence that you popped back into my life in my hour of greatest need.'

He smiled back at me. 'Oh, Jane, I wish I could have told you before. I was so close to it, so many times, but then that old training clicked back in . . .'

My mouth must have fallen open. 'You mean, you're . . .'

'Yes, one of us. Well, Security Service – at least I used to

be. I'm not sure how they're going to take this unauthorised leave.'

'You're not an architect? Did you know all along?' I felt
faint, as my mind raced to review the possibilities.

'I am, and no I didn't. I trained as an architect and, from
time to time, have worked for architectural practices. And
of course I didn't know about you, until I was too far in to
turn away. I started having suspicions early this year, when
you were so wary of talking about your job: you reacted as
I would have. Then I followed you to work and I knew. A
mate of mine from your outfit supplied the details. I should
have come clean then – that or broken it off. But I was in
love with you. I didn't know what to do, and everything
just started going wrong. There was that awful time when
you caught me searching your desk . . .'

'Yes, what was that?'

'Well, our boys had been following a couple of German
chaps, suspected agents. I happened to take a look at their
log-book and, to my total shock, saw that the Germans had
been clocked in Ennismore Gardens. Putting two and two
together, I guessed you were their target and thought I'd
better take a quick look round to try and see whether they'd
put anything nasty in your place. Unfortunately, you woke
up sooner than I'd expected.'

'And you kept it all from me?'

'Oh, Jane, I can't say how sorry I am. I was truly confused.
I couldn't say anything at my end – at that stage, I was more
scared that they would try to break us up than anything else.
Some irony, really. In the end, when things between us were
falling apart, I applied for a temporary transfer and was
placed in Berlin.'

'I really don't know what to say,' I told him.

'There's more, I'm afraid. My name . . .'

'Not Richard Hamilton?'

He shook his head.

I didn't know whether to laugh or slap him. 'I'm going to need some time to think about this. I suppose I am relieved you're not one of Them.'

'You thought that?' He chuckled. 'I'm so sorry.'

'You should be. You should be.'

Lying in bed last night, as I recycled through all the times we'd spent together, searching for clues that I should have picked up, my thoughts alternated between fury – at my stupidity and his deception – and amusement. But I couldn't stay cross for long: he did what he had to – what, I suppose, I would have done had I found out about him first. Then he saved me from Boris. He is really quite an extraordinary man.

Christmas Day, 25th December

I was at the hospital, sharing R's Christmas lunch (the turkey, predictably, tasted like a dry dishcloth), when I was called to the telephone. It was M. 'Miss Moneypenny, I'm sorry to have to do this to you again, but I'm going to need you out here this afternoon. Smith is on his way to collect the Chief of Staff. He'll be at the hospital gates for you in fifteen minutes.' He put the phone down abruptly.

The road to Windsor was clear – I imagine the whole nation was listening to the Queen's speech and I was not unhappy to have been given an excuse to avoid that particular feature of the traditional British Christmas. 'When did you find out?' I asked Bill.

'What? About your Mr Hamilton?'

I nodded.

'We got wind of it a couple of weeks ago. Tanqueray was checking him out in Berlin. We only had confirmation from Five the day of the er . . . incident. He was loosely connected to the Embassy in Berlin, and apparently went AWOL the previous day. We now know he was on his way to see you in London, but at the time there were fears that he could have been picked up by the other side. We received an All Stations wire asking for any information as to the whereabouts of one of their officers, followed by a list of his current aliases. Tanqueray picked it up and contacted me. I was going to tell you, once this whole thing was over. My best guess is that he heard on the Stasi underground about Boris's planned visit to you and came to warn you. Jolly good thing, as it turns out. Must say, you would have enjoyed the look on Troop's face when he received the news. Probably still wiping the egg off his not-so-smug face.' We both smiled at the thought.

'Do you know what this is about?' I asked, but he shook his head.

'No, the Old Man merely said he needed us. I'm guessing it might be 007 – he seems to have a knack for spoiling our Christmases.' As an attempt at levity, it crashed to the floor, leaving both of us to our private fears.

The Silver Wraith swept across the gravel and came to a stately halt outside the front door. Bill rang the old ship's bell and when Hammond opened the door he told us, 'The Admiral is just finishing his Christmas lunch,' and showed us into the library. It's a lovely room, with polished mahogany panelling, leather chairs and framed naval cutlasses hanging on the walls. Bill sat down while I walked over to the window and gazed out into Windsor Forest. Silhouetted against the trees in the pale-grey afternoon light, I could make out two grazing deer, so fragile, so beautiful. I made a vow to myself to visit Africa next year.

The door opened and M walked in. He was wearing a blazer over his habitual white shirt and spotted bow-tie. He looked grave. 'I received a signal from Henderson in Japan a few hours ago,' he began, without preamble. 'Three days ago, there was a tremendous explosion in the Fukuoka region. The house of a Swiss horticulturalist was blown to high heaven, killing everyone in sight. This morning, Henderson was contacted by the head of the Japanese secret service, Tanaka, who told him that he feared 007 had been killed in the explosion. Apparently, the owner of this fortress had cultivated a deadly garden of poisonous plants, which had become the favoured spot for suicide tourists. I know – sounds like bloody rubbish to me too. Tanaka wanted this man dead and had persuaded 007 to do his dirty work for him in exchange for the product of the MAGIC 44 – Chief of Staff will fill you in, Miss Moneypenny. And 007, reckless damn fool, rose to the challenge. The bodies of the horticulturalist,' he consulted a piece of paper, 'a Dr Guntram Shatterhand – what kind of name is that? – and his wife have been recovered, but there's no sign of 007, dead or alive. The Japs have been searching the area for the last three days, but didn't think to tell Henderson before today.

'We need to get someone over there immediately, Chief of Staff. Miss Moneypenny, send signals to all our stations in the Pacific; find out who's closest to the scene. Then contact Henderson and get him to wire over any information he can extract from the Japs, including whatever they've got on Shatterhand. Until we've evidence of 007's death, we must assume that he escaped. God knows, he's crawled from the jaws of death on countless occasions. Keep me informed of any developments.'

It was a dismissal and once we were back in the car Bill put his hands up to his temples and started massaging them. 'I hope to God 007's all right. The Old Man's obviously in a state about it. He was never intended to succeed at this mission − it was just something we cooked up on Molony's advice to try to get James to snap out of whatever gloom he was wallowing in. He's already achieved more than we expected with the intercept about the nuclear test. I can't believe he would have gone barrelling into the lion's den without some thought of how he was going to get out.'

Thursday, 27th December

Facsimiles of the passport photographs of Dr Shatterhand and his wife arrived today. They were on my desk, awaiting circulation, when 006 walked in. He took one look at them and exclaimed, 'By George, that's Blofeld and Bunt.' He peered more closely at them. 'He's had a nose job and grown a moustache, but it's definitely him − no doubt about it − and no amount of plastic surgery could make a difference to Bunt's ugly mug.'

By this afternoon, his identification had been confirmed by Q Branch, after they'd run it through their Image Comparison Determinator.* I felt the emotion that I've

---

* A photograph was inserted into a light box containing sensors able to calculate the exact dimensions, angles and planes of a human face

been trying to suppress suddenly well up: so 007 had taken his revenge on Blofeld for Tracy's death. If he'd died in the process, he would have thought it a fair bargain. Not for us, though. I can't begin to contemplate a world without 007. I do not want to.

New Year's Eve, 31st December

The clock is inching towards midnight and I'm filled with excitement. R fell asleep soon after we'd finished the hospital's execrable New Year's Eve 'Feast', still protesting that he was going to see in the new year. I stayed for a while, mulling over what he'd told me before he dropped off.

Pa did not die in 1940. R told me as he was shaving this afternoon – he'd discovered it the day before he leapt on a plane back to London to tell me. He'd been attached to the war crimes investigative unit. He was searching through the archives for the original blueprints of Colditz* when

---

– none of which are easy to alter using plastic surgery. When a second photograph was superimposed, its dimensions were compared with the first, making it possible to determine – to a significant degree of accuracy – whether the images were of the same person.

* Colditz Castle, a forbidding medieval edifice perched on a craggy hilltop near Leipzig, Germany. During the war, it was commandeered by the Nazis and used as a high-security prison for Allied officers and captured VIPs. Supposedly escape-proof, it was the only German POW camp with more guards than prisoners. The first inmates comprised a small group of Poles in transit after the fall of Poland. They were relocated in the early summer of 1940 and later replaced by another 140 Polish prisoners. In November 1940 a handful of British RAF officers arrived, followed by six British Army officers, and later by some French officers. More British, French, Belgian and Dutch

he found a list of names, tucked between the pages of a long document detailing the facilities installed in 1945 when it reverted to medical use. 'One jumped out at me: Lieutenant Hugh Sterling. I have to confess I did undertake a bit of independent research into your father's wartime activities after you told me about him. I've access into files you wouldn't have seen. One of them was the Ruthless file – and among the planning documents I found a list of the cover names they'd use in case of capture. Your father's was Sterling. Sterling – Moneypenny. You see the connection.

'It was a very thin piece of paper, and the writing had faded to a pale sepia, but it was definitely his cover name, halfway down a list of what I soon realised must have been Allied officers interned in the castle.'

I felt my heart swell and my eyes fill. I started grinning madly as I asked whether he was sure.

'Yes. And there was a date at the top of the page . . .' he paused and smiled gently. 'It was 13 April 1945. That's just days before it was liberated by the Americans.'

Does this mean my father was alive at the end of the war? That was the question that kept spinning round my head as I walked home through the cold winter night. It must. If so, I'm going to find him.

This has been an extraordinary year – for love, adventure, disappointment, danger, and now hope. I feel stronger,

---

officers were soon added to the prisoner population residing in – and attempting to escape from – the castle until its liberation on 16 April 1945. After the war, Colditz reverted to its former use as a psychiatric hospital, which was relocated only in 1996. The castle is now a tourist destination, housing a museum dedicated to its wartime occupation.

more alive more useful than ever before. And I'm excited about next year. Whatever it may hold, I'm ready for it.

I was suddenly seized by the idea that James is not dead. I don't know why, but I have this feeling, deep in my bones, that he escaped and one day will pop his face around my office door and say, 'Hello, Penny,' as if nothing had happened.

And if he doesn't, I'm going out there to look for him too.

Afterword

A diary, by its nature, is not a complete document. Life is episodic, but those episodes rarely conform to the cycle of seasons. In choosing my aunt's 1962 journal, I was fortunate that the central drama – the Cuban Missile Crisis and her role in it – did not bleed into the following year. But much else did. How much neater it would have been, for instance, had irrefutable evidence about my grandfather's final days surfaced in the dying gasps of December; had Prenderghast been tried and his contact within the service unearthed; had Bond not apparently disappeared without trace in a remote corner of Japan.

A diary contains one person's eye-view of the world, and is restricted to what he or she wishes to commit to the page. This, in turn, is influenced by their motivation for keeping a record of their lives. For some it is an outflow pipe for their emotions; for others a stab at immortality. My aunt, I suspect, used her journal as a trusted confidant in a world of secrets, a friend on whose shoulder she occasionally felt the need to cry, but who, when times were tense, did not require her to spell out her feelings.

The Moneypenny Diaries has marked the beginning of a major new episode in my life. The search for verification has consumed most of my spare time and a larger proportion of my thoughts. As that early lecture about the Cuban Missile Crisis brought so forcefully home, the diaries have spilled into my work. I find myself looking for an extra dimension to even the most well-worn of historical events. My aunt has introduced me to a parallel world of half-truths and subterfuge, adventure and peril – to the story behind history.

I am not sure I can ever return. Certainly I cannot leave now. I have taken a sabbatical from teaching to devote my full time to finding the answers to the questions raised in her diaries. And so it is with my aunt, hand in hand, that I will open the leather cover of her 1963 journal and plunge back into her world.